JIMMY DEAN'S LAST DANCE

A.K. ALLISS

Jimmy Dean's Last Dance
First published in 2021

Publisher: Spectrum Publishing

AUTHOR'S FOREWORD

JIMMY DEAN'S LAST DANCE is a work of alternative history fiction set in parts of the United States in 1962. While Jimmy Dean died in 1955, in this work, he is still very much alive, but never achieved the level of fame that he did in real life.

The reader with a keen eye will note many other splits from our timeline in this novel, whether that be through music, movies, people or events. I have tried to ensure that where this happens, there is a logical explanation for it, or that it serves a narrative purpose. I have also used it in instances where I felt it contributes to the colour of the novel in highlighting the spirit of the early sixties and celebrity and political culture of the time.

In any event, this is a work of fiction, and as such, the situations, characters, organizations and locations are strictly taken from my own imagination. At no time are they meant to imply an opinion or fact about a conspiracy, or cast doubt on the quality of a character's personality.

The people, organizations and situations in this novel are fiction and any resemblance or connection to their non-fictional counterparts is for the purposes of entertainment only.

For Janice, whom I have it on good authority,
would be "all over this book."

And now that you don't have to be perfect, you can be good.

East of Eden - John Steinbeck

Black velvet and that little boy's smile
Black velvet with that slow southern style
A new religion that'll bring ya to your knees
Black velvet if you please

Black Velvet - Alannah Myles

PROLOGUE

Mexico, 1957

THE CAPTAIN CRACKS JIMMY across the jaw backhanded, leaving a thick smell of stale cologne and sweat. He rocks in the chair and falls sideways. Two guards haul him to his feet, set the chair to rights and jam him onto it. Jimmy spits blood, a trail of it dribbling down the front of his white t-shirt. It's still trickling down the back of his neck from where they gave him a walloping with a nightstick. Hit him hard enough that time to make his vision swim.

"Where's the money?" The captain says the word 'money' hungrily, like it's a long awaited meal.

"I told you -"

CRACK.

Again. Harder this time. Across the temple and he sees stars. Jimmy doesn't fall, held steady by the guards. He looks up at the ceiling, blinking tears. His tongue finds a loose tooth at the back of his mouth. He spits, and it lands on the floor. Blood and bone catch the brightness of the dangling lightbulb.

Jimmy wonders if he should give in. Tell them. Decides not to. After all, it was Elvis who had hidden the money, not him. Better to play dumb. The plan had been to blow off some steam in Tijuana before crossing back over the border. 'Reward themselves for a job well done'. That's what Elvis had told him. And, like the idiot that he was, Jimmy had bought into the other man's chaos.

The TJ Police are the least of his worries. If they don't get the money and drugs back to Vegas, they are screwed. That's something the Captain doesn't know about. Frazini had sent them down here to bring back a shipment of weed and cash to Vegas, and what had they done? Well, not what *they* had done, but what Elvis had done. Blabbed off his big mouth about who they worked for, how much money they were carrying. At least Jimmy had the good sense to keep his mouth shut.

Who knew whether Elvis was suffering as bad as Jimmy? Most likely. His eyes blur again, but not enough that he can't see the Captain getting ready to give him another taste of his fist. He flinches, croaks at the Captain to stop. He holds his arm mid swing.

"I'll tell you... Just... Just stop." He hadn't meant to speak, but the thought of another blow makes his guts roil.

"Okay. I'm listening." The captain leans his bulk back on the table. It creaks and Jimmy wonders if the thing will support his weight. If it were to collapse beneath him, he couldn't be sure that he wouldn't burst out laughing.

Of course he can't just come out and tell the man where the money is. If he does that, he's as good as dead. Maybe as good as dead anyway? Hadn't Frazini given them clear instructions to bring the dope and the cash back pronto? Again, he curses himself for a fool. Should've stuck to the plan. He could be heading back to LA from Vegas right now if he had.

Jimmy blinks sweat and blood out of his eyes, croaks "Water."

The Captain looks at him, working his jaw with his calloused hand, the thick flesh of his neck corded. He flicks his head aggressively at one of his subordinates, grabs a chair. As the man leaves, he swings it around and sits on it with his gut resting against its back. He studies Jimmy, dark eyes glittering and sharp.

"Tell me."

"My friend..." He trails off. Coughs. Buying time. "He hid it outside of town. Buried it. We were gonna go back for it this morning. We... We didn't wanna get robbed."

Jimmy does laugh then. Bitterly. Lets it fall out of his mouth as easily as the tooth had. To his amazement, the Captain joins him with a thick and rich laughter that seems at odds with the room. When he stops, it's sudden, and the silence that follows in its absence is unnerving.

"You will take us to the money."

Elvis was going to be pissed, but Jimmy knows that their only chance out of this is to get outside of the police station walls. The Captain's man returns with a glass of water, and Jimmy sees that it's yellowed. Things float lazily in the water, magnified by the curve of the glass. He coughs as the guard holds it up to his lips and turns his head.

"I, uh, I changed my mind."

The guard shrugs, tosses the water on the floor. Clapping his hands, the Captain yanks Jimmy to his feet. As he is handed off to the guards, he is dragged through the room's doorway and sees Elvis being hauled out into the passage as well. His partner is kicking and swearing. One of his captors strikes him across the face. Elvis gives a low curse and Jimmy hears him say "I'll kill you, you son of a bitch!"

Jimmy has no doubt who the winner would be if it was just Elvis one on one with the guard. He'd seen his partner in action. That skill was what Jimmy was counting on when they got near to where the stash was buried. It's a risky choice, but the way Jimmy sees it, the only one that they have right now. Either that or rot in prison for the next however long. As he is pulled along and brought next to his partner, Elvis leans close, Southern drawl low.

"Heya Jim, how're you holdin' up?"

"I told them that we'd take them to the money." As Elvis glares at him, Jimmy is still glad that he'd made the choice he had, tries to explain. "It's our only option."

He gives a quick sideways glance at the Captain, hoping that Elvis can see that despite the man's size, he's out of shape. He can't tell whether Elvis gets it, but hopes that he does anyway. There's a lot of factors that need to come into play before he can make a call on whether or not he'd made the right decision or one that would land them in a desert grave.

The track where they had buried the stash isn't far outside the city. As good as Jimmy is, he's glad that Elvis is there. Damned if he could remember how to get them back there on his own. The Southerner leads the way unerringly. The Captain sits in the back, gun trained on Elvis' head. A guard sits behind Jimmy. He shifts in his seat as the man's hand grazes the back of his neck. He makes kissing noises, thick and unpleasant.

They pull up alongside a wooden stake with a red piece of cloth tied to it. As Elvis shuts off the engine, it makes a ticking sound, expelling heat. Jimmy is sweating as they exit the car. Low scrub and pale coloured rock spread out beneath the hot orange sun. Further back from the road, Jimmy can see disturbed earth where they'd buried the drugs and cash the day before. Frazini would be angry that they were late, but Jimmy was hoping Elvis would be able to talk their way back into his good graces. That's if they made it back across the border alive at all.

Elvis points out the upturned earth and Jimmy sees the Captain's eyes shining beneath the wide brim of his hat. The sun is baking now and he feels the full effect of it as if he had been struck around the head again. He slumps back against the car. Elvis points again and the Captain lets out a laugh. The guard laughs as well, mechanically, as if he is fearful of upsetting the Captain.

"You think I'm just a stupid beaner, Gringo?" He yanks his gun and points, indicating that Jimmy should go and dig. "You're little friend here can do all the work." He nods to the guard. "You, go keep an eye on him."

Jimmy swallows, but pushes himself off the car and starts walking towards the spot. The scrub tickles against his legs through the thick fabric of his jeans. He looks back, and the Captain waves the pistol at him. Jimmy starts digging with his hands, not taking long before he hits the duffel bag they had buried. He yanks it up and fumbles with the handle, sweat pricking his palms. He unzips the bag.

"What are you doing?" The Captain gestures to the guard standing behind Jimmy and barks in Spanish. "*Detenerlo*!"

Jimmy's heart is in his throat as he yanks the snub nosed .38 from the bag. Elvis deserved a medal for making him put it in there. The guard behind Jimmy clumsily goes to grab him. Before the man reaches him, Jimmy's finger slips against the trigger and there's a loud pop. He sees the guy clutch at his chest and topple.

As the Captain approaches in a rush, Jimmy falls back and yells wildly. Elvis runs at the man, lunges and tackles his legs. They both fall to the ground in a mass of limbs. Elvis growls as he straddles the Captain and digs his thumb into one of his eyes. The Captain screeches in pain and raises his weapon blindly, but Elvis is too fast. He grabs at the Captain's hand, twists it, and relieves him of the weapon.

Elvis and the Captain struggle with the pistol, the Captain's huge fist striking Elvis just beneath the eye. Elvis yowls, brings the weapon around and hammers it into the side of the Captain's head. He pulls back, pistol clenched in one hand. The Captain thrusts upwards, pitching Elvis back and staggering to his knees, before gaining his feet shakily. He surges forward, tries to yank the weapon from Elvis' hand. There is a single booming sound and then the captain's hands go up and outwards. A backspray of the Captain's blood and brains spatters the front of Jimmy's t-shirt. He lets out a yell and falls backwards. The Captain staggers, then slumps forward onto Elvis.

Grunting sharply, Elvis quickly rolls the Captain's body from off top of him. He shuffles back, then up onto his feet, looks in shock at the corpse. The gun dangles by his side. He backs away, but stops when the car blocks him. Silence descends, a low breeze picks up and the steady drone of insects lifts, becoming the only noises. Jimmy steps forward and picks up the duffel bag, moves to the Captain. He looks down at the mess of bone, scalp and black hair. He turns and spits as Elvis lets out a breath.

"Well... Hot damn." Elvis wipes at his face and Jimmy sees some of the Captain's blood, splattered on his cheek, gets smeared by his hand.

Jimmy says nothing.

"You know we can't go back to Frazini." Elvis finally says.

"What? No... We have to deliver this shit!" Jimmy's eyes widen.

"Listen to me Jim-"

"Listening to you was what got me into this mess in the first place."

"We go back to Frazini after killing Mexican Police officers, we are done. And by done, I mean dead." He gives Jimmy a hard look and when Jimmy doesn't say anything, he continues. "This is gonna fuck up his supply chain. They'll have our faces posted everywhere. Not only that, but the premiums on bribes goes through the roof when you fuck with the Mexican Police. So, there's that. Use your brain. We have royally fucked up his operation. Hell, even I can see this for what it is."

The funny thing is, what Elvis is saying makes perfect sense.

"What do you suggest then? We go back across the border, and don't show up with the stash, we're dead. "

"Think about it, Jim." Elvis leans close. He allows the silence to sit there, broken only by the buzzing of flies gathering on the captain's corpse. "We're nobodies. Not worth the effort to chase down. We just lie low. It's that easy."

Jimmy isn't so sure about that idea. Frazini could be a vindictive asshole when he wanted to be. But what Elvis said about them being dead if they did go back to Frazini rung true. Much more likely than if they just went into hiding.

"Okay. Lie low." He spits again. "Shit. What a mess."

"Come on, help me clean up and let's get the hell out of here."

HOLLYWOOD NIGHTS

Los Angeles, 1962

JIMMY'S LEANING AGAINST the studio wall, smoking a Chesterfield and watching Marilyn and Weinstein huddle. He knows that he shouldn't, but feels the stab of jealousy anyway. She's different when Weinstein is around. More closed off. He hates that in the same way that he hates most of the superficial veneer that comes with the studio landscape. He scratches at the itchy fabric of the coat that the costume department had shoved him into and takes another pull on the cigarette.

They've got him playing a shoe salesman of all things. The director of this piece of shit, Cukor, had argued with Weinstein, the producer, about casting Jimmy. Marilyn had stepped in, did her thing, and saved his ass, so here he was. The real reason Cukor wanted Jimmy gone was that he had made a pass at

Jimmy a year or so back at some party. Jimmy wasn't much for older guys and had taken a hard pass. It had been enough of a slight to make them enemies going forward, Jimmy guesses.

Cukor would've been pitching it another way of course. You weren't open about these sorts of things, even if everybody knew the score. Maybe he'd be saying that the role wasn't a good fit for Jimmy or something? He couldn't disagree with the guy on that, even if it was just an excuse. The role wasn't him at all. With his hair plastered against his head, and the square get-up, Jimmy doesn't feel anywhere near himself. The only benefits of the gig were the paycheck, and that he got to hang out with Marilyn.

She finishes with Weinstein and as she walks over to him, he sees that her eyes are red rimmed. She smiles at him and he pretends that he doesn't notice the way her mascara has run. He spins the cigarette butt between his fingers and makes it disappear. A simple trick but it makes her laugh all the same. It's a laugh that makes him feel a little giddy as she loops her arm through his and her perfume tickles his nostrils.

She has that way about her. A way that makes a guy glad that she's giving him some time. Not that he thinks about her like the others do. It's not her figure that gets him, or the way she wears her femininity like a disguise. Not really his thing. It's more like he gets her. Understands her quick mind as well as the sadness that she carries the same as other women carry a clutch. Pulling away, she excuses herself to the bathroom. Says she wants to powder her nose. He has enough sense to leave it at that.

As he waits, he lights up again. There are eyes on him. Cukor. Watching. Guy's face is blank like a statue's. It makes the hair on the back of Jimmy's neck prickle. He doesn't believe for one second that he is safe from getting fired, even with Marilyn's protection. Hell, she's not even safe. He'd heard enough to know that the sharks in this joint were circling, the smell of her despair like blood in the water. He gives Cukor a smile, and is met with cold indifference.

Running a hand through his hair, he grimaces against the feel of the gunk that they had used to flatten it. He shrugs out of the coat and drapes it haphazardly from one of the costume racks. Back home, home being the small pool house adjoining the mansion in Sherman Oaks that he leases from Hal Wallis, he can take a long shower. It will feel good to wash off the smell of this place.

First though, that drink that he had promised Marilyn. She returns and takes his arm again, looking as perfect as if she had shed no tears at all. That was another of her tricks, an illusion of perfection that acted like armor against her fragility. He could call her out on it, but he figures there's enough people doing that already

Dean Martin had given Marilyn some comps to his joint down on the strip. Neon paints Marilyn's face into some sort of beautiful Picasso. Her hair catches the brilliant white of the sign, that big lush Dino's megawatt grin leering down. He had barely spoken two words to the guy, but had heard enough to get his number. Still, a drink is a drink, and as long as he's with her, it isn't so bad.

Inside, the waitresses hustle tables and a three piece act are set up on a low stage at one end of the room. They're pouring out a cover of Sealed With a Kiss across the audience. Marilyn gets the eyes of the bartender and holds up two fingers before blowing him a kiss. The bartender nods and then looks him up and down. Champagne for her, obviously, and whatever the bartender decides fits Jimmy best, apparently.

They take a seat, wedged up against a wall where the shadows are deep enough that people will hopefully forget she's there. Some nights, she wants the glances, and the whispers, but tonight doesn't seem like one of them. The curve of the booth they hide in softens the music and the murmur of the crowd. A waitress glides through the patrons like a knife and dispenses a flute of champagne for her and a whiskey sour for him. He takes a sip, watching her over the rim.

She hasn't lifted her glass. Holds it between her fingers and stares into its depths as if it holds whatever it is she's looking for. Her nails look bitten and in the room's dim lighting he sees that circles darken her eyes. One quick breath in, then out, then a long sip before she settles the flute and toys with its stem. Jimmy waits. He could wait all night when it came to her. Every other man in this room would do the same or more, so why not him?

"They're trying to fire me, you know?" Her voice isn't the breathy one that everyone knows. A bit more precise. Less dreamy.

"They wouldn't dare!" He doesn't think that he had sold the lie, and he's right.

"Stop acting." She doesn't look at him, long lashes shielding the brilliance of her eyes as she looks down. "You're no good at it."

She knows him too well. Knows the situation better than anyone thinks. She was on the outs. No one liked a liability. What was true for her, is more true for him. As far as those studio types were concerned, he was nothing. Just a resource to put somewhere and say some lines. A moon to orbit around the majesty of stars like Marilyn. Both of them are skirting the edges now though. It reminds him of the Indiana winter. Out on the ice, where you were never as safe as you thought. He clears his throat before speaking.

"What for?" The words are quick and she glances up just as quickly.

"Nothing that you need to worry about." Her tone is soft, mothering almost, and she reaches across the table and takes his hand.

He wants to flinch away, can feel her slight tremor against his skin. He keeps steady.

"You alright, Norma?" Anyone else calls her that, they're likely to get slapped, but not Jimmy.

"Take me home, Jim. I'm tired." She pats his hand and pulls hers away, takes the flute and tilts it all the way back.

Standing, she walks around the table and rests a hand on his shoulder. The band has moved on to You Belong To Me and he thinks if only you knew. He hesitates before standing and taking her hand. Leading her to the door, he knows that the conversation isn't done. At her place, they'll continue talking, perched on deck chairs by the shimmering light coming up through the pool's surface. Anytime that happens, it's like a throwback to a youth that he had never experienced. It's electrifying. Right now though? It feels wrong to crave it at the expense of her uncertainty.

Sunset to Helena Drive in Brentwood. The place pretty much sums up her personality. Cul De Sac. Big wall fronted by double gates. Screaming that she wants to be left alone. A real Greta Garbo house. Inside, it's modest, and as they walk through into the kitchen, she fixes Jimmy another whiskey without him asking. Their fingers graze as she hands it to him and gives him a sad smile that he thinks is meant to be flirtatious. He doesn't know what to do with it, so he packs it away with the rest of his screwed up feelings.

He goes to say something, but she places her finger to his lips and purses her own into a drawn out shhhhh. Kicking off her shoes, she sways through a small study towards the back door and pushes him outside before turning and vanishing back into the house. Looking around, he spots a deck chair and sits splay-legged on its edge, nursing the drink. The pool is kidney shaped and with the lights off, it reflects the moon. When she rejoins him, she's wearing a pink kimono and nothing underneath.

Her drink remains clutched beneath her chin and her big, helpless eyes are pools of despair. Searching for something to make them fill with laughter, he comes up short. Never was much of a comedian. She gifts him a smile anyway, maybe seeing his struggle. Her lips map the glass's rim, forced into a bigger smile by its curve. Lowering it, she looks back into the house, and when her stare returns to him, he can see fear in it.

"I can tell you anything, can't I?"

"Sure." A longer answer might scare her, so he keeps it short.

"I've been seeing someone."

"Who?" Not as disinterested as he had meant to sound.

She flinches even as he goes to apologize, but then the mask drops into place and he knows she's retreated to that space that is hers alone.

"I'm not going to tell you if you treat me like one of your floozies." She huffs, anger masked by her movie star voice.

"I would never..." He deploys the boyish look that he uses to make the older guys swoon.

She takes a deep breath, folds her legs tighter to her knees, gaze drifting to cold stars hidden by city lights.

"I know you wouldn't... I just..." Trailing off, still looking to the heavens. "You know, when you're little, they tell you that you can be anything, but they never tell you how much it will cost."

Ain't that the truth?

He says instead "At least you're not living in a pool house."

Making a clicking sound with her tongue, she gives him a quick sidelong glance "You wouldn't want this."

Silence hangs between them, draped as loosely as her gown.

"So. You gonna tell me who it is? Or do you plan to keep me in suspense all night?"

She gives the house this look, like it's waiting to see what she'll say, then finally "It's just this guy, kind of a big deal right now... People call him Mist-er Pres-i-dent."

And she says it just like that. Drawn out and sultry. A big long breath follows, like it's a weight she's put down. Not for long, barely long enough for him to count to five before she's picked it back up. He hasn't even had time to react.

"You and..." He's not certain he should believe her, but can't afford to damage her trust by showing that distrust.

Slicing through his sentence she gives him a warning look, tinged with regrets if he's reading it right. Thing was, he was really good at reading things right.

"Just promise me one thing." She cups his narrow chin in her small hand.

"Anything."

"Promise you'll never believe what they say about me."

His long brow furrows, but he says "Sure."

One word, but it seemed to wash away everything that is troubling her. Looking back, he'll wish he had been more careful with his promises.

I FOUGHT THE LAW

NEXT MORNING, JIMMY IS SO HUNGOVER that the very act of trying to recall much of the night before brings pain. His lips are gummed together and making his way to the tiny bathroom is an exercise in patience. He realizes that he's forgotten to close the blinds when the bold Californian sun streamers its way inside and hits him in the face. Wincing, he screws his eyes shut, splashes himself with cold water from the faucet.

His eyes are bloodshot and tender beneath the lathing motion of his flat palms. Swapping the bathroom for the kitchen, he opens the refrigerator, revealing emptiness. Jimmy trades scrambled eggs for a cigarette, taking one from the crumpled pack left on the kitchen counter. It burns his throat as he takes a drag and claws a shaky hand across his midsection before stepping out the back door.

One advantage of living here is that the place is always quiet. The streets beyond the high walls sound empty, as if every person had worked out that West coast living wasn't as easy as everybody said it was. Grown sick of the perpetual hustle. Moved away. Dragging deeply again, he coughs and spits phlegm, turns and saunters back inside.

Before he can sit, a knock at the door makes him jump. It's heavy and abrupt, and he stares for a long time at the door before making a move to answer it. He's confronted by two cops, one medium build, the other shorter, bullish almost. They don't wear uniforms, but the cheap quality of their suits coupled with their stiff stares labels them as law enforcement even before they introduce themselves.

"Yeah?" He mumbles. His Aunt had always said that he sounded as if he had swallowed a bull-frog when he spoke.

"James Byron Dean?" The shorter one smirks, as if the very combo of his names is a pretty funny joke.

"Yeah?" Jimmy eyeballs both of them. "Who's asking?"

"Detectives Porter and Wyatt." Medium height says.

"Which is which?"

"What?" Shorty is bristling "What did you say?"

"Which one of you is Porter and which is Wyatt?" He squints. "You look like a Porter to me."

He shouldn't be mouthing off but he's feeling like he wants to vomit any minute and can't be bothered with their hassle.

"We'll ask the questions, wise-ass."

Shrugging, Jimmy steps to one side and gestures them both in with a flourish. He shuffles past them as they step inside, sits slouched back in the old armchair adjacent to a multi-paned window. After a few seconds, they join him on the long couch opposite the chair. Both of them perch on the edge of it like birds on a wire. Medium retrieves a notebook and flips it open. He taps his pen gainst his chin before setting both aside and leaning forward, hands clasped before him. He has a look of conspiracy on his face, like it's him and Jimmy against his bullish partner.

"Detective Porter here just has a few questions. Nothing to worry about." He winks, but then adopts a sombre look. "It's about your friend, Miss Monroe."

"Marilyn?"

"You know many other Monroes?" Porter's snarl never seems far from his lips.

"What happened?" Jimmy's neck is burning and his stomach clenched.

Porter's snarl turns into an unfriendly leer "We figure you were the last one to see her. That right? Why don't you tell us? "

"What do you mean?"

"You seem like a smart young man." Wyatt offers him a consoling smile. "I'm sure we don't need to spell it out for you."

Heart thudding now, he doesn't want to ask them to confirm what he already knows.

"She's dead?"

"Mmhm" Wyatt nods and gives Porter a sidelong glance. "Now why don't you tell us about last night?"

"Were you two fucking?" Jimmy winces at the vulgarity of Porter's question but stifles it. Wouldn't do to give these two anymore than what they might already have.

"She's a friend."

"We know you were at her house last night." Wyatt again. They were playing tag team.

"Who doesn't?" He plays it cool, despite how his skin has grown all clammy. "We were at Dino's place for dinner, then went back to hers for a drink."

"A drink? Is that all?" The sly grin on Porter's face makes him look lecherous. "Come on... Handsome guy like you? A girl like her... "

"Easy, partner." Wyatt holds up a hand. "What time was that?"

"Don't know." Jimmy shrugs, stretching his legs out in front of him, pushing his hand between his knees, trying to curl around the hollow feeling of loss in his stomach. "About Midnight?"

"Anybody else there with you?" Porter is not even looking at him now, his narrow eyes taking in the living room.

"No." He sits back, folds his arms, chewing his gum as he stares flatly at the two of them.

Wyatt sighs. "You know, son, this would go a lot easier if..."

"How'd she die?" He wants to scream the words, but instead they escape from him in a tired whisper.

"We can't tell you that." Porter angles forward, looks Jimmy in the eye. There was hunger there that made the man look more like a beast than anything else. "Did she mention if she was seeing anyone? Anyone other than you?"

"I told you-"

"Yeah, yeah, calm down, kid." He stands, brushes his hands lightly against the front of his pants. "I think we have all we need here, Bill."

"You go ahead, I'll catch up." Wyatt watches his partner leave, then leans forward, bony elbows in shirt sleeves resting on his crooked knees. A real friendly posture. "Listen, James... I can call you that right?" Jimmy doesn't answer and Wyatt gives a gentle shrug. "I understand that it must come as something of a shock. Maybe you want to get out of town for a while and clear your head? I would strongly advise you against doing that. Nothing screams guilt more than a person running. You get where I'm going?" He sighs, then scrubs a hand across his face, his eyes showing exhaustion that Jimmy hadn't noticed at first. "Marilyn was in some real trouble. Wouldn't do to get caught up in it."

He has to admit, the Detective is doing a fine job of selling an overall impression of somebody concerned for Jimmy's wellbeing. Jimmy stares just that little bit harder, and he can see that the man's warm smile can't remove the cold deadness behind his eyes. They sit, deeply socketed like glittering sapphires, observant and relentless.

Promise you'll never believe what they say about me. She's there, reciting the oath she'd made him take the night before.

Her ghost speaks in her movie-star voice. A deception. Just like everything else about her. Both he and Wyatt keep their eyes locked on each other for a few moments more before the Detective sighs and stands up.

"You call me if you can think of anything." The Detective hands Jimmy a card. He thumbs it back and forth as Wyatt turns and leaves.

He shuts the door softly. Turning his back to it, Jimmy lets gravity yank his body down. A yawning emptiness snatches at him. He is abandoned again. Just like he had always been abandoned. Just like what had happened after his mother had died. The tears when they come are hot and purposeful. They slide down his cheeks in torrents.

What had pulled her so quickly from life? He closes his eyes and takes a deep breath. Then another. Then another. Finally, he's disengaged from everything, dropped into a place that only he can access. Soon, the hollow feeling drapes a veil over him, but he feels calm. He struggles to his feet, gets a glass of water from the kitchen as Marilyn's ghost follows him into the small tiled space.

What are you going to do, Jimmy?

"What do you mean?" Must be going crazy, talking to an empty room the way that he is. "What can I do?"

Help me.

He can't answer. Doesn't know what she wants from him. Doesn't want to engage with her unwelcome spirit. As if sensing his reluctance, she falls silent. Changing out of last night's clothes, he hits the street intending to head to the studio, see if he still has a job. He remembers that he'd left the car at her place last night and cabbed it home. He would've driven, but she had taken his keys with that mother hen way that she had. That answered how the cops knew he'd been at her place. Biting his lip, he starts walking and hails the first cab that he sees.

He gives the cabbie her address and occupies the back seat in silence. Jimmy thinks of their last conversation. Maybe he'd taken it for more of her paranoia. They'd known each other a month at most, but it had felt like much longer. In that time, he'd seen her slide from the warm bubbly chaos he had first experienced, to a woman frightened of herself. Was it only the trouble she was in with the studio? Maybe something else?

LA's streets pass in the hazy smear of daylight beyond the cab's windows. The city was changing. The desperation that had always been there had sunk below the surface, replaced by an optimism that felt out of place. Maybe it was just him? He felt torn between two places, and that feeling was even stronger now that he knew she wasn't here anymore. Pulling up outside her house, he feels it even more in the pit of stomach. Police cruisers line the curb.

Neighbors mingle, sunglasses lowered over their curiosity. They cluster, heads bent close, murmuring theories no doubt. His car was back up the drive. It was gonna be a tough gig getting to it. He pays the cab driver and hustles out of the vehicle. Looking at the broad white wall, he considers scaling it, but then tosses the idea. Quickest way to get arrested. He spots an officer out front, watching the neighbors with a bored expression. Jimmy ambles up to him, smashing his expression into a friendly smile that doesn't reach inside of him.

"Hey buddy!" He would never have used the word buddy in normal conversation. "Hey!"

The cop eyeballs him suspiciously, holds a hand up.

"Sorry, can't let you come any closer. Crime scene."

"Oh, yeah?" Jimmy gives the cop this look that says *no shit*. He eyes the big gate. "Anyone in there now?"

"I'm not answering any questions." The cop stops looking at Jimmy and stares off into the middle distance with determined disinterest.

Jimmy sighs and reaches into his pocket. He produces a couple of dollar bills and holds them out. "How about now?"

The cop's eyes dart to the money, then up at Jimmy's grin. He holds it, then lets it drop. Wouldn't do to oversell it.

"What do you want?" *Bingo*.

"What all of us want in this town." He eyes the gate, then gives the cop a sly wink, bringing him into the conspiracy. "Just a little brush with fame."

Sweat stains the cop's collar, and he keeps looking at the cash like it could transform itself into a few cold ones after his shift.

"Whaddaya say? Just five minutes."

"Could be it's time for my break." The cop stretches and collects the bills with the downward sweep of his hand. "Besides, they've already taken her away."

That makes him start a little. The thought of Marilyn laid out on a slab somewhere. Jimmy pushes it down when the cop gives him a hard stare. He smiles. "Thanks friend."

"Yeah, whatever." The cop steps away from the gate, heads to the neighbors as if to do the job that people higher up the food chain in the department had already done.

Crime tape is stretched across the open front door and Jimmy ducks beneath it. Couldn't believe that he had actually made it this far. Inside the house, it looks much as it had the night before. The only difference was that she isn't there, and her absence permeates the space in a way that makes it feel haunted. As if he had summoned her, her ghost is back beside him. It's not like he can see her, but her presence loiters behind his shoulder and when she speaks, it's with a small voice.

Oh Jimmy, they've made such a mess.

He wants to comfort her, but then remembers it's just his imagination and shunts it to one side. He should just go and get his car, but maybe what he said to the cop was true. Now that he's in here without her, he can't help but look into her life unmonitored, if only to be closer to her. Sure, he had been closer than others, but there was always something missing. Like she was withholding the truth behind a dam of lies, a barrier that was in constant danger of breaking.

Be careful.

Everyone kept warning him, but no-one was giving him very good reasons to stop. Besides, hadn't she made him promise? He sees the door to her bedroom. Better be quick. The bribe wouldn't hold the cop's attention for long. He moves to the door, pausing briefly with his hand on it before pushing it open. He flinches a little at the tangled mess of bedsheets, can almost picture her curves wrapped up in them. A mess of bags and parcels sits messily against the wall. Was this where they had found her? He keeps away from the bed, like it's some kind of shrine that risks sacrilege if he disturbs it.

The cops had been in here. Traces of them left everywhere. No doubt they would've tossed the room well. No point leaving themselves open to accusations of a shoddy investigation.

Probably why Porter and Wyatt had paid him a visit. He shakes his head as he spots where they'd been. Can almost superimpose their presence here by the tell-tale signs. He had always been good at this kind of thing, picking up the little details. After a moment, Jimmy focuses instead on where they hadn't been. Easy to waste time on looking at what's already been looked at.

It takes him what's left of his time to spot it, but when he does, a small click of satisfaction escapes his lips. There, beneath a chest of drawers next to the bed. The corner of a small book, sticking out. Bending quickly, he snatches it up and eyes the black leather cover before slipping it into his pocket. He jumps as the cop's voice rings out from the front door.

"Hey! You better get out of here! Now!"

The cop's voice sounds panicked, and Jimmy sees familiar faces through the open front door. The cop vanishes, bustling towards Porter and Wyatt who have just got out of their car. Jimmy swears and heads for the back instead. He stops to scoop his keys from the glass bowl next to the back door.

Predictable Marilyn.

His car is where he left it, and he sees that the broad gate is mercifully open and the way down the driveway free of obstacles. As he slides behind the wheel, he catches raised voices from inside but the engine drowns them out as he jams the keys in the ignition and starts the car. He plows it out the open front gate. A quick glance as he swings out the drive reveals Porter, red faced and yelling, chasing after him. They'd know it was him, of course, but the little book burning in his pocket would be worth the attention. Just a little piece of her that might reveal answers to questions that he desperately needs to know.

PRETTY GIRLS MAKE GRAVES

HEADING TOWARDS THE STUDIO, he fumbles the book from his pocket and rubs his thumb across the cover. Plain black leather, nothing on it. A looped leather thong secures the cover shut. He tosses it onto the seat next to him, extracts another cigarette and lights it with shaking fingers.

His heart is pounding thickly in his chest and it makes his breath arrive in short little pants. Doesn't even know why he's going to the studio. There was no way they were going ahead with the picture now that Marilyn was gone. Or maybe they would? Typical Hollywood shit. Using her death to promote the film in a way that it wouldn't have been otherwise. Either way, he was certain that Cukor wouldn't be up for tolerating Jimmy's presence on set any more.

The guard gives him a lazy wave as he almost skips to the gate, still full of the nervous energy carrying him. The book is back in his pocket and he is burning to open it, but he just wants to finish with this mess first. Feels like once he does this, he can leave behind the system that had used Marilyn up and squeezed her dry. People are looking at him as he passes, leant close to each other and whispering. Probably theorising whether or not he had been there when whatever had happened, happened.

Let 'em talk. It made no difference to the end result. Someone who was better than most of them ever would be, was gone. He spots Cukor and Weinstein pacing through the crowd. Even though he had been given lines, he hadn't really had much to do with the Director, let alone the Producer. Not surprising given his history with Cukor. Cukor spots him and turns his back as he approaches. Jimmy decides to ignore the brush off, goes in hard.

"Hey George."

A liberty he might not have taken ordinarily, but nothing about today was shaping up as ordinary. Besides, he doesn't have anything to lose. George turns, broad face red beneath those thick specs he wears.

"I have nothing to say to you." Jimmy is startled by the vehemence in the man's voice. "You can collect your check on the way through the gate."

Cukor keeps walking, making it clear that the exchange was at an end.

"C'mon George, don't be like that." Pushing harder. "I just want to know what happened to Marilyn."

The man stops and Jimmy can see that his fists are balled. He takes a step back, not putting it past the Director to take a swing at him. Instead, Cukor swivels precisely, stalks forward and jams his index finger into Jimmy's chest.

"Listen here you little pissant." His breath is hot in Jimmy's face and smells of booze and eggs. "For all I know, you had something to do with it. I've had cops up my ass all morning."

"I didn't." Jimmy is still, brow lowered not in anger, but some ill-defined emotion that he couldn't explain. "Listen, I'm sorry. I just want to know what happened to my friend."

Cukor pinches the bridge of his nose, then runs his fingers through his hair. He flaps one hand ineffectually in the air then lets it fall.

"She killed herself." Weinstein is watching their exchange now, usual genial face hidden beneath a frown. "Now, get out of here kid. We're done."

Not much he could say in return. In his heart he had wanted it to not be that, but his head knows otherwise. The hangover was persistent, but the ache was more to do with the push of anger than anything else. He watches the two men walk away. Turns and heads back to the gate, stopping to collect his check. He grips it numbly as he heads back to the car.

He returns home and sleeps off the residue of the hangover and the adrenaline that had carried him through most of the morning. When he awakens, it's night-time and he's surprised the two cops haven't come calling. Maybe they'd gotten all they wanted from him? Or maybe it's like George said? Nothing to investigate because her death was considered a blameless one. The lights from the pool flicker like spectres on the ceiling. He gets up, puts on the same clothes he had worn earlier. His stomach rumbles, reminding him that he hasn't eaten. He grabs his keys and heads for the door, skirting the pool and heading for Wallis' garage, of which he has free reign.

Instead of the car, he straddles the bike that Wallis has loaned him. It gives an animal growl as he kicks it to life. The noise and the throbbing of the engine make him feel more alive than he has in some time. He rides the thing down Quebec Avenue. Skims the top of Beechwood canyon at breakneck speed, heading towards Stan Burke's on Van Nuys. The road ahead appears in splashes of his headlight and he half wishes he could lose control and plummet the thing like a comet into the darkness past the houses flashing to either side.

He usually takes a seat at the bar, but this time he slides into a booth. The feeling of it takes him back to the night before. Less than twenty-four hours had passed since he and Marilyn had sat together. The waitress arrives, gives him a brief smile that was probably meant to be cheerful, but was tarnished by his mood.

He orders a cup of coffee and leans back. Less than a day was all it had taken for her to go from being real, vivid and vital to this dull throb that occupies the back of his skull.

Don't think that, Jim. She is there with him as long as he has his eyes closed. *I'm still here.*

At that, he opens them. Recalls something that he is surprised to have forgotten. The book. He reaches into his pocket and there it is. Yanking it out, Jimmy places it on the table in front of him. It sits there, unassuming. Odd that such a small thing can instantly bring a person back to life, especially one like Marilyn. Jimmy pictures her hands holding the book, fingers writing neatly on the pages housed between its covers.

He reaches for it, then stops. The hairs on the back of his neck prickle. He can feel eyes on him. He looks up and sees two men staring from over steaming cups of coffee. Both men are dark featured, heavy brows set low over eyes that glitter in the dim lighting. Maybe they'd come in while he'd been sitting there, or maybe they'd been there the whole time, but he thinks the former is most likely.

He slides the book off the table and into his pocket. The two men keep staring. Jimmy decides to call it like he sees it. Rarely has his intuition failed him. He gets to his feet and so do the men. He walks backwards, colliding with the waitress. His coffee goes flying and the woman gives an awkward shriek. He runs, hits the door and causes it to fly open with a bang. There's yelling behind him, but he doesn't stop. His breath is heavy as he runs. Rounding a corner, he pumps his legs, but no amount of effort is going to be enough.

They get him good. There in the alley behind the diner. In tight, big rings flashing back streetlight into his narrowed eyes as their fists rise and fall. Later, he'll be nursing bruises, but right now, each blow is a percussive sting. Jimmy curls into it, waiting. It has to end. He knows it does. Takes him back to Indiana. Not him, but some other kid. Can't even remember the name now. But he can remember the piggish faces of the kid's attackers. Nothing like this though. This time, there's more than a beating on the horizon. Marilyn is dead and he can't help but feel it's all his fault.

One of the goons grabs his hair. Pulls at it like a trolley conductor pulling at a lever. The other man grabs at his pocket, tears at it and he feels it give, the book falling out. He howls, lands a punch, and sweet relief follows as he breaks free. Thrashing onto his back, he lances out with a foot, feels a throb of pain going into his ankle, but ignores it. Scrabbling for the book, he misses. No time to try for it anymore. Kicking. Swinging. Anything just to get away from the thugs. The sound of a door opening, and shutting just as quickly. It's enough of a distraction to allow him to get to his feet. A hobbled run.

Someone yells his name. Coarse and uneducated that voice. Back on the lot, the owner of that voice might have got a bit part as Heavy # 1, or something. Not bothering to even look. Maybe the next thing he'll feel is a bullet in his spine. Shouldn't have gone snooping at the house, but now he has a feeling that Marilyn didn't kill herself and he has to know if that's the truth. *Has to.* It's not enough that he should leave it alone. She was worth more than that. *Is* worth more. Peroxide blonde hair. Soft eyes. Desperate lips. Same as him in some ways. The two of them could've been parted at birth.

The bullet never comes. Sweet freedom not even that sweet after all. He can hear their uncertain shuffling behind him. Thinks to himself that they're probably wondering if they should follow him out onto the Boulevard or not. A woman passes, hair coming out of its pins, her eyes like two lanterns, locking onto him. Smeared lipstick goes into a big O of surprise. Using the wall as a guide, he staggers, dripping blood. Its crimson splatter trails behind him. He coughs, hawking an even bigger stain against already stained bricks. He makes the bike, winces as he kicks it to life and roars off up the boulevard.

Back home. Not home really. Just a place he came by through Wallis because of his day job when he wasn't hanging around the lots trying to score extra work. Carpentry, acting, whatever. Anything to keep him from having to go back to where he came from. Handyman work pays the rent for a little piece of this big sprawling Spanish hacienda.

He'd been hoping to move out of here in the Spring. The movie work had been growing, but that was gonna stop now. Now that she's gone. He was a fool if he thought any different. He would be tarnished by her death. That was how scandal worked in the City of Angels. There were those that ascended, and those that were cast down. What had Marilyn said to him last night? Not that good an actor? Water filtered lights from the pool smears ripples through the venetians, masking his bruises in the mirror. Leaning close, he sees his lips, pouty already, starting to swell. Then her soft, breathy voice is next to his ear.

Did they hurt you bad, Jimmy?

He shakes his head and smiles, but it quickly dips into a scowl. Can remember her leaning close at the craft table that first time they'd met and telling him not to eat the sandwiches because the eggs were bad. It had been a good voice. Real. Funny. Warm. Not like now. So maybe her speaking to him this way, from beyond the grave, is right. He balls a fist and presses the ice pack to his cheek. The sting feels good.

Swivelling, he moves into the living room and collapses onto the long couch. The wooden beams dissect the ceiling above. Who had sent the goons? The same person that had killed her? The message, then, was clear. *Stop diggin' kid, or you'll end up making a grave.* Just buy into the suicide angle. Didn't it fit the bill? Troubled and fading star ending it before she burnt out completely. Baloney. That's what it was. He sits up then. Grabs the phone. Thick black receiver heavy in his hand. Dial tone, then a lady's tired drawl asking how she can help. Help. Jimmy knows that he needs it now.

"Operator? Yeah, get me Mississippi 662, please. Presley."

MISSISSIPPI KID

THE TRUCK'S TIRES CRUNCH ACROSS THE ASPHALT as Elvis pulls to a halt outside the diner. Early morning light breaks clouds and paints everything gold.

Prettiest time of the day. He opens the door and slides out.

The rain had made everything clean. That old bell above the door that had rung a hundred times before, rings again as he enters. He nods at Red, who is drawing heavily on his cigarette as he slouches his narrow shoulders past Elvis and out.

April is behind the counter, and when she looks up, her eyes still hold that slyness he remembers from the drive-in. Boy, does he remember it. And that's not all he remembers. One look at the way her uniform tugs at her chest reminds him well enough of those other things. Gets him hot just thinking about it, and he gives her that lopsided, syrupy smile that has bought him many similar memories with a lot of similar girls. Mama always said he was gonna wind up on the wrong side of a shotgun if he wasn't careful. He stops himself thinking about that. Mama wasn't there to scold him no more.

"What'll it be, stranger? Your usual?"

He nods, yanking the cap from his head, running his hands through his tousled quiff.

"Haven't seen you around lately?"

He nods again, swinging himself onto a stool.

"Elvis Aaron Presley! Did the cat catch your tongue? Don't you know it's beyond rude to ignore a lady when she's askin' you a question!?"

"Apologies, April." He ducks his head and takes the coffee that she offers him. "It's been a long night."

Her cheeks flush and she taps at the locket around her neck, the one he'd given her without too much thought.

"Well... Never you mind that then. No harm done." She turns, busies herself with some pastries. "There's a message here for you. Bessie ran it down. Says some fella from the city was tryin' to get hold of you..."

"City?" He frowns, trying to think of whether he knows anyone in either LA or New York, and can think of no-one.

Picking up the paper, April slides it across the counter, next to the cup roosting between his hands, taps it.

"Says right here. Dean." She watches his frown deepen. "You know him?"

He knows him alright. Hasn't heard from him in over five years though. Not since that business down in Mexico City. Right after Mama passed. The two of them had barely scraped out of the whole mess alive. He's got a good mind to just screw up the message, but something stops him. He squints at the note's single sentence scrawled below Jim's name.

This is worse than Mexico. Call me.

Driving home he had sung low to the radio. Sam Cooke doing that thing he did. The rain beating the windshield matches his fingers drumming on the steering wheel. It's a nervous percussion, filled with none of its usual cheer.

Worse than Mexico? What could be worse than that?

Left it all behind. That's what he'd thought. Still could if he wanted to.

Baby boy. You know better than to get involved with this. Stick to what you know.

And what's that, mama? What do I know? Working my ass off for that S.O.B. Wilson down at Crown Electric?

Mama's voice in his head stays silent. She wouldn't have done so in real life, he knows. She would've given his ear a real lashing.

Pop's in the kitchen when he enters the house through the creaking screen door. He looks up as Elvis rolls in. He's dropped weight since Mama passed. His eyes are a little sunken, and they glitter as lightning flares, making bright the dim space of the kitchen. The storm that was threatening earlier had taken on a savage tone.

"Somethin' troublin' you Son?" The man's drawl is gentle, unassuming.

They lock stares, son to father. Elvis flashes him a grin, the same one that he uses on everyone when he wants to avoid talking. Pop probably knows better, but he says nothing. Grunts as he stands, moves out of the kitchen and through the front room towards the porch. He waits for the screen door to close. Later, Elvis will join him so they can sit in companionable silence, something adopted now that Mama had left them. For now, he's got to think about whether or not he wants to make a bad decision.

It's a long pause before he lifts the phone. He asks Bessie to put him through to Jim's number and she does. The phone rings, and rings, and just as Elvis thinks it's going to ring out and he'll be off the hook, Jim answers. There's a pause as he waits, hoping he won't have to be the first to speak. But he does, just like it always is with Jim Dean.

"It's me." Doesn't need to tell Jim who the *me* is. Boy was sharper than a barrel full of swordfish.

"Thanks for callin' back so quickly." He sounds jittery, like he's drunk too much coffee.

"Make it quick. I'm pullin' night shift and I gotta get some shut-eye."

"Hey E, how you been?" Jimmy's voice was all angles and points, but sounded like it always did, as if it was coming through a detuned radio.

Elvis nestles the phone between cheek and shoulder and looks through the front room to the screen door. Nothing. For the best really, wouldn't do to let the old man hear this.

"Listen Jim, I'm callin' you back as a favor. You saved my ass in Mexico, but I didn't think it would come with a price tag. Now cut the chit-chat and tell me straight. What is it?"

"Oh, I think I got some trouble... Maybe the kind that could see me wind up in a pine box, you know?

"That bad, huh?" Elvis plays it casual, not wanting to fuel nerves. Still, he has to know. "Anythin' to do with Mexico?"

"No." Jim says it and Elvis feels a little stab of guilt lacing the relief. He was still free. Just needed to finish this call and go to bed. Forget the whole damn thing.

Hang it up. Just hang it up, Elvis. Walk away.

"Well, at least that's somethin'." He grimaces. "Okay, so what is it then?"

There's a shaky breath and the clink of ice hitting glass.

"Friend of mine. She died recently. Suicide... Or at least, that's what they're sayin'."

"Hey man, Well, uh, I'm sorry to hear that."

"Thing is, I'm calling bullshit on the whole thing."

"How's that now?" Elvis frowns, listens to the sound of liquid splashing, a swallow and a sharp intake of breath.

"No way she would. No way." For a moment, Elvis thinks that Jim is talking to himself. The voice is distant, like the roll of thunder that follows in the silence. "It's Marilyn."

"Marilyn?" He asks as if he doesn't know, but Mississippi wasn't on another planet, regardless of what those on the east and west coasts thought. "You're shittin' me?"

"No."

There's a finality to the word, as tall and unbreachable as the Rockies.

"Are you okay, Jim?"

"No, E. I don't think so."

He looks out the window. The clouds are glowering and they set the tone. He sighs, hanging his head, dark forelock grazing his forehead, as soft as Mama's touch had been.

"I'm comin'."

He packs the truck. Pop stands behind him, watching Elvis with hands jammed deep into the pockets of his work pants. His face was worn, lined with the grief that had been there since Mama went. Now those lines look deeper. Like Elvis telling him his plans to head West had applied some pressure that was deeper on an unseen level. He tosses the shotgun in last.

"You expectin' trouble, Son?" His voice is casual, but Elvis knows his father better than to take things at face value.

Elvis shrugs, then turns, trying for an easy grin but not quite getting there. "Well... You know what those city boys are like?"

"Nope. I do not."

Elvis opens the door, then sighs. "No, I guess you don't."

"Don't do anything that'll make your Mama sad."

"I won't, Pop." Not that Mama would be happy with him going at all. Maybe that's why her ghost is keeping quiet.

He swings himself into the cab and then Pop is there beside the open window. He rests a hand on his son's, gives it a quick squeeze. Elvis reverses the truck, then drives, refusing to look in the rearview mirror.

Night time cloaks his route from Tupelo. The rural landscape, spattered with oaks, whisks past unseen. With the window down, his hair is untethered from its tight slick and whips around his head. He hums low to the radio, occasionally singing when he warrants the song good enough. It's a good voice, strong, low and clear. Mama said he should've done something with it, but he didn't have the money, or the motivation. Best he had used it for was gettin' girls like April into the sack.

Heading South and West, driving long diagonal miles as he zig zags across highways, but always striving for the coast. When he's hungry, he stops at 7-11s, always opting for a cheeseburger, sometimes washing it down with a Coca-Cola. The cheeseburgers all taste the same, and not really like anything at all. Night bleeds out into day and he blinks in the sudden emergence of light. The greenery is still there but Elvis knows it'll fade as quickly as the night as he forges past Texas.

Dallas is already awake as he pulls over and climbs into the bed of the truck to catch a few hours sleep. Wouldn't do Jimmy any good if he were to drive the truck into a ditch. The tall, clean buildings grazing the big Lonestar sky make him feel small. He rolls over and shuts his eyes, the noise from passing traffic becoming a lullabye. In his sleep, he dreams that his Mama is watching him. Her kind, sweet eyes look sad and she's talking but he can't quite catch what it is she is trying to tell him.

Coming to with a start, Elvis looks at the sun high above, thinks that he's slept longer than he should've. He shuffles out of the truck bed and smooths back his hair as he climbs into the cab. His stomach rumbles, but he has no desire to stay in Dallas any longer than he has to. The truck takes a couple of tries to get started, and he's glad when he finally gets it going and threads his way into the traffic. Long curving lanes carry him on. The sky is the same faded blue as his jeans and the sun pursues his journey Westward.

Short scrubby trees flash past as he comes and goes through Fort Worth. Elvis swings North, angling it towards the long asphalt snake of Route 66 that will carry him towards the shining beacon of LA. Didn't think it was possible that the land could become any flatter, but as the daylight starts to wane, it does. The flatness is contradicted by long shadows that spread out in a fan from the surrounding mountain ranges, breaking the plains like slumbering giants.

It hits Elvis, how a place could feel so empty, and how small he is amongst the breadth of the space around him. The tallest building in Dallas might as well be nothing but a pin. As stars start to pierce the sky's blanket, he pulls over to take a leak, and it strikes him a second time. This absurd act against the grandeur of the world. It makes him want to get back in the truck, swing it back in the direction he had come, and live out his life as his Pop was doing.

Snorting, he gives the dirt a kick, as if that would assert some kind of dominance over his misgivings. Sliding back behind the wheel he pushes on, New Mexico welcoming him as greedily as any lover might. The truck gives him some trouble and after splicing and patching the radiator hose with one of his mother's old pantyhose, he nurses it all the way to Albuquerque. A room for the night at the King's Hotel swallows most of his money, but at least he is able to shower, eat something other than a cheeseburger, and sleep in a real bed.

He hits the bar for a quick beer before bed, still tasting the road's heat in the back of his throat as he downs the bottle in three quick gulps. A soft, plaintive voice says from behind him "You look like you got a real thirst, Mister."

He turns and sleepy brown eyes give him a full appraisal as he hooks both his arms on the bar. He raises his hand, holding one finger up, then squints and points at her, cocking his head. She nods slowly and he raises another finger to order a beer for her too. The girl sidles up to Elvis like a wary doe, but shows her boldness by taking the stool next to his. She smells like Geraniums as she leans forward to take the bottle of beer. Taking his own, Elvis watches her, eyes hooded, a mixture of lust and tiredness.

"You travelling alone?" She drinks, nursing the bottle invitingly.

He says nothing, just nods, knowing how this will end up but surprised by her directness all the same. She puts her hand on his, and the bartender glances their way as they quickly finish their drinks and leave the bar. They're barely up the stairs and she's already working at his belt. He grabs her and pulls her in tightly, one hand cupping her breast through her work shirt, fabric coarse against his palm. Her hand is in his jeans as he fumbles his key in the lock and falls backwards into the room through the suddenly open door. On the other side, he kicks it closed and then his jeans are down and she's on her knees, working at him with her mouth.

His head bangs back against the wall, and he strokes her cheek unwittingly, fingers jerking. He savours her attention, then lifts her and carries her to the bed, fingers plying the space between her legs. She's wet but he takes his time sliding her panties to one side and entering her. He kisses her, tasting himself on her lips. She wraps her legs around his waist and they move rhythmically against each other. The firm pressure of her comes and goes and he groans and closes his eyes. Her fingers touch his face and he sucks at them.

"You want another surprise?" Her voice is loud in the quietness of the room.

"Mmhm" He mumbles, voice low and rough.

Light spills in and he grunts, pushing himself back from her in shock. A dull pain blooms in the back of his head and he falls, catching a glancing blow off the corner of the bed. His cheek comes to rest on carpet that smells faintly of cigarettes. He hears her voice as consciousness is stolen from him.

"What took you so long?"

Another voice, this one masculine "You didn't look like you..."

Then darkness.

THE FIRST CUT

LANCER IS IN A BAD MOOD. Just as Lancer isn't the President's real name, his isn't Bull either. It's just what the other guys in the Service call him. Maybe it made them more comfortable to deny who they were working with? His actual name is Bai Abdallah if you wanted to be neighborly about it, but Bull fit him about as well as the black suit he wore.

Some of the other agents in the detail were real social types. Would fit in well at one of Jackie's frequent cocktail parties, but Bull was not that interested, truth be told. He watches as Jack kicks a waste basket across the oval office, spilling trash as it goes. Seems like blackmail really put a dent in the Commander-in-Chief's mood.

"Goddamn it." Not very Catholic of the man, Bull thinks, but keeps the smirk to himself.

Bull says nothing. Gets the feeling that saying anything right now would be a very career-limiting move. Risky enough that he was Arabic. Bull held no illusions other than that Jack had brought him on board to appear more progressive. Just one more way that the great one could convince the people that he didn't care about where a person had come from. What did Bull care anyway? The work was good and only stressful when Jack decided that he wanted to get amongst it and put himself in harm's way.

Johnson steps in, thick neck corded. It was ironic they called Bai what they did with this guy around. About as subtle as a sledgehammer. As if to prove Bull's point, the Veep comes in swinging.

"With all due respect, Mister President, if you had kept your dick in your pants, we wouldn't be in this mess." His Texan drawl makes the insult sharper than it would be from someone else's mouth. He shakes his head. "A damn actress."

Jack's eyes become slits, and his jaw bunches, but he doesn't say anything. Instead, he strides purposefully to the oak desk and sits behind it. He places his hands casually together on its surface. When he speaks again, the angry edge has left his voice and he has his cool back.

"Well, Lyndon, that, ah, ship has already sailed, apparently." he sighs, leaning back in the chair. "So what I'm asking for here are solutions, rather than accusations." He turns away, closes his eyes and pinches the bridge of his nose, then says under his breath. "Christ. Blackmail of all things..."

Bull steps forward, Johnson watching him with narrowed eyes "Mister President, I can head out to LA? Sort this out for you?"

Jack cracks an eyelid, piercing blue eyes locked onto Bull, bearing down with all of their charismatic weight. He swivels and leans forward.

"Go on."

"The call was traced, yes?"

Jack looks down and taps his desk then back up at Bull, this time turning his full stare on the man before speaking.

"Yes."

"Give me an address and I'll take care of it. Make the blackmailers aware of what will happen if they were to continue."

Johnson goes to object, but Jack waves the Veep silent

"You do know how important discretion is in this? Don't you Agent?"

Bull nods simply. No point saying anything more. Everyone in the room knew what was happening here. Someone was trying to pull a fast one on the highest office in the land, and there was no way that could happen. Not now. Jack makes a show of thinking it over, but there was no need for it. What else could he decide?

"You have full authorization to deal with them as you see fit."

"Very good, Mr. President. I'll get it done."

Bull is fixing a sandwich in the kitchen when Johnson comes in. He stands there for a moment and they stare at each other. When the Veep finally speaks, his voice is low, but the current running through his words is jagged and sharp.

"You got a hell of a lot of nerve, you little shit-stain." He jabs a finger in Bull's chest. Bull ignores it, takes a bite of his sandwich. "I hope you realize you're on your own in this. Plausible deniability. You know what that is, right?"

There was a threat. Not a very good one, but one all the same. Johnson steps back, studying Bull from head to toe as if he is livestock. He snorts air and turns on his heel. Bull sighs, takes another bite, then leans back. Maybe he shouldn't have thrown his hat in the ring? Isn't certain why he had. As much as he took his role seriously, this seemed like it had the potential to blow into a scandal. Shaking his head, he finishes the sandwich.

He had an address, and regardless of what happened when he got there, he was still on the payroll. Surely protecting the

President meant handling reputational risk as well? He takes the elevator down, staring at the scrap of paper with the address on it. He had looked it up. A studio address in West Hollywood. He pockets the scrap. In some ways, LA was more of a political cesspit than DC.

Exiting the elevator, he heads to the motor pool and signs out one of the shiny new Lincolns. Taking the service driveway out of the basement he swings into late evening DC traffic and flicks the radio on. The news is full of the usual Cold War shit. Soviets doing Nuke tests. Lots of Americans getting worked up about the potential of a nuclear war, but it was all the same to Bull. You didn't grow up where he had and not develop a certain casual attitude towards life and death. You enjoyed what you got and when it was gone, you didn't bitch about it.

He settles in for the drive to Dulles. Brand spanking new airport to accommodate the influx of people that the Kennedy administration was expecting to flood in to greet his Holiness, John Fitzgerald Kennedy the First. It might seem that Bull held disdain for the man, but in truth, it was the opposite. He got it. You couldn't sit around waiting for power to fall into your lap. You had to go out and take it. In that regard, he admired the Pres. Just couldn't get behind all the grandstanding that went with it. But maybe that was just him?

Checking in, he sits and skims a back issue of Time Magazine. Same old, same old between the covers. They call his flight and he follows other passengers out the gate. Seems like security is a little tighter than it used to be. A guard eyeballs him, but lets him pass without incident. Stepping outside, rain catches the tarmac and turns it into a starfield, reflecting back the lights of the aircrafts and the terminal. He boards the plane. A generically beautiful stewardess gets him a glass of water and a newspaper. He reads a few columns, yawns, puts it down and closes his eyes. He is asleep within moments.

Bull blinks awake, yawns and stretches, then peers out the window. Coming in on the final approach to LAX. Just under seven hours in the blink of an eye. Not that he's complaining of course. A little sleep has got him feeling juiced and ready to go. The plane lands and it takes them about ten minutes to disembark.

He had made a few calls before he had left DC, old favors from some guys he had worked with in the intelligence community. Better to show up informed. There wasn't much, but he had a few names. People higher up the food chain. The rest he could find out by asking around and see what he could shake out. People loved talking, especially around Bull. He made it look easy.

He hires a car, throws the briefcase in the backseat. The car is nothing too fancy, just something to get him from A to B. He knew that a few of the other agents loved making a big deal that they were meat shields for the Pres. but Bull thought that the key to that part of his role was subtlety. The art of looking like you were there without being there. The other important part of the job was being observant. Spotting the things that other people missed out. He stops at a roadside diner and grabs some coffee and pie. It's good and he helps himself to a second cup.

If he were another sort of person, he might head straight to the studio, but Bull is who he is. Instinctual. He prefers to play with a full deck, and right now, he feels like there's something that he doesn't know. Easy enough to stick to the story that someone has something on old Philandering Jack, who just so happens to also be President Jack. It feels too simple.

What about Monroe? He had seen the anger in the President's face when the Veep had bought her up, but what about the fear in his eyes. Yes. Something was scaring the shit out of the man. Bull had seen plenty of variations of it in his lifetime. Enough to tell him that he should go with his gut and follow the thing that made the most powerful man in the United States, maybe even the world, afraid.

Bull consults a road map and marks out a route to Monroe's house. Not too hard to get to. They had built LAX centrally enough that commutes to and fro would be easy. Besides, LA was now a driving city, even if it hadn't started out that way. The freeways carry him North to Brentwood and he gets off. He's changed from his suit into civilian clothing. Subtlety. No point giving anyone thoughts about who he might be, and who he might be here on behalf of.

Monroe's neighborhood is typical A-lister. Clean. Stinking of wealth. He pulls up to the gate and parks, sitting in the car while the engine ticks over. He sees two men talking by some crime tape. One spots him, leans in low to the other, whispers something and they approach his car. He winds down the window.

"Gonna have to ask you to move your vehicle. This is a crime scene."

Bull opens the door, gets out and flashes his badge, holding it long enough so they can see the image of the white house embossed on it.

"And I'm not here." Bull gives both men an easy smile, but lets them stare at the badge before putting it away. A risky move, given Johnson's warning, but these two looked like they could be threatened to silence easily enough. He steps forward, using his full height to effect. "I need to have a look around inside."

The two men look at each other, then back at him. The taller of the two men offers a hand. Bull grips it and shakes firmly "Detective Wyatt. LAPD.

Bull doesn't offer a name. Wyatt eyes him and then swallows.

"Well, uh, Let me show you around."

"I'll stay out here." The shorter man's mouth is turned down as he watches Bull. Bull ignores him.

"Sure, Ed." Wyatt leads the way, and they both duck under the tape before he and Bull enter the house.

Out of the sun, the interior is cool and inviting. Plush furniture and ornate wall hangings. A step up from Bull's own apartment back in DC by a long stretch, even with views of the Capitol. He looks around the room but sees nothing of interest.

"Where'd she die?"

"In the bedroom. She was found by her housekeeper this morning." Wyatt's cheeks flame a little. "In the nude."

Bull doesn't know what that has to do with anything but just nods and then gestures for Wyatt to show him the way. Not that he couldn't find it himself, but the less confrontational he makes this, the less it will give the Detective to think about later on. As they enter the bedroom, Wyatt stands there, as awkward as a teenager. Bull looks around then turns.

"Mind if I have a look on my own?" Bull says it congenially enough, but makes sure that Wyatt knows it isn't a request.

Have to give the guy some credit for having some balls. He looks like he's about to object, but then gives out a long sigh. Maybe he's caught on that what's happening right now goes way beyond his pay grade. He turns and leaves, and Bull allows his posture to slump. Seems the sleep on the flight over hadn't been as beneficial as he had first thought.

He starts grid searching the room, eyes flicking each corner and space. Not that he's been told what to look for, but he has an idea. His eyes fall on a wastebasket propped next to the door to the vanity room. It looks untouched. Casting a quick glance at the doorway, he steps forward and leans down. He delicately sifts through paper and tissues. He starts uncrumpling some. A line of text catches his eye.

Dr. S. Knopf.

He yanks it from the bin and flattens it out, eyes scanning the paper. Folding it neatly, Bull slips it in his pocket as footsteps beyond the door announce Wyatt's return.

"Got what you need?" It's Wyatt's turn to make it clear that his time was up.

Bull gives him a smile.

"I think so." He offers his hand. "Thanks for being so accommodating."

Wyatt pauses, looks back over his shoulder towards the front of the house.

"Are you alright, Detective?" Bull doesn't know what the man is thinking, but says nothing else, waiting to see what plays out.

"I have some information that may be worth something to you."

Bull waits.

"It could help you."

Bull sighs, reaches into his pocket, pulls out his wallet and yanks out a Ulysses, handing it to Wyatt. "Go on."

"Kid by the name of Dean was hanging around with Monroe before she offed herself. You might want to check him out... Maybe he has some information that your bos- "

Bull holds up a finger to his lips and Wyatt gives a start like a fish yanked on a hook. He nods slowly, showing he understands the direction if not the context. The Detective reaches into his pocket and opens a notebook, scrawling an address on a page before tearing it out and pushing it into Bull's hand.

Bull holds the paper, waits.

Wyatt's cheeks flash scarlet again.

"Is that it?"

Wyatt nods, then, when Bull says nothing further, coughs and gives his hand a limp shake.

"I'll see you out."

As they step outside into the bright sunlight, it dazzles Bull and he quickly replaces his sunglasses. Porter is standing off to one side, conversing with a uniformed officer. Both men watch him, Porter glaring. He gives the shorter of the two Detectives a friendly wave and returns to his car. The interior of the car is hot as he maps out a route to Jimmy Dean's house.

DESPERADOES

THE POOL HOUSE ISN'T A SAFE PLACE to crash anymore. Jimmy thinks about options, feeling that there are too few good ones. Shoving a few possessions into a leather bag, he secures the heavy brass clasp, picks it up and heads back out. He runs into Wallis by the pool, explains that he needs to split. Truth is that he should never have come back here.

The two men who took the book from him weren't messing around and there were no guarantees the cops wouldn't come back with more questions either. Too many what ifs to contend with. Wallis is a little nonplussed, but doesn't ask for details. Probably better that way. Instead, he takes Jimmy out to the garage, points to the Porsche Spyder that he hasn't driven for months.

"You know what I call it?" he tosses Jimmy the keys with a rueful grin "Little Bastard. Makes sense that you should use it."

Jimmy hefts the keys, looks up at Wallis, working the corner of his mouth with his teeth. "This is a lot."

"Hell, kid, I'm not givin' it to you." Gives the car an appraising look. "Just try not to write it off... Or if you do, make it good enough that I can at least claim the insurance."

"Thanks Wallis."

"Don't mention it." Wallis slaps a hand on Jimmy's shoulder. "Oh... One more thing..." Wallis moves to a wall, pushes a painting of a Ferrari to one side then quickly dials a combination into the wall safe behind it. "You might need this."

Jimmy fumbles the catch slightly. It's a pistol, snub-nosed and compact, but a gun all the same, designed for one purpose.

"Uh... Wallis..." Of course he had shot rifles with his Uncle back on the farm, but this was different. "I-"

"Don't be an idiot, Jim." He nods at the weapon, then at Jimmy's bruises. "Better to have it and not need it, than need it and not have it, understand what I'm getting at?" He gives Jimmy a solid stare. "I'm not kidding. When the chips are down, and it's either you or the other guy... Well, you know what to do."

Jimmy nods, swallows, then slips the gun behind his back, wedged in the waistband of his pants. "Listen Hal, I've got a friend coming into town. Southerner. Good looking. He knows that I was living here. Tell him I'm staying at the Cecil. He's to ask for Demille at the front desk, I'll tell them to give him a key."

Wallis eyeballs Jimmy, sighs, then shoos him as he would an insect. "Get out of here. I'm about at the limit of my curiosity." Jimmy turns and jumps in the Porsche, starts the engine.

"You take care of yourself, James" Wallis calls over the roar of the engine.

The wind whips Jimmy's scruffy hair. It feels good, like it's blowing away most of his cares. Doesn't fix anything of course. His Uncle had always said that his curiosity would get the better of him. Sad to think the old man was going to be proven right. Still, he needed to get that book back, if for no other reason than it held something that people wanted, but wasn't theirs to take.

Whatever was in it was irrelevant. To Jimmy, it was just something of hers that should be kept private. The press and the studios had done a good enough job of destroying her life to the point where she had seen no way out. If nothing else, he could preserve her dignity. Strange to think of the lengths he would go to for someone he had only just met, but there was kinship there. Jimmy thinks of where to start and then the answer comes to him.

Ciro's.

It was where the LA underbelly and A-Listers came together. A melting pot of celebrity and corruption, and most likely where he could find some answers. Ciro's had been built down on Sunset back in the Forties, and was still going strong. He had been there a couple of times with Marilyn. Wouldn't be hard to get in. The door staff all knew and liked him, regardless that he was now *persona non grata* in the biz.

He swings the car down towards the Canyon, planting his foot, taking the corners tight. Big shrubs on one side, slopes lined with short trees, scrubby grass and retaining walls on the other. Just as he had with the bike, he pushes the car to the limit. It isn't that Jimmy had a death wish, he just needed this. The speed and the concentration required to keep himself tethered to the road are like a drug. Freedom within control.

Pretty soon he's at the bottom, low two-story buildings and palm trees replacing the hills. He sees the grifters and the wannabes doing their thing. Their eyes track his progress. The car is a stand out amongst the other traffic. The opulence of the car's upholstery feels unfamiliar and the sense of being an imposter gnaws at him. No matter how much time he spends in LA he can never get used to the feeling that he exists on its fringes.

He has a few hours to kill until Ciro's opens, swings the car towards Cecil's. His tank feels empty, like he's been running on too little sleep. Even without Marilyn's death, things had been getting more and more strung out. Sometimes he has to wonder why he had even come out here. Did he have any right to believe that he could make it big? There were plenty of others already cramming the audition rooms of this town that could outperform him. He remembers what Brando had said to him, when they had met at a party a month or so ago.

Get an analyst kid.

Wasn't too sure what the guy had meant by that. Maybe it was just his way of saying that this town was built for the screw ups? If that was the case, then he had every right to be here. What had his old man said to him? Barely could remember the guy's face, let alone anything he had to say. Still, it was there... buried behind all the bad stuff that came to the surface when he thought of his father.

You'll never amount to anything.

Sure showed you, Dad.

The Porsche looks out of place in the neighborhood surrounding the hotel. The Cecil doesn't. It looks like it had always been here and the surrounding slums had grown from it like branches on a dead tree. Whatever grandeur it had once possessed had faded long before Jimmy pulled up outside in the Porsche. Wallis' car insurance had better be substantial.

Orange and brown carpet gives the foyer a feel like the floor had been stained by dried blood. A big art-deco glass chandelier dominates the vaulted ceiling. It looks like a movie set, long forgotten and occupied by ghosts. A man with a thin beard scratches at needle tracks on his arms. He blinks yellowed eyes at Jimmy. Pushing towards the front counter, Jimmy can feel the man's stare even with his back turned.

The concierge could barely be called that. He wears his hair long, and it shields his acne scarred skin in a greasy fall. A circular cap is crammed onto his head at an angle and as Jimmy approaches, he looks up without a smile. He sighs, throwing the comic book he had been reading onto the counter. Jimmy gives him a smile that he doesn't feel, leans on the counter.

"Can I help you?"

"Yeah, you got any vacancies?"

The concierge looks around the lobby and its shuffling denizens. Just then, the elevator dings. The doors slide open and a squeaking repetition precedes the appearance of a stretcher being wheeled by a man in a white uniform. There is a formless shape draped with a white sheet resting on it. The man doesn't even look at them as he passes. The concierge watches the man disappear with his cargo, then flicks his attention back to Jimmy.

"Looks like we just had something open up." It's not a smile or sneer he gives Jimmy, something in between.

Ignoring the man, Jimmy checks in using the name Demille, just as he had told Wallis that he would. He lets the concierge know that he is expecting someone. The man eyes Jimmy speculatively and sucks at his gums, making a smacking sound. No surprises as to what would come next.

"Extra charges if you have someone stayin' with you."

Jimmy pulls out his money clip and peels off a couple of extra bills. He hands them over, gives the guy a flat look before releasing them.

"Anyone else comes asking for me other than my friend... I'm not here."

Any bets the money would do little to guarantee his privacy. He takes the key, turns to the elevator and rides it to the seventh floor. There is a rank odor in the confined space that pinches at his nostrils and makes him hold his breath. The elevator comes to a halt and he scurries out of its stinking grasp.

The hall beyond is not much more appealing, dingy and run down. Jimmy keeps alert despite his tiredness. He makes his way down to his room, slides the key in the lock and has to work it to get it to turn. Once through, he looks around. A poorly made bed bracketed by twin armchairs clad in deep mahogany leather that could use reupholstering. He drops his bag and sinks into one. A wash of exhaustion floods over him and he closes his eyes. Before too long he is wrapped in dreamless sleep.

HOUSE OF THE RISING SUN

THE SMELL OF EXHAUST BRINGS ELVIS awake as much as the sudden stop. The droning hum, that he guesses is an engine, falls silent. Damn, his head hurt fiercer than anything he could remember. He'd been in a few scrapes, but never had he been clobbered like that before. All his fault, letting his pecker do the thinking.

He hears the car's doors open and close and blinks as the darkness is replaced by a sudden wash of a flashlight. The torch's beam pins him straight in the face. He'd raise a hand to shield it, but they are both tied tightly behind his back. A thick gag in his mouth prevents him from cussing out the wielder of the flashlight.

A second figure becomes dimly present beside the first and two pairs of strong hands yank him from the trunk. He falls roughly to the ground, cool concrete bruising his cheek as he's slammed into it. The trunk clunks shut and he is hauled up, then dragged between his two captors. He tries to find his feet, but they tingle from long hours of inactivity and remain useless.

"No funny business, Redneck."

There it was, a thick brutish lilt to the man's snarl. Wiseguy speak. It tells Elvis everything that he needs to know about the situation he was dealing with. Didn't take a genius to put two and two together. Any bets these guys worked for Frazini. Seems like he hadn't waited long enough before poking his head out of Tupelo after Mexico. Should've listened to his gut and stayed put.

Dominic Frazini. The guy he and Jimmy had been running dope for. Also the guy they had screwed over when they had botched that last job that had nearly gotten them both killed. Stupid of him to think that they might've got away with it. Of course, he could be completely wrong, and this could be something entirely different, but he doubts it.

He's yanked into a service elevator. The three men are awkward passengers as they ascend. As the door opens, one releases Elvis and sticks his head out, looks up and down the corridor. He gestures for his companion and Elvis gets shoved out. They grip his arms again and half march, half drag him to a nondescript door. One of the men knocks, there is silence, and then the door swings open. A shame that he had to be right about what this was.

Frazini stands there, big nostrils flaring, small eyes glittering in the lamplight coming from the suite. He looks behind him, waves a hand. Elvis glimpses a blonde vanish into another room, bare skin catching the light. Frazini jerks his head towards the room and the two thugs drag Elvis in. They tug the gag from his mouth. Dried sweat feels gritty on his scalp as he is dumped into a chair. He rocks a little and one of Frazini's men steadies him, almost gently. Elvis can't help himself, lets out a low chuckle. Frazini's eyes narrow, squinted and piggy. He cocks his head to one side, examining Elvis. Elvis watches him carefully, as he might a rattlesnake.

"Something funny?" Frazini keeps that stare going, really using up every last ounce of mileage on his hostility.

"Naw, man." Elvis' hadn't meant to sound like anything, but Frazini could find insult in a breath.

"You think you're in a good situation here?"

"Know that I ain't."

Frazini sighs, turns and walks back to a table, picks up a big Cuban and clips its end. He lights it, swallows a big gulp of the blueish smoke, then exhales. The guy liked to dramatize things. He stops with his back turned to Elvis and the two thugs. A clock ticking somewhere in the suite really finishes off the scene. Finally, he relents, turns back and comes and sits in the yellow velour armchair set across from Elvis.

"Imagine you're in my situation? What would you do?"

Elvis makes a show of looking around the suite, taking in the glitzy decor. He kinda likes it, even if it's the complete opposite of his world. His life was one of mud, fields, dirt roads, open air and backbreaking labor. This was like someone had draped a veil over the real world, made it something that it should never be.

"Hell, Hoss." He shifts his shoulders, trying to ease the strain on his bound hands. "I wouldn't know the first thing about what it'd be like to be in your situation."

Frazini laughs at that, gives Elvis a good look over before getting serious again.

"Where's your boyfriend?"

Ain't no secret who Frazini is referring to, but Elvis plays dumb all the same.

"Who?" Elvis furrows his straight brow as if that would convince Frazini to leave it alone.

"What was his name again?" Sort of cute that the mobster would go to all this effort to put on a show for Elvis' benefit. "Oh yeah..." clicks his fingers around the cigar, sending ash everywhere. "...Jimmy, right?

"Haven't seen him in years."

"That so?"

"Yeah..." Elvis tries not to let any of the fear that he's feeling creep onto his face.

"You think you're clever?" Frazini puts the cigar down, lets it rest in the ashtray, still burning.

"Not really." Elvis knows what a rhetorical question is, but doesn't feel in the mood for humoring Frazini. "If you're gonna kill me, why don't you just shut up and get on with it already?"

"Kill you?" Frazini looks at his men, gives another short laugh. They look at each other, big dumb faces filled with confusion, then each laughs uncertainly. "You think I brought you here to kill you?"

Elvis keeps still. Seems like he'd found himself playing a different game to the one he thought he'd been playing. Frazini picks up the cigar, gives the end the zippo treatment, sucks in a big mouthful of smoke, then blows it into Elvis' face. Elvis coughs, then blinks.

"No, no, no, my friend. I'm not gonna kill you." He leans back, drapes the hand holding the cigar across the back of the armchair. "The way I see it, you owe me for Mexico. You and that little fuck up cost me money. Not a lot, mind you. Not compared to what I have already. I could've let it go, but... Now you're out and about, people might start to think that old Dominic is growing soft in letting you go wherever the hell you like. That would set a bad example. So here's what's gonna happen. You're gonna continue on your way to see your old pal, Jimmy. Yeah, don't look surprised. The outfit has a lot of dirt on a lot of people. Bigger people than you. We have our fingers in all sorts of info. Friends in higher places than you would assume. When you catch up with him... Well, I think you can work that part out, right?"

Why they weren't putting him in an unmarked grave somewhere as well is beyond Elvis. He wasn't much for thinking, but that didn't stop him wondering if all of this wasn't something else. Maybe tied up to Jimmy's thing?

"And if I don't?"

"How's your Pop, Elvis?" The way Frazini says it makes Elvis' skin crawl. "He keeping well?"

Elvis doesn't say anything.

"So we understand each other?"

"Yeah." Elvis' knows better than to hesitate.

"Good boy." Frazini nods and one of the men loosens Elvis' bonds. "You want a drink? You look a little pale."

Frazini stands and makes his way to a small circular table holding a bottle. What looks like expensive bourbon glistens deep amber. The mobster pours out a measure, holds it out towards Elvis. He glares at it dully before taking it.

"Listen kid, you do what we ask, you got no problems." He smiles. It's a warm smile, but Elvis figures that Frazini is a good actor. "We'll be square. You get that, right?"

Elvis takes a sip. First time he'd had bourbon that didn't burn in a harsh way. It glides warmly down his throat and, despite everything, takes away a little of the nerves. Frazini gets up, and Elvis follows suit. He hands Elvis a wad of cash and a stack of chips.

"Go downstairs, enjoy yourself before you head off." His grip on Elvis' shoulder is firm. "Take the edge off. When you're ready, Michael here will take you to a car."

As Elvis stands outside the door, free from Frazini, he's got this feeling like he's been thrown into a cage, one that there was no way out of.

Wandering from the elevator in a daze, he sees the main floor of the joint is heaving. A non-stop procession of people set to blow their dough at the tables or go home winners. A gaggle of dancing girls walks past, but he's too out of it to worry about them. That should've told him everything he needed to know about his situation. He angles for a bar and seats himself on a stool while the crowd's murmur and the sounds of gaming tables creates a kind of music.

The bartender is pretty, made up in a way that could keep a guy drinking for a long time. Elvis points to a bottle on the back wall, waits as she pours him a double. He downs it in one go, then holds up two fingers again. The second one he takes his time with. A quick glance behind him shows him Michael, standing attentively and watching Elvis. Seems like even if he tries to make a dash for it, he wouldn't get far.

Thinking on it, Elvis can't believe that he had been so stupid. Going back to Tupelo had been a chump's move. He had put his only family right in Frazini's crosshairs. Perhaps if he did run for it now? Get back to Tupelo before they knew what was up and... And what? Another dumb move. Frazini would have that possibility covered for sure. No. Seemed like the only way out of the fix he was in was to do as Frazini had said. Elvis doesn't know why he had been let off the hook and Jimmy hadn't, but he suspected there wasn't anyway that he would ever find that out.

He turns and raises his glass to Michael and the man stares at him with zero expression. Looks like his new companion would be a fun guy to hang with. Elvis drains the glass, leaves some bills on the bar with a generous tip. Not his money anyway. He walks out of the bar area, shoving his hands in his pockets. His rumpled clothing and unkempt hair draws some stares but he ignores the gawkers. Lights flash in his eyes and the noise becomes overwhelming.

He steps outside and looks up at the big sign that proclaims in flashing neon that the place is the Sands. Beyond the sign, the dark surrounding Vegas clutches at it greedily. Michael comes and stands beside him, a silent presence. Elvis takes a battered packet of cigarettes from his pocket, pulls out a broken one, then offers it to his new shadow. The man doesn't even acknowledge the offer.

"You like it here?" Elvis isn't expecting an answer, is surprised when he gets one.

"I don't get paid to like things."

"No, I guess most of us don't." Elvis finishes his cigarette, flicks it towards the curb. "Come on, let's get this done."

ROCK THE CASBAH

BULL REACHES DEAN'S HOUSE. From where he's parked, he's got a pretty good vantage point. He can see an older guy, former good looks running soft, sitting on a bench next to a brunette. The brunette has got some looks too alright and Bull watches the two talking. They seem to have the marriage thing nailed. Both lean into each other as if they are genuinely interested in what the other has to say. It's a rare little snapshot that he hadn't been expecting.

Bull has to wonder if he's chasing a dead end? Maybe the cop wanted him to waste his time? Still, if pulling President Jack out of the shit meant following every little lead, then it was his sworn and solemn duty to do so. He keeps watching. The brunette stands and gives the guy a peck on the top of the head before moving indoors. The guy picks up a paper and starts skimming it. It looks like he's reading an issue of Variety. A movie type then? That would make sense.

He gets out of the car and picks his way down a slope. The bottom of the slope meets a wall that wouldn't give Bull too many problems. He vaults the wall, pulling his piece at the same time. The guy peers up at him for a moment, sees the gun and raises his hands. He looks like someone had sucked all the blood out of his face. Big eyes track Bull's movements. He levels the gun, puts a finger up to his lips. Could've done this the official way, but this guy was not the cops. No need for a light touch. Didn't matter how much clout he had on a studio lot, it was just him and Bull. As far as power went, the scales were now tipped in Bull's favour.

"I'm gonna ask you some questions. Yes and no types. Just nod or shake your head... got it?" Bull keeps his voice low.

The man nods his head.

"Good. Just like that. James Dean? He live here?"

The man nods again, hands slowly lowering, clasping the edges of the bench as if it could save him from the situation.

"He about?"

The man shakes his head.

"You know where he is?"

The man pauses and Bull doesn't hesitate to push the gun just a little bit towards him. It's enough. The guy flinches and then nods his head. Just then, the woman calls out, her voice getting closer.

"Can I get you a drink, darling?"

The man's eyes widen and Bull nods quickly, indicating that he should speak.

"No, I'm fine." The man's voice tremors, but Bull is impressed by the way that he gets it under control quickly. "I'm just going to be taking a call. I'll let you know when I'm done."

"Oh, okay." She sounds put out, but her voice grows faint again, as if she had turned and walked away from the door.

"Smart." Bull gives the man a brief smile. It says: *Keep going this way and everything will be alright.* "Okay, I'm gonna hand you a pen and a notebook. You're gonna write down where Dean went, then I'm gonna be out of your and your lovely girl's life forever."

The man waits, whole body tense as if someone has put some serious voltage through him. Bull produces the pen and notebook, hands it to the man. He makes sure to keep the gun thrust forward, a reinforcement of what he wants. The man takes the pen, looks at it hard, then sighs as if he doesn't even realize he had. He starts scribbling and then hands the pen and notebook back. He leans back, watches Bull as he scans what's been written on the page.

"I'm gonna assume that you've done the right thing and this will check out, if not..." Bull gives the door a little glance.

He turns without waiting to see if the guy has got the message. Bull smiles. Always had a knack for getting to the bottom of things quickly. He tucks the notebook and pen back into his pocket and vaults the wall. Making his way back up the slope, he reaches his car and gets in. It's hot inside, but he sits for a minute, opening the map book. From here to the Cecil is a walk in the park. Bull cracks the window, dons his sunglasses and starts the car. Pulling away from the curb, his stomach rumbles. Food would be a good idea before anything else. No point going in on an empty stomach, regardless of wanting to get the job done. Something about the weather out here was playing with his focus. Too warm. Dreamlike almost.

Truth is, Bull doesn't want to hurt the kid, just wants to find out what he knows. Chances are that Monroe blabbed to him something, but Bull hopes that isn't the case. If Dean does know something, well... Bull would have to deal with it when he had to. That was the way of it. Duty before anything else. Bull had known what duty was before he had even met the Pres. It was what he had grown up with. His father had made it big during the oil boom in the Middle East, moved them out to the States ten years back. Lot of sacrifices. Always travelling back and forth internationally, leaving it to his mother to raise him. So he had that expectation to succeed riding on his shoulders the whole way through school. Keep the old man proud of giving his son a name.

Turned out education didn't trump racism though. Even with a degree in Political Science, the best Bull could manage was the Service. Guess at least the citizenship had helped with that. Heading West, he drives through suburban neatness, away from Sherman Oaks. Flicking on the radio, he hears that new tune that he likes. What was it called again? Can't remember, but one of the guys had told him that it was something to do with Heroin. His thoughts wander with the passing scenery. Tiredness and the weather again.

Los Angeles was a funny town. Polar opposite in some ways to DC. There was this weight of history in DC that LA didn't have, at least not in the same way. Sure, it had a lot of stories, but most of them felt insubstantial. Snapshots of history that lends the place more weight than what it actually possesses. The sight of a burger stand and his growling stomach interrupt his meandering thoughts. Yeah, definitely a good idea to eat. Pulling over the car, he gets out, mouth already watering.

Seems like he was always tired, no matter how much sleeping he did. Jimmy rolls out of bed, feeling the sweat lacing his back. He shrugs, looks towards the bathroom and decides against it. Too much of everything bottled up inside him right now to stop. Ciro's is the only thing on his mind. There's this feeling in his gut that is more urgent than anything else. Ciro's was where he'd find what he wanted. He was certain of it.

Jimmy feels friendless and it drives up his nerves. Even with the tension that was there in the phone call, he can't wait for E to get here. He fumbles getting dressed, like he's ready to rush out the front door now if he could get away with going to Ciro's dressed as he is. Maybe he should be making more of an effort, but in this town, nobody noticed a nobody. If you didn't have money, then forget it. You were nothing but an extra.

He unpacks his least rumpled suit and dons it. Exiting the hotel, he stifles a laugh. Little Bastard is still there, unmolested. He jumps into the front seat, glad to be doing something. He opens the glove compartment. Sees the dark mass of the gun sitting there. Quickly, he shuts it and swallows before starting the car. Planting his foot, the car roars and he feels guilty for trailing rubber. It's quickly forgotten with the speed. The car is quick. Exhilarating. He takes corners and pedestrians gape as he rushes past.

He evens out the speed, remembering the cops. Better that he doesn't draw any more attention to himself than what he has already. Ciro's. Gotta get to Ciro's. Marilyn might be at Ciro's, held in the grasp of some Gorilla. Somewhere she didn't belong. Just like she didn't belong on a slab. Everything about that was all wrong. Might as well be him lying there, all cold faced and stiff, they are that alike. Getting that book back was more important to him than working out why she had gone the way she had.

He pulls around back, where he's sure he can get some parking. Before he gets out of the car, he sits for a few moments. Stills his breathing. The evening light throws things into halves. Half light and half shadow. Sitting behind the club, he hears laughter. It's a little too much joy and he has to take a few moments more. Anytime that he had been here had been with her. Now it was just him and a feeling of loneliness that strikes at him like an unseen assailant. Has to get it together. No good to anyone if he falls apart now.

He checks his look in the mirror, straightens his mouth into that rueful, sad grin that he wears most of the time. It's what people know him for. Marilyn had called it his secret weapon. Right now, he's wielding it to full effect. Brings it into play with the doorman. The guy looks at him and nods, then gives him another hard stare that makes Jimmy think that the game is up. Then the doorman gets distracted and Jimmy takes full advantage of it, slipping past and inside.

Ciro's interior is all red velvet. A looping, baroque design that might have been at home in a dance hall sixty years ago. Overstuffed chairs and a broad stage dominate the room. The smile he uses as a disguise keeps trying to slip, but Jimmy holds it in place, looking from face to face, working hard to keep the intensity in check. He makes a beeline for a subtle door set to the left of the stage. A big guy in a tux stands next to it, completely removing any secrecy. He eyeballs Jimmy before a veil of recognition drops across his broad features. Jimmy shoves his hands in his pockets, not making eye contact with the guy.

He holds his breath, but doesn't need to. The doorman admits him, and he ducks through, not believing his luck. A long hallway leads him towards the rear of the building, lighting dim and oppressive. Breaching the entrance to the gaming room at the back, he surveys the neat rows of tables. The patrons were digging the place, but Jimmy finds something almost toxic about it. The Club's guests stood, transfixed by the games, watching their money come and go in tides of chips.

Scanning the room, he tries to keep it casual, but even now, Jimmy feels as if he is standing on the brink. Big men that looked like they lived hard lives peppered the crowd. He switches his focus, watching them, trying to pick out a familiar face. His eyes land, pausing on each one before moving onto the next. He freezes when his eyes skim past and return to a single person. His heart thuds, and sounds in his ears like waves crashing upon a shore.

That was the guy, or one of them at least. The one that counted anyway. He had been the one that had taken the book. Marilyn's captor in a sense. He's leaning in and talking to someone. Jimmy squints and then recognition sets in. Not just someone. That was Weinstein. Jimmy quickly turns, shielding his face, while still keeping both men in his sights. The men lean close to each other, watching the table while talking. He sees the thug glance away from Weinstein, towards where he is standing.

Something about the man's gaze is magnetic and Jimmy is drawn to it. He can't help it. He knows that he should try and hide, shield his face... Anything, but they stare at each other. The other man reaches the same place of recognition that Jimmy had only moments ago. He moves forward with the glacial mass of an unavoidable iceberg. Ordinarily, this would be a good time for Jimmy to run, but instinct roots him to the spot. Was this goon really gonna take him out in front of all these people? He has to dig his nails into the palms of his hands to stop from shaking.

The guy comes to a halt in front of him, movements ponderous. They lock eyes. He can still remember the tight grip of the thug's hand on his leg. Now that he has an opportunity to look, he can see the bruise that his kick had left on the man's cheek. Yeah. He'd got him a good one. The thing was a deep shade of purple that was oddly satisfying. Jimmy feels compelled to reach out and touch it. The thug is handsome in a brutish way. All these little details reduce Jimmy's fear, turning the man from a monster into something more human.

"Mr. Weinstein has asked that you leave." The clipped civility of the man's voice sounds awkward. "I suggest that you do."

The tone leaves no doubt about what would happen to Jimmy if he refuses. He bristles.

"Not leaving until you give me back what you took."

The man's fingers twitch, as if he isn't in full possession of them. Cricking his neck, he puts his chin forward.

"I don't know what you're talking about. Now, do I need to have security escort you outside?"

Familiarity aside, Jimmy had no doubt that the doorman would see him on his way if he didn't get wise and split. Jimmy glances past the man's shoulder, sees Weinstein watching the interaction. No point pushing this out any further. He has the who, now he just needs the why. He shrugs as if the whole thing is a huge misunderstanding, turns on his heel and struts away. He can feel eyes on him, tracking his departure. Kind of wishes that he had brought the gun. Who knows whether this will get taken any further once he has left the club.

The whole way back to the car, he is tense. The hairs on the back of his neck prickle and his stomach roils sourly. He gets in, turns the key in the ignition and revs the engine. Time to check back at the hotel, see if Elvis had finally rolled into town. It was a long shot. Mississippi to LA was no quick thing. Pulling out onto Sunset, he heads back towards the Cecil and its uncertain safety. The whole way he checks his mirror, worry gnawing at him that he may have poked the bear a little too hard.

Don't give up, Jimmy. Please don't give up.

Maybe Marilyn was as lonely in the afterlife as she had been here? Maybe she was just pushing him so that he could join her that little bit faster? Either way, she won't leave him alone and

Jimmy can't answer those questions. In a way, he doesn't need to, Marilyn does a good enough job for the both of them.

Hurry Jimmy. You're running out of time.

UNDER THE BRIDGE

THIS WAS THE THING ABOUT LA. You just couldn't match it for sprawl. While New York thrust its way out of the earth as if it had always been there, LA clung to the coast like a glamorous parasite, low and flat. In New York, the buildings obscured line of sight, but out on the West Coast, the city laid it all out for you, bookended by the mountains behind it. Six hours driving with Michael had left him stiff. The mobster's stolid presence was like riding with a brick wall. When they finally pull into a gas station driveway, Elvis is glad to get out of the car and stretch.

Any thoughts of splitting while the guy is in the restroom are quickly dissolved. Michael pockets the keys and takes them in with him. Elvis leans against the car, watching the headlights weave their way down the flanks of the San Gabriel Mountains. At the base of the range, the cloak of LA's lights spreads in an uneven fan. Elvis watches the traffic, mind drifting in his tiredness. His head still hurts from where he had been clobbered. He eyeballs the 7-11 attached to the gas station and wonders if Michael will shoot him if he goes and gets some Tylenol. He decides to risk it.

Way he figures, if Frazini wanted him dead, he would be already. Maybe him getting Elvis to ice Jim was just a convenient way of distancing himself from being implicated? Maybe once Elvis was done, it would be his turn next? As he enters the store, the bell rings. The clerk is an old guy and he looks up from a car magazine, eyeing Elvis as he places a packet of painkillers on the bench between them.

"That'll be eighty cents." His voice holds a dry croak of failure.

He rings up the sale as the door crashes open and Michael strides in. Both Elvis and the clerk look at him as if he has arrived from outer space.

"What?" Elvis holds up the packet of Tylenol, gives it a shake.

"You gotta go anywhere, you clear it with me first." His hand is near his jacket and Elvis doesn't need to see the bulge to know what he's concealing.

"Sure thing, chief... I just thought we were cool by now is all."

Michael grunts and stalks back outside. The clerk is studying Elvis with a keener eye.

"You alright, son?"

"Hell if I know." He thanks the man, turns and strides out. He gets in the car, waits in the passenger seat as Michael seethes. "You gonna be pissed all day, man?"

Michael says nothing, starts the car and they're back off on their way down the mountains. If he looks up high enough, beyond the diffused glare coming off the city, Elvis can see a faint spatter of stars. Back home, they were on full display. Would Pop be out on the porch now? Elvis wishes he could be there with him.

As LA draws closer, he tries as best he can to puzzle a way out of the mess he'd become involved in. Didn't help that he had Michael's immovable presence there in the car beside him as a constant reminder. The man's face is lit ghoulishly, the dash's green light turning it vile. Elvis reaches forward, switches on the radio. A broadcast is playing.

"*Hollywood is reeling after learning of the death of one of its most iconic stars. Marilyn Monroe was found dead by apparent suicide in her Brentwood home. The actress' body was discovered by her housekeeper. Several persons of interest were interviewed, but foul play was ruled out. More recently, Monroe had found herself in trouble over photographs of an erotic nature. She was 36.*"

The radio falls silent as Michael twists it off savagely. Elvis looks at him sidelong. Nothing there on the man's face to suggest why he had moved so quickly to shut it down. Suspicion lodges itself in the back of Elvis' brain and refuses to be budged.

The more he thinks about it, the more he starts to believe that all of this is more than just some big coincidence. Hell, if they had wanted to, they could've come for him or Jim at any time. Why wait? Why now?

Mexico wasn't something that he liked to think about too often these days. The way he and Jim had been busted down there like that had stunk of a set-up. Big time. Like an easy way to get rid of them, without the dirty work. There was usually only one way a gringo made it out of a Mexican prison and that was in a pine box. Still, Jim had gotten them out. The little S.O.B. had done it. Then they had made for the border like a couple of jack rabbits. That had been the last time that Elvis had seen the other man, so who knew what had happened between then and now. Was it something else that had brought Frazini into the mix? Something to do with Jim's relationship with Monroe, maybe? By Elvis' reckoning, it had to be more than just payback for Mexico.

The outskirts of the city are vanishing beneath layers of brick and asphalt as they delve further into LA, heading North. Even though the buildings that pass are low, he feels that same tightness in his chest that he had experienced in Dallas and Vegas. Not enough open landscape for his liking. The city lights whisks around his head as if a flock of birds is swooping at him. They hit a dark patch, a rare undeveloped part that hadn't been suffocated by the urban sprawl yet. He looks over at Michael, sees the man staring straight ahead, not even acknowledging him. Elvis makes his decision. Hell if he knew if it's a good one, but... He owed Jim. Wasn't about to let a two-bit wannabe Capone threaten him.

"Hey, uh... Michael? I gotta take a leak." Michael keeps his eyes locked in the road ahead. Damn if he wasn't a single minded type of guy. "I mean it man, I'm gonna piss my pants if you don't pull over."

Michael looks over at him. "You should've gone at the gas station."

"Sorry, I uh, had a hell of a headache. Damn slipped my mind is all." He softens his eyes. "C'mon. Help a fella out?"

Michael glances at him, then exhales heavily, starts pulling the car over. A thrill runs through Elvis' body. Could be the dumbest thing he's done in a long time, who knew? He gets out, back turned to the car. Michael has gotten out of the car as well, is walking around towards Elvis.

"You mind giving me some privacy?" Michael steps closer. "Oh well, have it your way."

Elvis parts his legs slightly. He's aiming for some bastardized version of a *musubi dachi*, just like Juergen had shown him back in Germany in `58. He hears the crunch of gravel beneath Michael's loafers. He focuses his breathing, waiting. The mobster moves closer. Elvis supports his weight on one leg, then pivots. His other leg lashes out high in a *mawashi geri*, a roundhouse kick that catches Michael in the side of the head. The mobster grunts and drops. Elvis settles back, takes a breath then quickly moves to the other man's prone form. Not bad for the amount of lessons he'd had.

Crouching, he rifles through Michael's jacket. The guy's packing a huge revolver that looks like it could bring down an elephant. Elvis hefts it, gives a smirk. A lot of good it had done the guy. He pulls a money clip stuffed with bills and the car keys. He grabs Michael by the collar and hauls him towards a slope covered with shrubs with some vacant looking buildings at its base. The man is heavy. With a grunt, Elvis rolls him down the slope. Michael would be cut up some, and madder than a wildcat when he came to, if he didn't break his neck on the way down. Not Elvis' problem. Maybe he should've made sure that the guy wouldn't be coming after him, but that wasn't his deal if he could help it.

Getting back in the car, he adjusts the seat and the mirrors, then pulls off faster than he had intended, leaving a spray of gravel. He cranks the radio and scrubs a hand across his face. He lets out a low whistle, heart thumping a little faster than usual, making his breath catch in his throat. His knuckles are white against the steering wheel as LA's lights flare up through the windscreen. With the windows down, he feels the tension pressing against the back of his neck loosen. He scrambles in the dark of the glove box, swerving as he fumbles for a map book. He flicks through hard to read pages, eventually finding what he is looking for.

The address Jim gave him is a little ways off, and he pushes down on the accelerator. After a few moments, he forces himself to ease back. No point getting pulled over by the cops and winding up in the can. Seemed like the trouble had already started before he was ready for it, but no need to add to his woes. If this was any indication of how this whole thing was gonna play out, then he definitely should've stayed at home.

Getting closer, he sees the quality of the neighbourhood start to change. It's as if someone had just decided that this was as good a place as any to inject some wealth. The houses become grandiose rather than wealthy, the hills behind them creating a majestic backdrop. As he pulls up outside the address Jimmy had given him, he raises an eyebrow. If Jim was living here, Elvis had to wonder why he had bothered getting himself mixed up in something that had forced him to leave. Pulling up to the gate, he shuts off the engine and gets out of the car.

Walking over to an intercom panel set into the wall near the gate, he presses a button beneath the speaker grille and waits. There's no answer. Looking back over his shoulder, he lets out a heavy sigh. Well damn. All this way and no sign of Jim. He looks back at the intercom, then up at the wall. No way he was gonna try and climb it. People spoke about how Southerners were trigger happy, but there was a reason the West was called wild once upon a time. Even if Jim had split, Elvis would still have to find him, and he wouldn't be doing that dead from getting shot by some edgy homeowner.

He leans on the intercom again, not really sure why he's doing it, but not certain of what else he can do. The intercom remains stubbornly quiet and Elvis waves a hand at it, turns to head back to the car. He stops in his tracks when the thing crackles to life.

"H-hello?" A hesitant voice cuts through the static and Elvis jogs back, leans on the button.

"Yeah, uh, is this Jim Dean's house?" He curses his drawl, thinking there was no way the owner would open up for...

He jerks back a little in surprise as the gate slides open and the long, sweeping driveway beyond beckons him towards the house. Giving a quick backwards glance and rubbing the back of his head in confusion, Elvis strides up the driveway. He sees that the door is open and an older guy is standing at the entrance, hovering behind him is a pretty brunette. Her eyes are a little wider than they should be under normal circumstances. He smiles at her but the guy's words stop him.

"Okay Mister, that's far enough." Elvis sees a small pistol in the man's hand and swears under his breath. "What's your name?"

"E-Elvis." He stutters a little. "Uh.. Elvis Presley." He holds a hand out, sees the gun jerk a little. "Hey, would you mind lowering that thing? I'm just here to see my friend. This was the address that he gave me."

The man looks down at his hand, jumps a little as if he doesn't remember what he was doing with it in the first place.

He lets it fall and hang at his side. He runs a hand through his hair, and Elvis sees that it's shaking a little. Turning to the woman behind him, the man waves her inside then beckons for Elvis to follow him inside. Elvis hangs back a bit, wondering what all the fear was about. Maybe something to do with Jim? Had he gotten here too late? He realizes the man is waiting for him at the door and follows him into the house. Before he can stop himself, he lets out a low whistle. The interior of the place made his home in Tupelo look like a woodshed.

A big chandelier graces the entrance, glittering in faux candlelight. Through a large arch is a stately living space with a broad fireplace dominating one end. A fireplace in California? It's like he's stepped into a place where money is something a person can get from a faucet. Sense, however, seemed in short demand the same way that water was during a drought. The man leads him into the room.

The woman had vanished to somewhere else in the house, maybe up the curved staircase that was wide enough that Elvis could've driven a truck up it. Elvis takes the seat he's offered, thinking that for how much it's probably worth, it should be a whole lot more comfortable. A double of whiskey is thrust into his hand and when he drinks it, he thinks he hasn't ever really had real whiskey before. It trumps the stuff that Frazini had given him.

The man takes a seat across from Elvis, holding his own drink in both hands. Thankfully the gun had pulled a disappearing act because the guts have a tremor to them that isn't givin' up. Elvis' companion takes a long drink and then places the tumbler to one side. He leans forward, steepling his fingers and resting his elbows on his knees. When he looks up, he's studying Elvis carefully. He reaches for a silver cigarette case, flicks it open and pulls one out. He offers one to Elvis, who takes it, puts it between his lips and allows the man to light it for him with a monogrammed Zippo. The flame wavers slightly with the Guy's shaking. Finally, the man grows more calm, some of the tension draining from him like water down a partially blocked drain. As if he has suddenly remembered his manners, he leans forward, offering a hand. Elvis takes it.

"Hal Wallis." He releases Elvis' hand, leans back against the high back of the chair. "Sorry about before, it's been a strange sort of day."

"Mister." Elvis releases a lazy drift of smoke. "You have no idea."

HOTEL CALIFORNIA

BULL LOOKS UP AT THE SHITTY HOTEL, thinking that the broken lighting gives it even more of a hellish look than it might have had otherwise. He waits in the car for a few moments, watching bums push their meagre belongings along cracked sidewalks in shopping carts. Even in broad daylight, this place would look desolate. Reminds him a little of the Northeastern section of DC. Less green, but then that seems to be the way out here. Seems to be that the only trees worth talking about in the heart of LA are those fake-ass palm trees the city planners were insistent on putting everywhere. Getting out of the car, he shrugs off his jacket, works his neck and heads into the hotel.

The lobby has seen better days and the night clerk watches him approach with a slack jaw. A couple of bums argue. He ignores them and pushes forward. He leans on the counter and studies the man for a minute. The clerk eyeballs him right back, then picks at the acne scars that riddle his cheeks. Bull smiles, holds up the headshot of Dean that he had gotten from the casting place. Had taken a while to get it too. As many hopefuls as palm trees in LA. Bull thought he had seen hustling before, but this was on another level. The clerk peers at the photo.

"You seen this guy?" The clerk gives the photo another look, this time like he's really trying to place Dean.

Bull thinks maybe he could get lucky, but the kid shakes his head. Sighing, Bull turns, scans the lobby. Nothing. The occupants look like they've all had much harder lives than Jimmy Dean. It makes Bull think of a different approach. Turning, he leans in and casts a conspiratorial look over his shoulder before whispering to the clerk in a low voice.

"How much for a peek at the registration book?" He looks at the big ledger resting next to the guy's elbow, raises an eyebrow.

The clerk gulps. Like a full on swallow that sends his big Adam's apple bobbing. "We aren't supposed to..."

"C'mon..." Bull gives the clerk a big smile, amping it up. "You really think your boss is gonna find out?" Money appears on the counter as if magicked there. Bull taps it. "Hey. Look at that. Someone left this ten spot here. You thirsty kid? There's a shitty bar across the street, maybe if you just give me a look at that book, I can mind the counter for you. Any prestigious looking clientele show up, I come get you. What do you think?"

The clerk eyes the money, then his hand lashes out almost as quickly as Bull's had when he had placed it there, snatches it.

Lifting the book, the clerk slides it between the narrow opening set into the bars. They look as if they offer only scant protection. Bull gives him a grateful nod and smile, then scans the pages. He spots it almost straight away. Dean's script is far neater than its neighbours. Just as Bull thought that he might, Dean had used an assumed name.

Demille. Guy has a sense of humour. His broad face creases into a slow smile. He taps his finger on the room number. Despite Bull's suggestion, the clerk has hung around and is watching him, a hungry expression on his face. Bull knows exactly what the kid wants, but the little dweeb is gonna have to work for it. He pushes the book back, but as the clerk goes to grab it. Bull clamps his fingers closed on its edge, holds it tightly. The hungry expression flees the clerk's face, replaced by uncertainty.

"You want some more booze money? That it?" He gives the clerk a wink and the guy side-eyes Bull. "You got spare keys for all these rooms? Right?"

Jimmy is dead tired when he makes it back to the Cecil. The bed in the place can only loosely be called that, but right now it's as alluring to him as a siren. He shuffles into the lobby and the clerk gives him a sidelong glance. When he sees Jimmy look his way, he quickly goes back to reading his magazine. Even through the tiredness, a sense of alertness spikes within Jimmy and he watches the clerk for a few moments more as he keeps walking towards the elevators. The guy's eyes flicker up, lock with Jimmy's gaze as if it is a magnet. Jimmy stops, looks at the elevator, then back at the clerk. He starts heading towards the concierge desk.

"I don't want no trouble, man!" The guy's voice cracks as Jimmy pulls Wallis' pistol from where he's shoved it into his waistband.

The lobby seems suddenly a lot emptier than it had been, its residents scattered as if they possessed a supernatural aversion to risk. The clerk is already reaching for the metal shutter that he can pull down as needed, but Jimmy is faster, making the desk in three long strides. He blocks the shutter with one hand, while he shoves the gun in and through the grille. The guy flattens himself against the rear wall behind the desk, both hands raised. He goes to speak, but Jimmy brandishes the weapon. There's more risk of it going off by accident than him actually firing it intentionally.

"Why're you lookin' at me?" Jimmy's voice is tight and punchy, striking out at the clerk.

"Nothing man... I-I... Nothing!" Jimmy's face contorts as he jams the gun forward again. This time the clerk lets out a quick, high shriek. "Alright, alright... there's a big guy up in your room.

He paid me some money... Man, I make like a buck an hour." He's shielding his face with his hands. "I don't know what he wants. I just let him up there. I swear. Just leave me alone!"

Jimmy steps back, lowers the gun, then looks around quickly as if the guy in his room might appear at any moment. His mind is racing as the clerk squirms back, sitting now in a swivel chair that squeaks as he shifts. Jimmy turns, looking back at the entrance, then at the elevators again. He feels a hot thread running through him. It jerks him up as if he is being manipulated by a puppeteer. This was never gonna stop unless he did something about it right here and now. A cold fist clutches at his heart, but is quickly overridden by the anger.

Giving the guy a warning glance, Jimmy turns and heads for the elevators, tucking the gun back into his waistband. As the elevator gives an unsteady lurch, a worrying little sphere of apprehension nestles itself into his gut. He has no idea who it is that is waiting for him, and he is certainly no brawler. The black eye that had sprung up on his face was testament to that. No. He has to be smarter about it. Any other way will probably see him wind up as fish food. Something that Elvis had said to him once came flooding back.

If you know what they expect you to do, then you're already one step ahead of 'em.

And he did know. He knew that there was an unknown person waiting for him in his room. He knew the way into and out of the room, and that his unknown guest was expecting him.

So why make it easy for them? He thought about the layout of the room. A narrow space began immediately beyond the entrance. No point just walking right in then. No, better that he make them come to him. At least that gave him some sort of advantage, no matter how slight. What better way to make that happen than to act as if he wasn't Jimmy?

The plan has the potential to backfire, but what else is there? Go on the run? They'd track him down eventually. Whoever *they* were. The elevator comes to a halt and he exits into the dimly lit hallway. There is the faint sound of a hacking cough coming from one of the rooms, but no other signs of life. His pace is steady, even if his feet do want to spin and turn him in the opposite direction. It's not that Jimmy isn't brave, it's more that he's cautious. What other way was there to be? His friend Martin liked to say that he was like a cat. Well, here's hoping he got the nine lives side of the deal as well. He reaches the door to his room and knocks as if it's the most ordinary thing in the world for him to be doing.

"Housekeeping." He makes his voice indistinct, as if he could be anyone. Anyone but him.

There is silence.

He hadn't thought that part through. What if the guy didn't-

"Come back later." The voice is deep, rumbling and considered.

There is one thing he knows now. The guy isn't anywhere near the door. Jimmy can work with that. He pulls the gun and puts the keys in the door, unlocking it and pushing through.

"I thought I..." The guy is big, dressed casually but looking like that wasn't the norm for him. "Oh. I see."

He's not even looking at the gun and that tells Jimmy a lot more than he knew a few seconds ago.

"Who sent you? Weinstein?"

"Hey, James, why don't you put that thing away before you get us both killed?" He's standing now, posture relaxed.

Jimmy isn't buying it. The guy seems like he could go from nothing to action in zero seconds. He hangs back.

"Tell me." Jimmy keeps his voice flat, thinking that if he allowed any emotion in, that it might betray the cold flood of fear that he was feeling.

"I just want to ask you some questions." The intruder's face is calm and his tone is as casual as if they were two friends chatting over a couple of beers.

"Is this about Marilyn? I told your friend, I just want the book back." Jimmy is edging back now, thinking he had made a huge mistake in coming up here.

There was a flicker then, a slight ripple that disturbed the implacable stillness of the other man's features. He holds both his hands up, showing that they are empty. It's like he's trying to calm a snarling dog.

"You want to protect her legacy, don't you? You know what this town is like? They'll say anything." The guy holds one hand out, palm forward. "I can help you with that."

Jimmy steps back but he's misjudged his retreat and his back bumps into a wall. He falters and the gun dips. It's all the opportunity the other man needs. He's lurching forward with incredible speed. For a big guy, he is fast and decisive. Letting out a wail, Jimmy falls back, but the wall blocks his escape and the man is upon him, skilled precision in his movements. He quickly removes the gun, then grabs Jimmy by the arm and twists it behind his back. Jimmy is panting, face pressed against the dirty carpet now, the smell of it tickling the inside of his nose unpleasantly.

Elvis hears the shout before the doors of the elevator are fully open and wishes he had brought the revolver. More of a dismayed cry really, but he recognises the voice all the same. He's rushing headlong down the hall, not really taking into account any need for caution. His boots strike the grimy carpet as he runs, and it muffle any noise he might've otherwise made. He sees the open door, rushes towards it and through. There's Jimmy, face down on the floor, a big guy restraining him. He looks up, eyes slightly widened, confusion peppering his expression.

Elvis doesn't go with anything fancy this time. Karate was more about defence anyway. This looked like it needed some good old fashioned brawling. Elvis slams into the guy, feeling his weight and thinking that he might have just launched himself into some trouble. The guy grunts but comes back strong, his solid blow landing in Elvis' ribs. It nearly takes his breath away, and as he darts out of reach, he notices the lean hardness to his opponent's physique. They are watching each other warily now, and Elvis sees the gun on the floor. Jimmy is gasping, sitting up, pale and sweaty.

"Jim, grab the..."

The other guy doesn't let him finish, lurches as if he is going to grab the gun. Elvis moves in, but realizes too late that he's been duped. The other guy is up on him again, moving with lightning speed and the accuracy of someone who knows his way around boxing. Elvis darts back, takes a graze from a blow that would've knocked him out cold. He decides that it's time to fight dirty, because that seemed the most likely way of winning against someone who clearly outmatched him. As the guy moves towards Elvis, he steps to one side, and as predicted the guy goes in the other direction, as if anticipating a trick. Bringing his knee up, he shifts into a *mae geri* side snap kick.

It's a good one and catches the man in the groin. He lets out a low groan, then an explosive burst of air and drops. Elvis isn't finished with him. He brings his knee up, catching the falling man on the chin. He brings his foot back to deliver a kick, but as the toe of his boot swings toward the guy's head, he feels an iron fist clench around his ankle and pull. Suddenly Elvis is falling backwards, letting out a whoop of surprise. The man gets to his hands and knees, blood weeping from a graze on his cheek. He starts crawling towards Elvis but stops, eyes locked past him. Craning his neck and looking up from his prone position, Elvis sees Jimmy standing above them, gun aimed at the man.

"We're getting out of here." Jimmy's voice is strained and he watches the man carefully. "You try following us, you know what you're gonna get. Think about your odds."

What Jimmy didn't realize was that his threat was as empty as an old lunch sack. This guy had known exactly what he was doing and Elvis didn't think that round two would come off quite as this one had. Hell, he was certain of it. There was no way that he could take this guy on again. He struggles to his feet, starts backing away.

"C'mon Jim. We gotta go." The guy has slumped back down, but looks up at them, a hard glint in his eyes.

They back out of the room together, the man watching their departure the whole time.

THE CHAIN

THIS WAS WEINSTEIN'S DOING. Had to be. Some kind of thing he'd done to insulate himself against anything that came out of Marilyn's death. It couldn't be anyone else. At least it seemed that way to Jimmy. Anyone in Hollywood that knew Jimmy, knew that he had been living at Wallis'. It was an easy enough leap for someone to find out where he had gone from there then. If Wallis had spilled that info, then Jimmy couldn't blame him. The guy was in the biz, and the biz was all about keeping your friends close, and your enemies closer, especially when it came to producers. People might think that Hollywood was there for entertainment, but it was really just a big racket.

"You okay?" They're in The Little Bastard and Elvis is watching him steadily.

Jimmy doesn't even realize that he had been muttering until Elvis had interrupted his rambling train of thought "Yeah. Fine. You?"

"Oh yeah, never better." Elvis goes to lean his head back but there's nothing there to rest against, the seats too low with no headrest. He looks around the interior of the car, as if noticing what they're driving in for the first time. "This is some piece of work, how'd you wind up with it?"

"It's not mine." He loosens his hands on the steering wheel. "A friend is loaning it to me."

"You've sure got some generous friends." Elvis rests his arm against the curved side of the car. He touches a finger to a cut on his cheek and winces. "And some not so generous enemies."

"Thanks for pulling me out of that." Jimmy gives Elvis a swift glance, then returns his focus to the road ahead.

"So you gonna tell me more about what this mess is you've gotten yourself into?"

"Don't know the full picture yet. Might be bigger than I first thought." He shifts his shoulders, trying to loosen a knot of tension. "Have to go speak to Weinstein. He's in on this for sure."

Elvis sits forward, half twisted in his seat. "Are you serious, Jim? That guy meant business. We should get out of here. Lie low."

"And you think they're just gonna stop because I leave it alone? Huh, E?"

Jimmy gives the other man another quick look and sees that an odd expression has settled upon Elvis' face, one that Jimmy is unable to translate.

"Yeah... Maybe you're right..." Elvis pulls a toothpick from his shirt pocket, wedges it between his teeth and adopts a thoughtful expression.

Jimmy steers one handed, fishes around the glove compartment for a pack of cigarettes. He finds a half-finished pack of Marlboro, takes one out and lights it. His nerves unspool as he takes a drag and lets out a long drift of smoke that's whipped away into the LA night. There's an awkward silence between the two men until Jimmy breaks it with a question.

"You hear anything from Frazini?"

There's a slight pause before Elvis answers "Uh uh. You?"

"Nothing."

Something in the way that Elvis answered makes Jimmy think that maybe he's not telling the truth. He thinks about drilling down into that, but then stows it. Better that he focus his energies on resolving this mess before dredging up another that had been long dormant.

"So this Weinstein guy? What makes you think he's involved?"

"Marilyn had this book. I got hold of it, but I got rolled. I saw Weinstein and one of the guys that took it from me talking."

"You really think he's just gonna give it up to you if you ask him for it?"

"I'm not planning on asking."

"Is this where I come in?"

Jimmy feels the back of his neck flush hotly. Guiltily. He doesn't look at Elvis and floors the accelerator. The car surges forward as his partner leans back as best he can in the sports seat, closing his eyes. It's late, and Jimmy is feeling the fatigue bleed past the rapidly dissolving adrenalin. He thinks that it'll be easier to get to Weinstein at this time of night. The producer would be working late, and security was less tight at nighttime. Guy might as well sell his house and live there for all the time he spent at work. They head West towards the studio lot.

Pulling up outside, they get out and head towards the guard hut. Jimmy is relieved to see that Bill Devereaux is on duty. Bill looks up from his magazine, squinting to see who's coming, then breaks into a broad smile. They had shared a smoke break now and then. He gives Elvis a curious look. Elvis smiles at him, showing his perfect teeth and Bill smiles back.

"Jimmy!" He puts the magazine to one side. "I heard they let you go?... How're you holding up?"

"Oh... fine." He makes a show of looking bummed out. "I just swung by to pick up some stuff I forgot to take with me earlier."

Bill looks about, as if checking to see if anyone is watching. "Well, I'm not really supposed to let you back on the lot, but... Go on in. Just be quick, okay?"

"Sure thing, Bill." Jimmy gives Bill a brief smile.

"Eh... think nothing of it, kid. They don't pay me enough to be an asshole." Bill winks and Jimmy and Elvis leave him to return to his magazine.

The studio lot is bustling with regulars as Jim and Elvis make their way through looming sets. Enough people working at night to make Elvis wonder what was so important. They push their way towards the back. Elvis is barely paying attention, worried that someone might point out that they're not meant to be there anymore now that Jim had been fired.

They reach the production offices and Elvis is relieved to see that no one sits behind the receptionist's desk. It seemed odd based on Jim thinking that the producer would be here working late. If that was the case, then no assistant didn't add up. Didn't seem to make a difference to Jim though. He boldly pushes his way through the office door. Elvis follows and stops, staring. Hollywood opulence collected all in one place.

Floor to ceiling bookcases stacked with awards. A large desk made of what looked like walnut at the back of the room. A stack of bound papers towers on one side of it. Jim makes his way quickly to the desk, and starts rifling through the stack. Elvis hangs back at the door, one eye peeled outside, watching to see if anyone comes. His nerves are jacked. This felt dangerous in a way that he wasn't used to. It kept him looking out of the office, then back in at Jim. The other man is frantically pawing through the papers, strewing them on the floor as if not caring about any mess that he made. Elvis didn't think his nerves could get wound any tighter. It's not helping that Jim seems to be pitched at the same level.

"I'd help you, but I don't know what the hell it is you're looking for." Elvis throws his hands up.

"The book! Weren't you paying attention?!?" There's a tightness to the set of Jim's shoulders and a snarl in his voice. "Gotta be here. I saw Weinstein talking to the guy that took it from me."

"And if he doesn't have it?

"He has it."

Jim moves to the drawers, yanking them out and spilling the contents onto the floor, but they fail to yield the book. Jim studies the desk's surface, as if hoping it would show him something that he was missing. Suddenly he bends forward. Elvis sees what Jim had. A piece of paper, stuck to the one corner of the desk's edge by cello-tape. Jim picks it up, snatching really, reads it.

"Palm Springs." He half mutters, crunching the paper in his hands and stalking back towards the door.

Elvis watches him for a moment, then scurries out, having to hustle to keep up.

"Wait, where are you going?"

"This says Weinstein's in Palm Springs. So that's where we're gonna go." Not turning back, Jim is already at the edge of the reception area.

"We're gonna drive four hours to Palm Springs based on a scrap of paper? C'mon Jim... You're all worked up. Not thinking straight."

Spinning, Jim thrusts the piece of paper towards Elvis, right into his face. His features are contorted.

"You don't get it, do you?" He brandishes the paper as if it were a knife. "This guy could've killed Marilyn... Hell, for all I know, he could be trying to kill me. What am I gonna do? Screw this up and throw it away? Pretend like none of this happened?"

"I thought you said Marilyn killed herself? Or are you still tied to this crazy conspiracy thing you got stuck in your head?"

"Sure. Maybe she did, maybe she didn't. But there's a bunch of stuff here that feels off. More than off. I can't just leave it... I can't, E!" Jim pauses, licks his lips then gives Elvis this sidelong glance. Elvis knows what's coming before Jim even says anything. "Besides, I think you owe me."

There it is. The truth is finally coming out. His part in this wasn't because Jim actually needed him, it was because he thought he was owed some kind of payback.

"That's a cheap shot. Mexico wasn't my fault." It's Elvis' turn to get worked up now and he can feel the anger boiling to the surface.

"Yeah. Sure. It wasn't your fault. Play it the way you always do. Not. Your. Fault. But remember, I had to get us out of that mess." Jim stays quiet for a long time. When he finally does speak, Elvis has to strain to make out his words. "Why'd you grill me about Frazini before?"

There's a sharp stab in the back of Elvis' neck. He shrugs, trying to come up with a response quickly and mostly succeeding "Why wouldn't I ask about him? First time I've left Mississippi except for deliveries in nearly four years, you think I'm not nervous about that?" Jim squints at him, head clocked to one side but says nothing. "Look. I'll come down to Palm Springs with you. We'll talk to the guy. If he has this notebook you're so riled up about, we'll get it. Then we get out of there before anybody else catches up with us. Deal?"

Jim places his hands in the crook of his back, arches it and looks up at the ceiling. He releases a huff of air. Finally he lowers his head, and starts to head back the way they had come, out of the studio.

"Come on, we should get out here before whoever that was back at the hotel works out where we've gone. If he knew that I was at the hotel, there's a good chance that he knows that I'm here."

Elvis frowns. He doesn't want to say that if the guy had followed them here, then they were screwed. Jimmy seems wilder than three cats fighting in a sack, so he keeps quiet. He turns to follow and they are both stopped by the appearance of a birdlike woman. She stands there, blinking at them, holding a thick file in her hands and eyeing Jim up and down.

"What are you doing here?" She asks Jim coldly.

"Uh... I'm here to see Mr. Weinstein... See if he can get Mr. Cukor to change his mind?"

"Mr Weinstein is in Palm Springs..."

"Oh yeah. Yeah yeah yeah, I - I forgot. He told me he was going there."

"James. I don't think-" Elvis watches the woman's face flush.

"Now now, uh, that was all a misunderstanding. I am totally fine... totally fine."

The assistant straightens herself.

"You are acting very strange, Mr. Dean." The woman's tone had turned even icier, if that was possible.

Elvis could see that if they didn't get out of here, the woman was going to call security on them. He grabs Jim by the shoulders.

" Sorry to bother you, we'll be on our way." Elvis aims for his most apologetic look. "He's just upset is all... You understand? Marilyn and everything else."

The assistant seemed to thaw a bit, but her murmur is barely audible. "Yes... A terrible waste."

Elvis hustles Jimmy off quickly before the assistant changes her mind about causing a scene.

Of course Bull was going to follow them, and if he had to make an educated guess, he knew exactly where they were heading. Dean had told him as much. Had practically handed it to him.

Who sent you? Weinstein?

The producer.

The blackmailer.

Any bets that's where Dean, full of anger and accusation, would head next. If he was quick enough he could get there before them. Kill two birds with one stone. He rubs a hand at his groin. That redneck knew how to handle himself. Bull would have to be more careful when and if a next time came around that they squared off. He limps to the elevator, enters, and leans against the wall. Ignoring the clerk's nervous stare, Bull leaves the hotel and gets in his car. No sign of the men, but he wasn't concerned.

He pulls off, allowing the streets to carry him away from the desperation of the slums. Not that he can see much of it. Night-time rests upon the city, turning it into a haphazard collection of lights. Tiredness washes over Bull and he blinks lazily. It was turning into more effort than he had originally anticipated. Providing there were no other hiccups, he'd put in a call to his boss so it could be fed up the chain to the Pres. once he was done at the studio.

Twenty minutes from the hellscape of skid row and this part of town feels like Bull has been transported to a different city entirely. Even if it was a collection of glorified warehouses, the studio lots stunk of the wealth that their industry had created. He finds the place easily enough, but rather than barge in, he pulls up in the street. Not quite across, but close enough that he has a good vantage point. For the most part, the street is quiet, and Bull leans back in the seat to wait.

No point putting himself in a situation where he might have to fight again. They were either already here, or going to be soon enough. Either way, let them come to him, see what they wanted with Weinstein. What Weinstein might be holding on Jack. Let them bring whatever that might be straight to him. Less chance of causing a scene. He could tidy up any loose threads once that was taken care of. He turns on the radio. Pres. Jack is doing his usual. Downplaying Castro's relationship with Russia. Trying to save face after he royally screwed the pooch in that Bay of Pigs debacle. Not that anyone saw that. Jack and his brother had managed to come out of the whole thing looking like heroes. But it had been close, of that there could be no doubt.

Then it's little brother Robbie's turn to take the platform, talking about growing concerns over organised crime. In some ways the younger Kennedy had an earnestness that Jack never quite pulled off. Bull smirks. Everyone thought that the

Kennedy boys had been funded by their father's bootlegging, but that wasn't it at all. No, Joe Kennedy might've been a lot of things, but that wasn't one of them. He just had a savvy business mind. Sure, he might have played it fast and loose, but that didn't make him a criminal. Still, people talked, and what they were saying now, despite whether it was true or false, could very likely end up costing the Kennedy brothers down the line if people listened. Bull has to wonder if the image that both men put forward was an indirect response to the public's fascination with Kennedy conspiracy theories.

Robbie finishes, then it's back to Jack to deliver a sweeping *coup de gras* of assurance that the US was entirely safe from getting nuked to hell by Russia. As long as Jack remained in the hot seat that is. Bull admires the long game. Or maybe he should call it the long con? Whatever the case, it was several thousand pay grades above what he would ever know. His job was to keep President Jack safe from any bullets that might have his distinguished name on them as well as off the books shit, like this. He switches off the radio and waits to take care of this relatively small scale dilemma that also has the potential of ruining Jack's ambitions.

Ten minutes pass and then they're there. Bull can see them clearly in the bright lights positioned at the studio's entrance. The Southerner follows Dean, a frown pinching his straight brow. For his part, Dean has a dour, but determined, cast to his expression. They move to a sporty looking Porsche. Bull bites his lip. He could follow them, but what if all that they had gotten from Weinstein was zip? He watches as the Porsche's tail-lights flare to life. Something about it sparks that old feeling of intuition that he gets sometimes. Could be completely wrong, but it was there in the way that both men had looked when they had come out of the studio. As if they hadn't found what they were looking for but knew where to go next to get it. Bull makes a decision, waits until the Porsche is moving. He starts his car and pulls off, careful to keep some distance between himself and the car ahead.

PAINT IT BLACK

JOSHUA TREES, YUCCAS AND SAGE BRUSH are featureless shapes against the darkness of night. They've long left the city behind, taking the highway West and slightly South to Palm Springs. Out here, the air has developed an intensity that the city can never match. The sharp and fragrant smells of the desert snatch at Jimmy's nostrils. Elvis has fallen asleep awkwardly in the seat next to him. Even with the wind's whip, Jimmy can hear the other man's snores. Couldn't blame the guy really. If he could afford to sleep, Jimmy would do the same as his friend.

Do you know what you're looking for Jimmy? Marilyn's voice is unaffected by the rushing noise of asphalt. *Do you know what to do with it once you get it?*

It's the book right? Jimmy doesn't speak the words out loud. *There's something in the book?*

Yes. Remember what we spoke about?

He remembers. The President. And then she had shushed him. That fearful look back at the house. Enough to make him wonder what it was that she was afraid of. He doesn't like to think about how he had let her override his concern for her. Bad enough that he's got this gnawing sensation that her death might have something to do with Weinstein and he might've stopped it if he had known more. But what if it did go higher? What if that was what she had wanted to tell him, without explicitly saying as much? It took on angles that were too high and vertical for his reasoning to scale. The implications loomed over him like the cliff faces of the mountains sitting dark hued across the desert's flat surface.

On either side, slumbering communities rested, peacefully ignorant of the machinations of more powerful forces than themselves. Jimmy, however, is awake. Perhaps for the first time in his life. The road ahead spears its way through the darkness, feeling like a magnet that draws him closer to an answer. Occasionally, he thinks he sees a glimmer of light behind them, but it is so inconsistent that he partitions it away as something manufactured by his tiredness and paranoia. It feels like he has been carrying those things a lot longer than just the last few days. Shrugging in his seat, he tries to rid himself of the discomfort.

They get closer to Palm Springs, the desert slowly tamed by golf courses and palm trees. It's like someone had lifted a piece of LA and dropped it right in the middle of a wasteland. Wasn't that what LA was anyway? A city that shouldn't exist where it did, surviving purely through engineering and the human capacity for sheer stubbornness? It's heading into dawn now, the first light grazing the sky and pinching at Jimmy's eyes painfully. Maybe they'll get to Weinstein's place before he awakens? Get the book without the producer being any wiser until it was too late to do anything about it.

The streets are deserted, millionaire holiday makers sleeping while Jimmy and Elvis make their entrance. The only concession to Palm Springs' place in the desert are the cacti that dot front yards. Not much sign of grass, with the exception of rolling golf greens that layer the hills surrounding the community. Everywhere Jimmy looks he sees the hubris of wealth. Without any of the trappings that pass to either side of Little Bastard, the occupants here would be at the mercy of a parched and unforgiving landscape. Weinstein's house is no different.

It's an L shaped structure, white and glistening in its modernity. A broad driveway leads up to a fascia dominated by large windows which defy the rising sun. There are a couple of cars in the driveway, one a solid top, the other a convertible. The curtains are drawn, but Jimmy can still catch a glimpse of a broad swimming pool at the rear of the house. As he brings the Porsche to a halt, Elvis snorts, blinks, and then comes groggily awake. He blinks again, taking in the house and it's opulence.

"Damn." Elvis opens the door, gets out and gives a huge stretch. "What are you guessin' a place like this would set you back, Jim?"

"Oh... More money than either one of us will ever see." He's humouring the other man. He doesn't really care what the place is worth, just about the answers that might be found within its walls.

Jim moves up to a window, peers through, and then comes back to Elvis "We need to get in there."

"We what now?" Elvis frowns. "Come on, Jim. We've been driving half the night and now you want to get busted on a B&E charge? Let's just look around out here. That was the deal, remember?"

Jim shakes his head "You split if you want, I came here to find answers."

He moves off around the side of the house. After a minute, he hears the crunch of Elvis' footsteps on rocks as the other man follows. Around the side of the house, Jimmy finds a door leading into the laundry. He grips the handle, and then steps back quickly as it pushes inwards. He gives Elvis a long look, and his partner looks back, dark brow beetled. Jimmy ignores the obvious annoyance on his partner's face, turns and slowly opens the door. Inside, the house is quiet. He keeps his footsteps light as he moves across the tiled floor. He hears a huffed sigh from behind him and then the tread of Elvis' feet on the tiles as the other man follows.

The interior of the house is open plan. Airy. The slanted ceiling is high and globe light fixtures dangle in asymmetry. A long island bench separates the space in its centre. There are empty wine bottles and used glasses strewn across its surface. A dim glow comes from the corner where a silver lamp on a curved support hangs over a large, L-shaped modular lounge suite that sits beneath a large window, looking out across the front yard. There are papers strewn across the lounge. Jimmy moves to them and starts searching.

"Jim!" Elvis hisses.

Jimmy waves him quiet, eyes roving over the papers. He sees nothing related to Marilyn. He spins, studies the space, eyes landing on a doorway leading into a dim office. He gestures for Elvis to follow, moves quickly across the living area. At the office's door, he hesitates, peering into the gloom. The blinds have been lowered. A dark, heavy looking desk sits against one wall. Jimmy moves to it, yanks a drawer. It's locked. He looks over the surface of the desk.

"What are you doing?" Elvis mutters, looking back into the living area, anxiousness clear on his face. "We need to get out of here."

"Wait a minute." Jim grabs up a heavy looking letter opener.

He yanks on the drawer again and a small gap appears, enough so that Jimmy can jam the opener in. He pries at the drawer until there's a single crack and the drawer slides open completely. Sifting through the drawer, Jimmy scatters papers.

Elvis lets out a frustrated grunt. Jimmy ignores him, spotting something. He extracts it from the drawer. It's a stack of papers held together by a clip. He scans the writing on the cover page and releases a long breath.

"Goddamn bastard!" He swears.

"What?" Elvis leans forward. "What is it?"

"They were blackmailing her..." Jimmy hands the paper to Elvis. "They were threatening to spill the beans on her thing with the President."

He turns and stalks from the office, all semblance of stealth forgotten.

"Where are you going?!?" Elvis watches him pass, expression incredulous.

Jimmy heads towards the rear of the house and the bedrooms.

"I'm gonna wake that son of a bitch up and ask him some questions."

Jimmy hears Elvis come after him, voice still low, but more urgent now "Jim! Wait!"

Bull is tired as he pulls into Palm Springs. He had seen the Porsche ahead, its tail lights a red smear. The oppressive darkness begins to lift as both cars pass the city limits. He is starting to feel the effects of not enough sleep and too many miles. Four and a half hours. He'd been lucky that he hadn't driven off the side of the road and crashed in the desert.

Bull watches the sports car zoom ahead. His foot feels heavy with an impulse to close the gap. It wouldn't do. Early hour traffic is sparse, affording low opportunity for cover. He keeps a whole lot of road between himself and the other car, his headlights switched off now that slow morning light is starting to eke into the sky. Once they get into the city centre, Bull uses old tricks to stay hidden. Turning down side roads that run parallel to the other cars path, but with enough line of sight that he could keep tabs on them. Switching from one side road to another, falling back and speeding up. It was all a game of cat and mouse.

He sees the car pull down a side road and hangs back. No point getting spotted. The road looks like any other road, but as he cruises past, he sees that it ends in a cul-de-sac. He keeps driving, gets to the end of the road, then does a u-turn and heads back. As he pulls into the cul-de-sac, he sees the Porsche is parked in front of a large house. It's built with clean and angular lines. Bull sits in the driver's seat and clicks his tongue against his teeth. Risky confronting them here. If the producer was at home, then the commotion might spook him. It was the producer that was blackmailing the Pres., whatever Dean and his friends' involvement was second to that. No point bringing them any further into it if he didn't have to.

Bull sighs, not liking the situation, but unwilling to let it go any further. He opens the car door, gets out and walks towards the house. The broad driveway affords little cover, so he sticks to the edge of the property and goes in through a rocky garden dotted with cacti. Behind a low wall, there is narrow space with concrete slabs acting as a path. Bull is able to scale it easily.

He drops down into the space, hugging the wall. He moves to the rear of the house, and as he gets closer, he can hear hushed whispers. They're delivered in a furious overlap, both men firing back and forth at each other. He stops, straining to make out their words, but with a low morning breeze blowing, they are obscured, snatched away and rendered meaningless. He moves forward, making sure to keep himself low and out of sight.

Weinstein's body is slumped in a deckchair. One arm dangles down, as if reaching to touch the cool blue of the pool and the red streaks that drift lazily through the water. There is a bullet hole neatly placed in one side of his head, and a messy ruin of hair and bone fragments on the other. Elvis gapes at the scene, then turns angrily to Jim. The other man's eyes are flat as he looks at the dead producer.

"What the hell is this?" Jabbing angrily at the corpse, Elvis rounds on Jim, snatching at his arm. "This is insane, man! We need to get out of here! Now!"

He's keeping his voice low, but it's an effort.

Jim doesn't reply. He gives the body one last look and then pushes towards it. Weinstein is wearing only boxers, some slip-ons and a gown. As Jimmy touches him, his head lolls to one side and his body droops in the chair. Elvis grabs at Jim to pull him back, but the other man shrugs him off, rounds on him.

"Get off of me!" His voice is a low snarl. "It has to be here."

"Jim." Lowering his voice, Elvis holds his hands up. "Listen to yourself. You're not thinkin' straight."

"I have to - " Jim stops talking abruptly, eyes landing on something. Moving back to the producer, he grabs the corner of the robe, snatching it up and shaking it. A small black book drops out of an inside pocket. He grabs it off the ground, gripping it as tightly as if it were gold. "This is it, this is -"

"Hand it over." Elvis' stomach drops away when he hears that voice, knowing who it belongs to. *Stupid. We should've just run when we had the chance.*

He isn't sure whether he was talking about now, or when they had managed to get out of Mexico. Either way, not thinking ahead in both situations had landed them here. Jim looks up quickly, eyes like saucers, panting low and fast. He's still in a crouch, book brandished in one hand like a weapon, seeing what Elvis was already looking at. The guy from the hotel stands at the corner of the house, gun levelled at the two of them. Jim starts backing away and Elvis, left with no other options, does the same.

"It doesn't have to be like this." Despite the tension that crackles in the air between them, the guy's voice is level, as if they were talking about sport. Elvis recalls the weight of the man's punches, isn't keen on experiencing that a second time. "Just hand it over and I'll let you go on your way."

"Did you kill her? Huh?" Jim thrusts the book forward, stabbing it in the air towards the man.

The man's eyes get this sad look to them, like he's about to do something that he isn't looking forward to. He never gets the chance. There is a sharp cracking noise, like thunder, then the guy jerks back, eyes wide, the calm facade vanished. He clutches at his shoulder, falls against the wall and then slides down, leaving a red smear. Red blooms beneath his fingers, staining the fabric of his shirt. Elvis doesn't hesitate, clutches Jim's arm and yanks him away. There is another gunshot and he flinches but keeps running, Jim pulled in his wake. They make the Porsche, and Elvis vaults into the driver's seat.

"Keys! Now!" He's yelling, breath held a little, waiting for a third shot that never comes.

Then the keys are in his hand, then in the ignition and then the car is roaring to life. He reverses, tires leaving a dark trail of rubber as they spin on the immaculate drive. Then they're roaring down the street, lights flickering on in the houses as they speed into the dawn.

BAD GUY

BULL SCANS THE ROOFTOPS of the neighbouring houses, trying to make out where the shot had come from. He grits his teeth, pressing a hand against the dull pain in his shoulder. Bringing it back, he sees the blood on his palm and realizes how badly he's screwed. His legs jut out at angles from where he's slumped on the ground at the base of the wall. He closes his eyes. Only a matter of time before another bullet gives him a hole in the head similar to the corpse slumped in the deckchair.

A warning meant for the Pres. maybe? One of Jack's opponents?

Not too far from the realms of possibility. Bull was informed enough to know that not every US affiliated agency had his boss' best interest at heart. Jack hadn't been exactly shy about making a heap of enemies on his climb to the top. Bull got it. Nature of the beast. Still, he wasn't a hundred percent on who the most likely culprit could be. That Bull couldn't see his attacker indicated a sniper. That it was a sniper pointed to the CIA. Those shady fucks were always playing different sides of the fence depending on how best it served their own interests. Still, he couldn't believe they would actually be so forward. Guess he shouldn't have been so naive.

He was feeling colder now. In fact, his shivering had gotten so bad that his teeth were chattering. Of all the ways Bull had thought that he would go out, lying in a backyard in Palm Springs next to a dead movie producer was the farthest from it. Better that he had not volunteered for this gig. Could almost picture the smug satisfaction on Johnson's face when he received the news. Maybe Johnson had had something to do with it? Wouldn't that be funny?

Wouldn't what be funny? It's all foggy now. Can't even recall what he'd been doing down here. *Oh yeah. Monroe. Blackmail. Dean.*

Maybe what they had on the Pres. was bigger than what any of them had thought? Maybe a lot bigger than the shakedown that Jack had seemed to think was going on. He'd walked right into a lion's den, the way that he saw it. No business getting involved really. What had he hoped to prove? To become Jack's right hand man? Pres. already had plenty of those, including his brother. And you know what they said about blood. Speaking of which. He coughs and there's an unpleasant thickness in his throat. Opening his eyes, Bull finds the effort required is something monumental. Seeing the dead producer, Bull laughs.

"I'll be joining you soon en-"

"You should save your energy, friend." Bull frowns and looks over.

There's a small man, thin and unassuming, standing there with his hands in his pockets. He wears a work shirt and khakis, as plain as the rest of him. The only thing out of the ordinary is the big beard he sports and a pair of gold-rimmed aviators. The man bends down, pulling big, splayed hands from his pockets and resting them on his knees as he crouches. He has a smile, though it's humourless and grey. Give Bull an ounce of strength and he'd wipe that smile straight off the man's face. Still, he'd hate to give the guy any satisfaction by acting afraid, even though he was.

"Don't seem to have any energy at all." Blinking, it takes Bull far longer than it should to open his eyes again. "So what's the going rate at the Agency for assassinations these days?"

The guy smirks "Good guess, Sport. Shame about all this. You could've made a good asset. We're always looking for people on the inside that we can use"

"Tell me something." Bull has no strength left for cracks, so cuts to the chase. "Your boss, whoever that is, are they planning on taking out Jack?"

"That's what you want to know on your way out?" The guy stands, turns his back and lets out a huge sigh. "You're thinking small. Maybe you wouldn't have been such a good fit after all."

Bull isn't listening any more. The man turns and looks down at his body. He lets out another sigh, scrubs a hand through his beard. Shielding his eyes against the rising sun, he raises a hand, waves to some unseen recipient. He points down at Weinstein's corpse, then at Bull's, gives the signal to come collect them.

Jimmy flicks through the book with his breath in his throat and his heart pounding in his chest. At first the lines of text scrawled within make no sense. Forcing himself to calm down, he looks at the words more carefully. Dates. Names. Some sort of appointment book? He flicks forward, seeing the dates getting closer to the last day of Marilyn's life. There's Weinstein's name. Cukor. DiMaggio. Jimmy. He frowns at the last date. Nothing. He flicks the page, sees that it's blank. Flicks back. His scowl deepens as he stares at it. After looking at it for a few seconds he pops the glove box, pulls a pencil from it. Starts running the lead tip across the space on the page next to the date.

There. He had been right. Only the smallest of indentations, barely visible. If there had been less light, he might not have seen them. Whatever had been written there must've been erased, but enough remained that Jimmy could bring it back to life. The bright sun cresting the horizon illuminates the page brilliantly. Marilyn pointing the way, maybe? As the pencil reveals the letters, Jimmy's breath catches again, but this time for entirely different reasons.

JK. He turns to Elvis, opens his mouth to speak, but isn't granted the opportunity. Something slams into the back of the car and he is flung forward, head glancing painfully off of the dash. He wipes at the bloody taste in his mouth and swivels in his seat. Looking back over his shoulder, he sees a black sedan coming in for another bite of Little Bastard's rear. He braces himself, yanking the gun from his belt. Elvis gives him a quick glance, grips the steering wheel and plants his foot. Not quick enough. The sedan nudges them again and this time the Porsche swerves. Elvis snarls.

"You gonna take a shot or hold that thing all day?"

Jimmy swallows, levels his arm over the rear of the car and squeezes. The gun's pop is whisked away by the flapping wind that envelopes the open space around them. Doesn't matter. The shot completely misses the sedan and now it comes again, eager for a third strike. It connects with the Porsche again and this time the swerve yanks the car one way, then the other. Elvis fights with the wheel to regain control, but fails. The car starts to tip. Jimmy grabs Elvis' head, yanks him down, ducks himself as far into the small space afforded as he can.

The car lifts and suddenly he's weightless. Then gravity reasserts itself, pushing him down as the car strikes the dirt. There's nothing now but a confusion of dust and rock. A sharpened stone or a busted piece of the Porsche strikes and cuts his cheek. Jimmy isn't certain which as his mind becomes a tangle. He hears Elvis shouting unintelligibly as the car slides before finally slowing, tilted up on one side. Jimmy has his eyes squinted tightly shut. Somehow, miraculously, he is still clutching the gun and hasn't managed to put a bullet in either himself or Elvis.

Silence falls and Jimmy realizes that he is half in and half out of the car. He rolls over, glimpses patches of blue smeared through the chaos of dust still obscuring most of the sky. He coughs, then hears Elvis do the same. Just because both of them are coughing doesn't mean that they're going to be alive for much longer. He can't feel any pain, but that also means little. Trying to reorder his thoughts, he stops. What was that? Straining to hear, catching the sound of footfalls on gravel. He thrusts the gun forward in the general direction of the footsteps without really seeing what he is aiming at.

"Hold it!" Jimmy's voice holds a lot more confidence than what he is feeling.

There's a sound like someone spitting on the dirt, then a metallic click.

"Put it down." The voice is a dry whisper, a match for the desert wind that whips past inconsistently. Jimmy refuses. "You really want me to shoot you, don't you?"

Anger flares within him then. Who the hell was this son of a bitch to tell him what to do? Without thinking he squeezes the trigger. The weapon bucks in his hand awkwardly from his prone position.

There is thud then that dry whispering voice again, fainter than it had been. "Damn... You shot-"

Then nothing.

Jimmy wipes at his stinging eyes, trying to make out something. Anything. Finally, his vision clears and he sees a body sprawled where it fell, a tan coloured bundle. He crawls out of the vehicle, gains his feet, gun dangling limply. A noise from behind him makes him spin jerkily, gun outstretched again, arm trembling with jacked up nerves. Elvis is there, one hand held to his face, the other stretched out placatingly.

"Cool it, Jim... Just..." More coughing. "Just cool it. He's dead."

"You seriously think that's it?"

"Naw, man. No way. But just... Uh... I don't know... Just take it easy, is all." Elvis spits, moves to the body and rolls it over. "Let's see what we're dealing with."

Jim's hunched over the body while Elvis looks back at the mangled wreck of the Porsche. They should both be dead. That they're not and the guy who tried to kill them is, borders on divine intervention.

This your doing mama?

He looks up at the sky as if the answers he's looking for will magically appear there, but there is nothing. Not even the softly remembered voice of his mother admonishing him for not taking her advice. He can remember that as being her way. Never scolding. Just guiding in that gentle manner that she had owned. Maybe that had a lot to do with the loss of his brother? Like Elvis being the only son she had left had made him that much more precious in some way? Guess he'd never know.

As Jim continues looking, Elvis watches the horizon. Before too long, someone was going to come up that road and then they were going to be in an even bigger world of trouble. He moves over, stands above Jim for a few moments before breaking the silence.

"C'mon man, we gotta get out of here."

"Just gimme a moment. It's got to be here."

Elvis scratches his head "What's got to be there?"

"Something that will tell me who this asshole was working for." He glances back briefly over his shoulder at Elvis. Jim looks just like a kid. A scared and lost kid. "This proves that Marilyn didn't do it. She didn't kill herself."

"Huh?" Elvis tries to keep the doubt out of his voice. "How do you figure that?"

"That other guy? The one who showed up at Weinstein's pad. That was one thing. But then someone takes him out? What does that tell you? Lots of people interested in what is going on. And all of it kicks off with Marilyn's death. That can't be a coincidence. So I work out who all these interested parties are? Then I can start working out what their connection to Marilyn was. Maybe that tells me who killed her."

"And what's that gonna achieve? It ain't gonna bring her back"

"I know that." Elvis expected anger, but didn't get it. Jim just stands, back turned to Elvis, staring down the road as if the answer will come along at any second. Next time he speaks, his voice is soft. "But someone has to answer for what happened to her."

Where Jim hadn't gotten angry, Elvis did. They had nearly been killed just for going after some damn book, and here Jim was, talking crazy again. Hold people to account? Get them to answer? That was just asking for a shallow grave somewhere. He had to wonder that if Jim knew about Frazini, about what Frazini had wanted Elvis to do, whether he would be making the same choices. A little stab of guilt pricks him and he decides that it's better that the other man doesn't know. It would only make a messy situation that much worse. He's about to start talking again, try to convince Jim to see some reason, when he stops.

There's the low drone of an engine approaching. Jim turns, gives Elvis a wide-eyed look that says that he's reconsidered his burning desire to continue searching the body. At least he had enough sense to know that they couldn't stick around here any longer. The dead guy's car is parked too far up the road for them to reach it in time, even if they had the keys close at hand. Grabbing Jim by the arm, Elvis yanks him forward, making for the scrub at the edge of the road. It wouldn't offer much in the way of somewhere to hide, but it was their only bet at this point.

Lying there, chin pressed to the dirt, he narrows his eyes as he watches the black sedan come to a halt behind the dead guy's car. It sits there for long moments, then a little skinny, bearded guy gets out. He has a gun held loosely in one hand and he walks up, careful to keep the dead guy's vehicle between himself and the scrub. He stops, not approaching the body. His eyes aren't visible behind his aviators, but the lenses are fixed on the body. The direction of his gaze doesn't deviate as he speaks.

"You boys should come out now." He waits, sighs, then continues. "You come out now, we can cut some kind of deal. You don't? Well... Let's just say we've got that scenario covered as well."

Elvis looks quickly at Jim, their eyes locked. Before he has a chance to stop the other man, Jim calls out, his voice uneven.

"How do you know that we won't make a corpse out of you like your friend there?" The threat sounds as empty as it is.

"I don't." Elvis thinks the guy is smarter than he looks, playing to Jim's threat not by acting scared, but acknowledging its potential. "But, you want to find out what happened to your girlfriend, I'm probably the best bet you've got of making that happen. You take me out, that opportunity goes away."

If he was quicker, Elvis might've been able to stop Jim, but there was no time. Jim stands and Elvis is surprised when he isn't dropped immediately. For his part, he stays put, not willing to trust blind luck as much as his partner.

"Tell your friend this only works if he puts himself where we can see him too."

We? Another smart move on the mystery man's part. Nothing got the fear working overtime than the spectre of multiple threats.

Jim looks down at Elvis, frowns as Elvis stays glued to the ground. He gestures for the other man to stand. There's a pause, then Elvis lets out a low grunt before getting to his feet.

Mystery man's posture shifts, a little more relaxed, he beckons. "Now come on out where we can continue this conversation like adults."

Jim leads as Elvis follows, both men picking their way over the scrub. As they get closer to the mystery man, he leans back on the hood of the car. He raises his hand, and Elvis isn't certain but he swears he catches the flash of something catching the rising sun, way off in the scrub. He swallows, thinking that it would be better if he hadn't seen that, but knowing full well the reason that he had. A good way of lending weight to the guy's unspoken threat.

Mystery man gives the dead body another glance, dismissive almost "Dwight always was a hothead."

"'Dwight' huh?" Elvis folds his arms, the skin between his shoulder blades crawling. "And what do we call you?"

"Well, you can call me Hank." Hank smirks. "Yeah... that's got a nice ring to it." Jim is staring at him, eyes flat, mouth working as if he's chewing on something sour. "What's the matter son? You upset that we had to put a bullet in the President's man?"

Jim's eyes widen. "President's..."

"Oh? You didn't know? How else did you think Jacky boy was going to clean up his mess?"

Jim flashes a pinched look at Elvis, before turning back to Hank. "So he was responsible for Marilyn's death? For Weinstein's."

"You're a smart guy, I'm sure you can figure it out. But here's a story for you that might help fill in a few blanks." Hank pulls out a stick of gum, unwraps it and pops it in his mouth, chewing as he continues. "Say you were a high profile politician. Say you had made a few questionable decisions which might result in some negative press, chief of which was knocking up a Hollywood actress. Now take it one step further. What if that actress was emotionally unstable? What if she had threatened to expose the whole thing? It sort of makes it less certain that you're going to be able to hold onto that little taste of power that you'd managed to grab. If that was really you, what would you do?"

"Pregnant?"

"Guess you weren't as much of a confidante as you thought you were, huh?" Hank's shoulders roll in a gentle shrug.

"You're lying." Jim's voice is flat.

"Am I?" Hank reaches into his pocket, tosses a folded square of paper towards Jim.

It lands on the ground between them, a baited hook. Picking it up, Jim reads it, mouth moving soundlessly. He blinks, swipes at his eyes. Lowering his hand, the paper dangles from his fingers. Hank gestures for Jim to pass it back, and he does without protest. He looked deflated.

Elvis watches Jim watch Hank. He knows that whatever the man says next is gonna be lost in the white noise brought on by whatever his partner had read, real or imagined. Best he can do is put in his two cents and hope it tempers things.

"That still doesn't tell us who you are."

Hank turns his aviators on Elvis, and he sees himself reflected in the mirrored lenses.

"How's Frazini these days?" Elvis' blood runs cold as Hank chews his gum. "Seems like you guys had quite a conversation, although, judging that you weren't a good little dog and did as you were told, the next conversation won't be as pleasant."

Jim turns, mouth gaping "What's he talking about, E?"

Hank clicks his tongue "Huh. You haven't told him? What kind of a partner are you?"

Elvis rounds on Hank, snarling. "Quit this bullshit! You tell us who you are and what the hell you want."

Hank smirks "As you command... Doggy." Leaning further back on the hood of the car, he puts his hands in his pockets. "I'm assuming you gentlemen have heard of the CIA?"

BETTER THE DEVIL

JIM LISTENS AS THE MAN calling himself Hank continues. His mind is still reeling over hearing Frazini's name. If he is honest with himself, he had suspected that Elvis had been in contact with Frazini, even if his partner hadn't said as much. Regardless, he would have to take it up later. Right now, Hank was saying more things and Jimmy figured that their continued health depended heavily on his ability to listen. It's hard to push through the buzz that has been present since Hank had shown him the test results, but he manages.

"Let's just say that the Company and the current administration do not see eye to eye on more than a few things." The man chuckles, low and dry. "Personally, I think playboy Jack has some good ideas, but at this point in the game, good ideas aren't worth much. Being the pragmatists that we are, the Agency has decided to take matters into their own hands in light of bigger concerns. If we don't do something about the Russkies, none of this shit will matter a whole lot. Not that Jack seems particularly concerned about that. He's become a little gun shy since his error in judgement with Cuba. Which is where we reach our dilemma, but also a possible solution. We can't do a whole heap about Russia, but there's quite a bit we can do on the home front to swing things in the direction they should be heading."

"And you think the President is gonna let you cowboys get away with killing one of his men?" Elvis' face is still painted in hostile shades, full lips twisted.

"Now hold on a moment, let's clear some things up." Hank holds up one finger. "We didn't kill that fine agent anymore than we did that movie producer."

"What do you mea-" Hank keeps talking over Elvis.

"The way I see it, we came along at the right time. Who knows how many poor innocents you two psychopaths might've taken out on your little killing spree?"

"What the fuck're you talkin' about!?!" Elvis is shouting now, veins thick in his neck as he thrusts forward, but Jim has already worked it out.

Jimmy restrains Elvis, pushes him back "It's just like he said. They're planning on pinning those murders on us... Unless we do something for them. That about it, Hank?"

"See." Hank points pistol-fingered at Jimmy, pretends to fire. "I knew you were a smart guy."

"So, what is it? You want us to help end Jack's presidency early? Is that it?" Jimmy squints at Hank.

"Something like that." He looks over at Elvis. "Am I right in thinking you got some military experience?"

Glaring at Hank, Elvis remains silent.

"I'll take that as a yes." Hank spits out the gum. "So assuming you know how to handle a rifle, that means we've got some use for you. Jimmy here can come along as an insurance policy."

Watching the man, the realization of what Hank was getting at fell over Jimmy "You can't be serious..."

"Hey, two for two kid. You really got some brains up there, huh?"

It doesn't take long for Elvis to play catch up. His eyes glisten and his jaw is clenched tightly. Finally he snaps "You're insane."

He lunges forward and this time Jimmy is too slow to stop him. Elvis' blow lands squarely on Hank's jaw and the man falls backwards. He sits in the dirt, rubbing at his face. He removes his aviators, gives Elvis an appraising stare with hazel eyes. "You got a mean hook, Slick. They teach you that in the army?"

Elvis stands above Hank, fists bunching at his sides "I'll show you some other things they taught me as well."

"Relax. It's not as big a deal as what you're making out." Hank stands, dusts off his pants as if Elvis isn't standing in front of him ready to strike again.

"So, let me get this straight? You're asking us to kill the President of the United States, and if we don't you're going to frame us both for murder?"

Hank switches his attention to Jimmy, gives him a speculative stare. Finally, he shrugs "When you put it that way, it does sound like a big fucking deal, doesn't it?" He takes out another stick of gum, pops it in his mouth and starts chewing. "But yeah, that's about it."

Jimmy turns from the man, feels his face flush as if noticing the sun's heat for the first time "Why us? Why not just use one of your own people?"

"Plausible deniability. You know what that means?" Hank waits, but when both men remain silent, he continues. "Plus, you two came along at the right time. This thing with Marilyn gives you motive. You're close to her, you want revenge. Frazini gave us the skinny on both of you. We know you both got priors down in Mexico, not to mention that business with the *El Capitan*. It's quite a nice package really. Saves us having to create something from nothing." He sighs before finishing. "You're in the hole on this one, boys. You don't do it for us, you're going to prison for murder. You do it for us, there's a chance you get out of it in one piece... Unlikely, but you got a chance."

"Aren't you meant to be protecting the interests of the United States? How's this fit into that?" Jimmy turns back and watches as Hank puffs his cheeks.

"What do you think we're doing?" Hank blinks, sighs before continuing. "You think you got it all sorted in your head about the way the world runs, but in the grand scheme of things, you, country boy here, Jack, Marilyn... Hell, even me, we're pieces on a board. Most of the time, the game is playing you. But sometimes, just sometimes, you catch a break, and you get to play back." He comes close, ignoring Elvis' glare on his back, leans in so that his voice is just above a whisper. "Question is, do you want a seat at the table? Or do you just want to keep on getting pushed around? Think about what he did to Marilyn..."

"Jim..." Elvis' voice is a junkyard dog's growl.

Jim holds Hank's stare "Fine. What do we need to do?"

"Hold up there." Hank looks over his shoulder. "We should take care of Dwight. He's starting to draw flies."

Elvis wasn't much for politics. In fact, most of what Hank had said had gone over his head. Yeah, he got the general gist, including the kicker that good old Hank had decided to throw their way about what he had in store for the President. But all that hoo-ha about Russians and whatnot? Forget it. All he knows is that Jim was allowing them to get drawn into a spider's web. If his partner thought that it was their only chance of getting out of things alive, Elvis had to think that he isn't as smart as what Hank keeps saying he is.

Which makes sense. Seems that anything that came out of the guy's mouth was worth about as much as that old truck he'd lost on the way to LA. No, the way Elvis is seeing things, he ices the President, he's gonna find himself iced as well. Him and Jim both for that matter regardless of that 'insurance policy' bullshit. But right now, with Dwight stored in the trunk and Hank sitting behind him with a gun trained on his neck, he has to play it cool. Jim sits in the passenger seat, gnawing at his lower lip. Once they had put the body in the trunk under Hank's watchful eye, his partner had fallen silent and had stayed that way on the drive to wherever Hank was taking them.

The way Hank had put it, both of them were Agency assets now. Elvis had quizzed him on that, not liking the sound of it one bit. If they were assets, how did that plausible deniability factor in? Couldn't someone, somewhere down the line, link them up once the deed was done?

Off the books. That's how Hank had replied, which put a bit more fat on Elvis' theory that they were only alive as long as Jack was still breathing.

"You're both pretty quiet for the amount of questions you were throwing my way earlier." Elvis gives the rearview mirror a quick glance, sees that Hank has donned his aviators once more, and is chewing another stick of gum.

"Excuse me if I don't feel chatty, Hoss." He grips the steering wheel, forces his hands to relax. "The situation isn't heading in a direction that lends itself to much conversation."

"Oh, come on... Don't be like that. You boys are about to make the history books."

"That implies we're going to get caught." Jim's mumbled words catch Elvis off guard.

"Well, there you go again. Overthinking things."

"It's what us geniuses do." Jim is staring straight ahead.

"Ha!" Hank lets out a burst of laughter. "You're a real funny guy, you know that James?"

Now that Elvis had let Jim's words settle into his mind a bit, he's starting to think that maybe his partner hadn't bought completely into Hank's bullshit after all. If that's the case, then maybe they have a chance. If not? Well, maybe Frazini had been right and he should cut his losses? He didn't want to think about what that would be like should he need to make such a decision. Shrugging his shoulders, he settles in and lets his focus rest on the road ahead.

Hank's directing him from memory it seems, and hasn't told them much beyond that they're going to an airfield. He gives the lefts, rights and straight aheads pretty confidently which means that he's been this way plenty of times in the past. Before they hit the city, they're turning off onto a side road. It's narrow and unpaved and at every bump, Elvis prays that the gun doesn't go off.

"Hey Hank?"

"Mmmm?" The guy has this lazy way about him that bleeds into every action and word, like he's lived on the fringes and been exposed to so much threat that nothing can touch him.

"You mind taking that pistol out the back of my neck?"

"Sure, sure." Real, casual, like he's forgotten it was there.

Elvis feels the pressure ease as Hank moves the pistol's barrel away. He swallows his sigh of relief, clutching the wheel and trying to make out the road ahead through the dust. A stiff wind has picked up and is blowing it haphazardly. It holds steady as they keep driving, Elvis figuring another forty minutes. Some buildings pop up on either side of the vehicles. Utilitarian. Nothing of note to mark their purpose.

"Take that right coming up."

Elvis swings the car onto a paved section. Up ahead is a gatehouse and his foot eases on the accelerator as an armed guard appears. He'd been on enough bases in Germany during his time there to realize that they were coming up to a Government facility. As he pulls the car to a halt, the guard approaches, weapon ready. He eyeballs the black sedan's plates, standing back but gesturing for Elvis to wind down the window. Elvis casts a quick glance back at Hank.

"Let me handle this." Hank murmurs.

The guard looks at Elvis with doubt on his face. He jerks a little as he hears the rear window being wound down, swivels the barrel of the gun in that direction.

"Take it easy, Private." Out of the corner of his eye, Elvis sees Hank extend his arm out the window, flashing what he assumes are his Agency credentials.

The guard leans forward, studies the black leather wallet, then stands up straight. He re-enters the gatehouse and then the boom gate is swinging up.

"Go on through." Hank thumps the back of Elvis' seat and he drives forward.

As they enter the base, Elvis catches a glimpse of a sign with the words *El Toro* painted beneath some other military designators. He's never heard of the place before, but judging by the low rumble of jets taking off, he figures it's an air force base. Through a gap in the buildings, he spots a row of soldiers marching in unison. Jim is craning his neck, studying the base with all of his usual quiet intensity.

"Take that road to the left." Hank's pointing out a road that leads away from the other buildings, to another fenced off section within the main barrier surrounding the base. "Stop when you get to the gate, I gotta go make sure everything is set up for you boys. We weren't expecting to have to change tack like we have."

Elvis brings the car to a stop at the gate leading beyond the fence and the car shifts on its suspension as Hank gets out. He walks to the gate house and a man in civilian clothing wearing aviators similar to Hank's comes out. He has a clipboard in his hands. Hank says something to him which Elvis can't hear even with the window down.

"Well ain't this some shit?" Elvis breathes under his breath.

He looks at Jim, but the other man is leaned over the steering wheel, chin resting on its top. He's looking at Hank, eyes hooded. Elvis isn't sure that he likes the fire that's burning in that stare, has to wonder if maybe it's gonna immolate both of them.

Y RUSO COMO YO

PAST THE GATEHOUSE, INSIDE THE COMPOUND, Hank walks ahead of them. Guard towers sit at each corner, and Jimmy sees their occupants, attentive and watchful. If it was possible, Hank is even more relaxed than he had been in the car. Maybe being on his own turf has something to do with it? A stiff wind has picked up, and it pushes at his back as Hank leads them to a small Quonset hut.

The door squeaks on its hinges as Hank heads on inside. Elvis follows and Jimmy gives a quick backwards glance. The compound looks deserted. He shrugs his shoulders against an uneasy feeling. It makes everything feel heavier than usual as he follows Hank and Elvis into the hut. A table occupies the centre of the room and he sees a balding guy, young, big liquid eyes looking up at their entry. He's seated on the table's opposite side. Hank moves on up to the head of the table, pulls out a chair, swings it around and then straddles it, arms laced over its back. He's produced a toothpick from somewhere, works it between his lips as he speaks.

"Lee. How's things? They been treating you alright?"

Lee gives Hank a cursory glance, then switches to studying both Jimmy and Elvis. His eyes are expressive, deep set in a triangular face, receding hair swept into a side part. He remains that way for a few moments, then stands up and reaches across the table, extending his hand. Elvis doesn't move, but Jimmy leans forward, grabs the man's hand and gives it a quick shake. His grip is strong, but his hands are soft. He holds Jim's hand longer than what is comfortable before releasing it. He swings the extended hand to Elvis, holds it there. When Elvis finally takes the offered handshake, he goes to make it quick, but Lee holds it for that same, awkward length of time. Elvis gives him a hard stare. Finally, he releases Elvis' hand and sits.

Hank is watching, a smirk on his lips. He leans back and folds his arms across his chest "You boys play nice."

Lee clears his throat and bows his head a little at Hank's words. Jimmy can't work out the dynamic between the two, but guesses that it's deferential from Lee's side. There was a definite dominance to the way that Hank holds the room. Sitting at the head of the table. Calling them boys. That sort of thing. So that made Lee an asset too? Before he can think about it, Lee speaks.

"Can we please get down to business?" His voice is quiet. Considered. The type that you might not notice in the company of stronger men.

"Sure, Lee." With his genial manner, Hank comes across as everybody's friend, but Jimmy thinks that the man wouldn't hesitate to put a bullet in any one of them if needed.

Lee frowns. Maybe there was a layer of doubt there that Jimmy would be able to exploit? He notices Hank watching him, eyes hooded, and he relaxes. Wouldn't do to let Hank catch on to what he was thinking. For his part, Elvis still hasn't sat, opting instead to lean against the wall, arms folded. He looks down at them, surly good looks creased in a frown that mirrors Lee's. The atmosphere hangs oppressively and Jimmy hunches over, feeling its weight.

"Okay gentlemen, first things first. Before we get to any of the technical details, we're gonna have to test your aptitude with a rifle. Lee here is a trained marksman and has kindly offered his assistance in that regard. He'll handle any upskilling you boys need."

He gives Lee a thumbs up, but the other man doesn't react. His face looks rigid, as if he is unaccustomed to showing much of anything. A real cold fish by the looks of it. Hank shrugs and continues.

"While we get you both up to speed in that area, the Company is going to give you three squares, and beds to sleep in. Pretty good deal, huh?"

"What about my family? I'd like to see them." Lee asks suddenly.

"I'm afraid that's not possible. Not right now, at least." Hank gives Lee an apologetic shrug. "You said I'd be able to see my girls." Lee shows only the slightest trace of annoyance. "That was part of the deal."

"Well..." Hank pauses. "Let me float it up the chain, maybe we can work something out?"

Lee coughs again, falls silent.

"Okay, so I have some business to deal with. In the meantime, you boys all get to know each other better. Lee can get you settled in."

Hank stands and moves around the table towards the door. He gives Jimmy a wink as he heads out. As the door closes behind him, Lee looks between the two men. There's a distracted quality to his gaze. Like he's trying to think about several things at once that have nothing to do with Jimmy and Elvis. Jimmy guesses the only way to find out what they were, was to try and get to know the man better.

"You smoke, Lee?" Jimmy leans back in his chair, legs stretched out beneath the table, as if he isn't seated in the middle of a heavily guarded military compound.

"No." Lee stands and moves to the door, opening it and holding it for the other two men.

Jimmy gets to his feet, watches as Elvis gives Lee another heated stare on the way out the door. He was gonna have to get on top of his partner's attitude if he wanted to make any inroads to getting in Lee's good books. If Elvis didn't like someone, he made damn sure that he let them know about it. He catches up to the man outside, leans in close.

"Keep it cool. Isn't that what you told me to do?" He hisses. "So take your own advice... Keep it cool."

The mess hall hut is not much different than the meeting hut, with the exception that it's bigger and contains a large kitchen built into one side. White clothed chefs work behind big industrial pots and the smell of army grade food tickles at Elvis' nostrils. It smells no different than the mess hall at Friedberg. Even the spattered collection of military personnel sitting at tables in small groups is the same. He follows Jim and Lee over to a long table.

The guy seated at it is definitely not military. Not by a long shot. He looks up from a bowl of steaming chili and Elvis can see that his eyebrows have been drawn on with makeup and he's sporting a toupee. It's an odd effect and he can't work out what the guy's deal is. He's wearing a loose shirt and he gives the three men a heavy once over, then gestures for them to sit. Lee gives him an assessing gaze of his own and then takes a seat. Jim sits down as they're introduced.

"This is Dave."

Dave looks up sharply, drops his spoon, spattering chili on the table's surface. Some of it narrowly misses Elvis. He was starting to get the feeling that everyone in this whole sorry mess was an asshole.

"Goddamn it, Lee! How many times do I have to tell you?" Dave's voice is aggressive, with a Cajun lilt. "It's David. Fellas, don't listen to a thing this knucklehead tells you. He's..." David taps his head.

Elvis might've thought that Lee would get up, take a swing at David. Instead, the guy sits there, hands clasped before him, his mouth quirked in an odd little smile. It reminds Elvis of a rattler, right before it strikes. David Stares back, then picks up the spoon and keeps eating. Lee continues speaking as if nothing had happened.

"David's got a plane. When we're ready, he'll be flying you to where you need to go."

Elvis notices that Lee doesn't elaborate on the where. Decides to take a stab at finding out "You able to give us an idea of where that might be? Or are we gonna treat us like damn mushrooms?"

"Too risky." Lee doesn't even look at Elvis, and that little spike of irritation flares up in him again, same as it had back in the meeting hut. The guy is an arrogant jerk. "Hank wants to keep things locked down."

"You worried we might fly the coop? Go and spill the beans on Hank's big plan?"

"Not that you'd get far, but yes, something like that."

Lee has a prissy way of speaking, like he's a lot better than everyone else. Elvis can't see it, personally, but Jim doesn't seem to mind the guy. In fact, since they had gotten here, his partner had been acting a whole heap of strange. Like right now. He's leaning forward, watching Lee intently.

"How long have you been here, Lee?"

"I came in a couple of weeks ago." He watches Jim carefully. "But I've been working with Hank and his crew a bit longer."

David has the spoon in his hand, stopped halfway to his mouth and he lowers it, his face darkening "Lee, you best keep those thin lips of yours better secured." He jabs the spoon in Lee's direction. "Remember what happens when you go speaking out of turn?"

Lee does this swallow and slow blink, then stands "I'll show you to the bunkhouse."

Outside, Lee walks them along the fence, past a firing range. Jim jerks a little at the infrequent peppering sound of rifle fire. Lee doesn't even seem to notice it. He walks with a long gait, every step carrying him as if he's on very important business. They reach the bunkhouse, a long building that looks like every other part of the camp. Elvis is starting to get that heavy feeling he got back in Germany, the monotonous architecture of camp life leaning on him.

"The bunkhouses sleep thirty, but there are only a few of us in the camp. Usually there'd be more, but everyone is out on assignment." He says it like it's a big deal. He stops at the door, turns to a smaller brick building set behind a low fence just beyond the bunkhouse, points it out. There's a large antenna array set to one side of it. "Over there's off limits. There's fatigues and t-shirts in the bunkhouse lockers. Get changed and I'll come back and get you in an hour."

Without waiting for an acknowledgement, Lee turns and strides off.

"Friendly bunch." Elvis drawls.

Jim has his hands bunched in the small of his back, watching as Lee disappears around the corner of another building. He turns back to Elvis and points at the fenced off hut.

"We gotta see what's in that building."

"You aimin' to get us killed, Jim?" Elvis leans in close, voice low, eyes on one of the guard towers.

Jim's not even looking at Elvis, eyes flickering over the other buildings in the camp.

"Fine, have it your way." Keeping his voice low, Elvis keeps the heat in it. "Bad enough that I'm here at all! Killin' the damn President? That's what we're talking about here Jim, and it's damn lunacy! You can go poking around if you want, but keep me the hell out of it. I'm gonna get busy trying to work out how

I can get out of here. You're more than welcome to join me if you want, or stick around and see how long you last." He pokes Jim in the chest. "I didn't sign up for none of this shit."

Elvis doesn't wait for Jim to respond. He spins and pushes into the bunkhouse.

DOWNWARD SPIRAL

JIMMY HAS CHANGED HIS CLOTHES and is sitting on a folding chair outside the bunkhouse when Lee comes striding back towards him. He's toting a rifle and comes to a stop at the bottom of the stairs. Shielding his eyes with one hand, he looks up at Jimmy.

"Where's the other guy?" His voice holds suspicion.

"Sleeping." Jimmy stands and opens the door, looks inside and calls into the dim space. "E?"

There's a low curse and springs creak as Elvis' dim shape rises from a bottom bunk. He looks towards Jimmy, then waves him away. Jimmy goes back outside, shrugs apologetically.

"We've had a rough couple of days."

Lee doesn't say anything, lowers the rifle so that its stock is resting on the ground and the barrel is leaning parallel with his hip.

"You ever shoot before?"

"Some." Jimmy comes down the stairs. In the heat, the thick drill cotton of the fatigues is itchy against his skin. He scratches at his leg. "Used to live out on a farm with my uncle. Been hunting with him a few times."

"I suppose it'll have to do." Lee looks up as Elvis makes an appearance. "What took you so long?"

Elvis grunts by way of response, tucking his white t-shirt into the fatigues. The guy could make a pair of mechanic's coveralls look sexy.

"I asked you a question." Lee's voice doesn't really get much above normal speaking volume, but it's evident that he's pissed.

"And I didn't feel much like givin' you an answer." Elvis smiles at Lee, a real shit-eating grin.

He saunters down the stairs, comes over to stand in front of Lee, thumbs hooked in his belt loops. He's chewing gum and exaggerates the movement of his jaw. Jimmy puts himself between the two men.

"Hey, hey, cool it you two."

Lee looks at Elvis and Elvis gives a gentle shrug and extends one arm as if graciously conceding to the other man.

Lee turns brusquely, lifting the rifle and hoisting it over one narrow shoulder by its strap. "This way."

Jimmy gives Elvis a warning look, then follows after Lee. Leading them through the camp, Lee speaks rarely and when he does, only to point out amenities. There's an ablution hut, a recreation room, and a library amongst other things. Jimmy notices that there is a distinct lack of anything resembling a way of communicating with the outside world, with the exception perhaps of the antenna array.

They reach the firing range and Lee starts setting up. His movements are mechanical, more machine-like than human. There's a rustle, and Jimmy looks up to see that David is sitting in a deck chair, leaned right back so that his toupee is slightly askew. He's smoking a cigarette and watching Lee work with a bored expression on his face. Was he watching Lee just as Lee was watching them? One big paranoia chain?

Elvis moves over to Lee, sticks his hand out for the rifle. Lee maintains his hold, but then relinquishes it after a few terse moments. Elvis checks it over, then grabs some cartridges from the box that's sitting on a folding table. He loads the gun expertly, rests the stock against his shoulder and takes aim. He fires. A bullet casing hits the concrete as he grabs the rifle's bolt and slams another round into the chamber. He fires again. Then again. Then a fourth, fifth and sixth time. Jimmy watches Lee move down the range to where the targets are set up at one end. Elvis reloads the rifle.

"E!" Jimmy hisses. "What the hell are you doing?"

He moves quickly to the other man, grabs him by the shoulder. Lee's walking back and stops. He's looking straight at Elvis. Elvis has the rifle's stock resting in the crook between his shoulder and chest, barrel raised and pointed at Lee. The other man puts his hands on his hips and stares at Elvis peering through the scope. His voice carries clearly in the stillness following the last succession of shots.

"If you point a gun at somebody, it usually means you want to kill them."

Elvis moves his eyes away from the scope and Jimmy can see that there's sweat beading on his forehead. He blinks, then lowers the rifle.

"Naw, man." He puts the rifle on the table. "Why would you think that I'd want any of you assholes dead?"

David smirks, gives a loud guffaw, then gets up from the deck chair "You guys are crazy."

He wanders off. Elvis stalks after him and Lee comes back to the shelter with the target. As he rests it on the folding table, Jimmy sees that each of Elvis' shots have hit dead centre. Lee doesn't look at it again once he's put it on the table. Instead he picks up the rifle and hands it to Jimmy. Jimmy holds the weapon awkwardly. He'd never been fond of guns. With the knowledge of what he was supposed to do with this one, he's even less so. Lee is watching him handle the rifle. He comes over and takes him to the firing position. He helps Jimmy adjust his grip on the rifle so that he's holding it properly.

"The trick is to make it feel as if the rifle is part of your arms. You're not so much holding it, as letting it rest naturally. You said you've done some shooting? How did you manage that?"

Jimmy recalls the red splash of blood on snow, flinches a little.

"Not very well." The gun still feels awkward in his hands, but he forces himself to relax.

"It's just a paper target."

Sure it was, and they weren't using it to train Jimmy or Elvis to put a bullet in Kennedy's skull, either. Nevertheless, he does as instructed. The first shot goes wide, but by the sixth shot, he's managed to hit the target several times.

"There you go." Lee gives a brief smile and Jimmy thinks it's the first time that he's actually seen the man show any real emotion. "Just keep at it, you'll be a pro in no time."

Jimmy showers and, instead of returning to the bunkhouse, takes Lee up on his earlier invite, joining him in the mess hall. There's a small bar at one end, and Jimmy sees Lee sitting at a table reading a paper as he grabs a beer and joins him. Lee has a Coca-Cola next to him, a pool of condensation at its base. As Jimmy sits, Lee doesn't acknowledge him, keeps reading the paper. After a few moments he looks up as if noticing he's got company for the first time.

"You don't want a beer?" Jimmy gives his bottle a little shake, suds splashing against its insides.

"No thanks." Lee doesn't elaborate. "How're you feeling?"

"Fine, I guess?"

It's like they're tiptoeing around the reason why they're both here. Jimmy decides to leave it, not even sure how much Lee knows. Could be his part in the whole thing is just to train them up and nothing more. Hank hadn't been exactly forthcoming during their introduction. Speaking of which, where was the slimy bastard? It made his skin crawl to think of what the guy was up to.

"Your friend is difficult. Hank won't tolerate that."

"Elvis? He's alright. Just gets a little hot under the collar from time to time." Lee gives him this hard stare so Jimmy changes the subject to something they both have in common. "How well do you know Hank?"

"Not very." Lee cocks his head to one side. "How well do you know him?"

"Oh, about the same, I reckon."

"Has he told you much about the operation?"

Jimmy licks his lips, takes a long sip of beer, decides that being vague is probably the better option "A little."

"Enough to let you know that this is going to change the course of history, right?" Lee's stare has turned predatory again.

Something about Lee's words makes Jimmy think of Lincoln in a way that he hadn't before. What if Wilkes-Booth had landed his shot when he took it instead of missing? Had he thought about it as he had stood on the gallows, preparing himself to swing? There were so many ways this could go wrong for him and Elvis if somebody blabbed. The thought makes Jimmy clam up real quick and glad when the door bangs open and Elvis comes slouching in.

His hair is freshly slicked, but there are dark circles beneath his eyes. Lee sees him, grabs the paper and can of coke and excuses himself. Elvis doesn't even acknowledge Lee as the other man exits. He saunters over to the bar, grabs a beer and then joins Jimmy. Kicking back the seat that Lee had occupied, he swings his long legs up onto the table and crosses them at the ankle.

"Glad you showed up when you did." Jimmy takes another sip of beer.

"Getting sick of your new friend?" Elvis rests the beer bottle against his stomach.

"Just didn't want to answer some of the questions that he was asking."

"Such as?"

"You know what."

Elvis sighs, pulls his legs down, scoots the chair forward, and rests the bottle on the table. He hangs his head over it, looking down at the beer inside as if it holds solutions. He sighs again "Guess I do." Taking a drink, Elvis looks up at Jimmy. "You think that what Hank told you about JFK and Marilyn is true? That S.O.B. really ice her because she was pregnant with his kid?"

"I -"

As much as it is the whole reason that he and Elvis had found themselves in this mess, Jimmy finds that he had not thought about it much. Feels a measure of guilt at that. Was he avoiding it because of what it could mean? Was it really a possibility that Marilyn could've posed that much of a threat to someone of the President's status? He can't see it. Can't bring himself to see it more like it. If he does, then it means that he had to admit his own motives for wanting the President Dead, and that sits completely separate to those of Hank and whoever else is working with him. But the initials in her book...

His initials.

Maybe that was another reason why he hadn't thought about her? Everytime he did, there she was, begging him to find a resolution to her unhappy end.

Look at what he did to me. You have an opportunity to make this right.

"- I don't know." Whether he's answering Elvis or Marilyn is unclear. Even the one beer he's had is starting to blur his thoughts. The tiredness hits him like a sledgehammer and he slumps in the chair.

"You don't look so good, Jim."

It's not just him though. They're all responsible.

Now Marilyn's voice has taken on a hard edge. Accusatory and frantic. It twists inside of him like something living, gaining strength the more he listens to it.

Jimmy's finding it hard to breathe. He stands and pushes the chair and it falls backward, clattering loudly in the stillness of the mess hall. The bartender looks up at him. As he staggers to the door, Elvis follows, grabbing him by the arm.

"Hey, Jim!" Elvis goes to grab him again. "Where're you going?"

Elvis' voice fades as he rushes towards the door, pushes out into the fresh air. The pale floodlights over the camp wheel like stars and then he's pitching forward, face sweaty like he's just run a marathon. He hears Elvis' voice coming from a long way away, but he can't answer. He's falling. A myriad of images assault him.

Dean Martin's big leering face.

Detectives Porter and Wyatt, coming after him.

Hank with his casually cruel smile.

Marilyn, lying on her bed, tousled blonde mane in disarray over her bare back, eyes staring into the void.

Somewhere, a phone's ringing and Jimmy thinks that's strange. No phones in the camp.

No phones.

Then blackness swallows him.

RADAR LOVE

ELVIS IS STANDING NEXT TO LEE and a medic, Jim lying weakly on a bunk as the medic checks him over. He's come to, but his face still holds a waxy look, and his breathing seems shallow. Elvis folds his arms while Lee stands to one side watching over things. The medic presses a stethoscope to Jim's chest, listens for a few moments then stands. He moves to a basin and starts washing his hands.

"He's dehydrated and needs bed rest, but there's nothing to suggest anything more serious. Let him lie up until tomorrow."

Lee gives a brief nod and the medic heads out of the bunkhouse.

"Hank gonna be okay with this?" Jim's voice is a rasp.

"Who gives a goddamn what *Hank* thinks?" Elvis feels heat on the back of his neck.

Right now he's ready to throttle Lee, get himself and Jim the hell out of here and take their chances getting as far as they could. As if he can tell what Elvis is thinking, Lee turns to him.

"Make sure he stays in bed until tomorrow morning. I'll come get him for more target practice then." He heads to the door, then stops, jabs a finger at both of them. "Don't either of you leave the bunkhouse."

Elvis drops heavily onto the bunk opposite Jim's, runs his hands over his face. A beam of light skewers Jim, making him look even paler. He doesn't look well. Elvis' father had suffered a terrible fever when Elvis had been young and Jim has that same look about him. He looks away, but his attention is brought back as the other man speaks.

"Did you hear that phone ringing?"

"Huh?" Elvis looks back. "What phone?"

"A phone. I heard one ringing right before I blacked out."

"Uh uh." Elvis grunts. He hadn't heard a thing, but then, he'd been more worried about what was happening with Jim to notice anything else.

"I swear I heard something..." Jim trails off then adds, almost as if to himself. "I haven't seen a phone in this place since we got here."

"Coulda just been in your head... Like the Doc said. You're exhausted." Could be more than that, if Elvis thinks about it carefully. What if the whole thing with Marilyn was just something Jim had made up to satisfy his own needs? Could happen. Elvis had seen it a few times in guys that he had served with. Coming up with things that could get them home to their families sooner through early discharge. Was that it? He watches the other man sit up, holds up a hand to stop him. "Whoah, whoah! Where d'you think you're goin'?"

"Gotta get in that building. Something in there that we need to see."

"And what makes you think there's not some guard in there waiting to pop you the minute you stick that pig-head of yours through the door, huh?"

"There won't be." How Jim knows this is beyond Elvis, but he doesn't have time to dwell on it as his partner continues. "It's something to do with Hank. Betting that place is his office while he's on base."

Well, maybe that makes a whole heap of sense, but it still doesn't give them any sort of reason for why they should be poking around in it. Better that they just see if they can't up and get the hell out of here.

"You go snoopin' around there, you're gonna be doin' it on your own." Elvis rests his hands on his knees. "I ain't wantin' any part of it, you hear?"

Jim gets off the bed, sways a bit, like he's gonna pitch face-first towards the floor. He collects his fatigues, pulls them on while leaning against the pole that supports the upper part of the bunk bed. He sits down heavily, laces his boots up. Once he's done, Elvis watches him move towards the window, peer out of it into the night. What he sees apparently satisfies his curiosity, because the next thing Elvis knows, Jim's moving towards the door at the opposite end of the bunkhouse from where they usually enter.

Elvis sits on the bunk for a few moments, then groans. Standing abruptly, he hurries after Jim. Wouldn't do to let the stubborn fool get himself shot. Two pairs of eyes are better than one, right? Besides, maybe Jim *will* find something in there that would help get them out of here. Elvis carries heavy doubt of that actually happening, but sitting around waiting feels just as pointless.

As Elvis joins Jim at the door, the other man gives him a doubtful stare "Thought you didn't want any part of this?"

"If you're gonna get yourself shot, I wanna be there to say 'I told you so'."

Jimmy leads and Elvis follows as they use the shadows to move up towards the brick building. Closer up, it's sitting in darkness. Maybe that was something he should be worried about, but having made up his mind, he can't spare the energy. As it turns out, when they reach the fence line surrounding the building, he sees a spot at its rear where he could scale it easily without being seen. He turns to Elvis.

"Keep a lookout."

Without waiting for an answer, Jimmy moves in a half crouch to a stack of crates placed at the rear corner of the fence. Whoever had put them there obviously hadn't got the memo about this place being off-limits. Jimmy clambers up one crate, and the next, until he reaches the topmost in the stack. He gives a quick glance down then clambers over the fence and down. Fortunately, the razor wire that dominates the base's perimeter fence is not present here. Maybe Hank figures people are scared enough of reprisals not to go snooping around. Dropping from the fence, he beckons Elvis over. The other man gives a furtive glance back the way they had come but the area between here and the bunkhouse is deserted. He grips the fence, leaning his face in close.

"Hang out here." Jim's whisper is hurried, his throat feeling tight. "You see anyone, make a bird noise."

"A bird noise?" Elvis has this incredulous look on his face. "What sort of bird noise?"

"Uh, you know..." As Jim goes to make a bird noise, he realises how ridiculous it is. "Scrap it. Just throw a piece of gravel at the window."

Elvis gives Jimmy this shrug, like that suggestion is only slightly better than the first. Jimmy shrugs back, then turns, heading towards the building. He sees a solid looking door and stops in his tracks, cursing his stupidity that he didn't think that the place might be locked up. He scans the front of the building, then lets out his breath in relief. A window sits on one side, and through whatever sheer luck Jimmy possesses, it sits ajar.

Scurrying over, Jimmy stops and peers through the crack. The interior of the building looks like one open space, and his luck seems to be holding because it sits in darkness. The only light coming into the room beyond the window is that bleeding in from the outside. He holds his breath as he pushes the window up. As he does, he can see why it hasn't been shut properly. It takes a lot more effort than it should to open. As the window squeals upwards in its frame, he hears Elvis swear from the fenceline. He turns back and scans the area behind the other man, but there is nothing there. Giving an apologetic wave, he braces himself and then slides through the open window.

Inside, he has to crawl over a desk. He's careful to pick his way through the scattered paperwork on its surface, disturbing it only slightly. In the diffused light, Jimmy sees scuffed linoleum and wood panelled desks set up around the space. Cork boards and blackboards line the walls. Papers pinned and scribbles in chalk. Jimmy moves to the first one, but there's nothing on it of interest. It seems to be a collection of interdepartmental memos with dates and personnel movements. Maybe if he knew exactly what it is that he should be looking for, they might mean something, but right now, they're incomprehensible.

He moves to one of the desks, and has the same experience. Nothing. He gives a grunt of frustration until he hits the next desk. That's when his eyes land on it. There's a tray and he spots the word *Helena*. He stops, eyes burning, locked onto the document like the word is a lodestone. His hand is shaking as he picks it up, and he has to force it to stillness. *12305 Fifth Helena Drive*. He scans the document, reading each line twice to make sure he gets its true meaning.

There's a lot that doesn't make sense, but what is clear is that it's an order of some type that instructs the service provider to wire-tap the premises at the address noted. Not just any premises. Marilyn's. He lets the document fall back into the tray, as if the piece of paper is hot. He stands there, staring at it, trying to mark its significance to everything else. The report he had seen at Weinstein's house backed up this. At first he had thought that it was the studio using the information to drop Marilyn from her contract without a legal blowback. This, though... This seemed to line up more with what Hank had said, about a blackmailing attempt on the President. Had the studio put Marilyn in the firing line for some type of clean up operation delivered on Jack's orders? He thinks back to that night by the pool, a time that felt like a hundred years ago.

I told you.

He remembers that shielded fear as she had looked at her house. The place that was meant to be her refuge. If he is honest with himself, Jimmy can't say that he had believed her at the time. It had felt too much like paranoia, and yet he was where he was and with the evidence in front of him. It made it feel a hell of a lot more real. He can't afford to think too long about it with the wealth of information surrounding him. He goes back to scanning the boards around the walls. If there's something else to find, it's going to be easier to find there with whatever short time he has available to him.

Moving from board to board, he sees the same as what he had first seen. But then, his eyes land on a photo. It shows a solid looking man getting out of a car. He has dark glasses on, and a hat, but Jimmy would recognise the man anywhere. When Hank had mentioned his name before, Jimmy had thought that maybe it was a bluff, but here he is. The photo is grainy, but there can be no doubt.

Frazini.

If Hank really had been in contact with Frazini, then Jimmy has to wonder in what other ways his former employer was involved in this thing. He starts lifting papers pinned next to the photo. His eyes land briefly on the name Kennedy. He scans the line. The memo wasn't concerning the older Kennedy brother this time. Had something to do with Robert. Robert Kennedy and Frazini somehow linked? It was no secret that the Attorney General had an obsession with eradicating organised crime. But what was the angle?

He's about to lift the paper from the board to better scrutinise it, when there is sharp pinging noise on the window.

His blood runs cold. He moves quickly. Heart thudding, he scurries for the window, slipping through it. He moves to close it, but remembers the noise. If Hank or anybody else asks, he'll just have to deny having anything to do with it, as unlikely as that was.

Elvis is jigging on the spot by the fence like he has to go to the bathroom. Jimmy looks at the fence, then runs at it, scaling it not as easily as he hopes but managing without scraping himself up too badly on the sharp ends at the top. He lands awkwardly, head suddenly spinning. He takes a breath, forces himself to calm down. Elvis points back towards the bunkhouse silently and Jimmy's half scared that he'll see Lee heading towards it, but it's just a guard. Sticking to the darkness, Jimmy and Elvis head back.

Inside, Elvis doesn't say anything, quickly returning to his own bunk and lying down. As his head hits the pillow, Jimmy rolls over, staring up at the bottom of the mattress above his own. The bunkhouse creaks in the wind, sounding haunted. Jimmy tries to shut out the sound, thinking that there were already enough ghosts in his head without inviting more. He thrashes and tries to stop any more unwelcome visits from Marilyn, but it seems that she's found access anyway, despite his best efforts.

They killed me, Jimmy. All of them took their piece of me.

And with the paper that had held her address still fresh in his mind, he can't disagree. The real question though, was what was he going to do about it?

WALK THE LINE

IT HAD BEEN A MONTH SINCE JIM had broken into the building and Hank had come back. If he had noticed anything amiss, the guy hadn't said anything. Right now, he's leaning against a pole, watching as Elvis practices. He seems satisfied with the progress both he and Jim had made under Lee's instruction. Speaking of the cold bastard, Lee watches Elvis, thin mouth a straight line that makes his opinion of the other man's shooting unreadable.

For Jim's sake, Elvis had kept things neutral with Lee, dialling back on the hostility so that they could at least work together. There still wasn't a clear way out of here, so biding his time was all he could do, it seemed. Maybe it's better just to wait until they have an opportunity off base to make their escape? Sooner or later, they would have to be left to their own devices. It isn't clear whether Jim has any opinions on the matter. In fact, ever since he had come out of the building, Elvis hadn't been able to get much of a read on anything that Jim was thinking.

What he did know was that Jim and Lee had become as thick as thieves. Elvis had his concerns on what that might mean, but he had made the decision to keep any tension with Lee tuned low, so he said nothing. Instead, he hung out with David. Whatever the guy's deal was, he had come to ignore the make-up and the wig. Figured that everybody was entitled to do whatever they felt like doing in this world that had turned all topsy-turvy.

At times, he wishes he could call Pop. Just a few minutes to chew the fat with the older man. Maybe be offered something that would help him out of this mess. But Pop isn't here. In fact, he had no idea if Pop was even safe. Frazini's words kept ringing in his ears.

How's your Pop?

Well, if he had the opportunity to see Frazini again, Elvis would let him know exactly what he thought of the bastard's concern for his father. Maybe take Lee's rifle and jam it up his ass. Hank had mentioned Frazini. Elvis had to wonder what the connection was. How did a two-bit mobster get caught up with the CIA? From what Jim had told him, there was a truckload of information inside the building behind the bunkhouse. Elvis kind of wishes he had gone in too. Maybe the answers he needed were inside?

He finishes up and hands the rifle to Jim. Raising the weapon, Jim sights down the scope and fires. The shot strikes true and Elvis thinks his partner has taken to it like a pro. Who knew? But some people just had a natural aptitude for things. It was like Elvis and the guitar. The first time that he had picked up the instrument, it was like he had known exactly what to do. A little rough, mind you, but still... It was like it had formed part of his spirit or some such. Just like his voice. Maybe if he had invested more time in that, he wouldn't be where he was now? Wonder what old Brother Frank would make of the whole situation? Probably look down on him and just shake his head. Make that disapproving noise he sometimes made, the one that came from in the back of his throat.

He thought about what Mama would think, but couldn't picture it. Truth was, she probably wouldn't have been able to comprehend any of this. She had been a lively woman, full of warmth and love, with not a mean bone in her body. At least, that's the way Elvis remembers her. To see her baby boy with these men? Preparing to do what he was gonna do? Well... It would probably just break her gentle heart. He puts it out of his mind, watches as Hank walks up.

"You got a lot of skill. They teach you that in the army?"

"Among other things." Elvis keeps it casual. He didn't like the guy, but there was no point bringing that up in the here and now.

"That'll come in handy later on."

Elvis takes out a stick of gum, starts chewing, gives Hank a thoughtful look. "So when're we gonna learn about this 'later on'?"

"When I'm ready to discuss it. You got the basics, what else do you need to know?" Despite his laid back demeanour, there's an edge in Hank's voice.

"Hey, no big deal, man... You take your sweet time."

Elvis decides to back down. No point riling the guy up when they were so close to a point where both he and Jim might find a break to get away from the psycho. He offers a stick of gum to Hank who gives it this long look before accepting, taking the gum and chewing noisily as he moves away to speak quietly to one side with David. Together, the two men wander off into the open space next to the practice range. Hank looks back over his shoulder once, but then becomes engrossed in his conversation.

Jim finishes and Lee gestures for them both to come close. He looks at each of them steadily, keeping his voice low and looking over at Hank "You both think you're ready?"

"As we'll ever be." Elvis nods. Maybe a little too quickly judging by the cold stare that Lee gives him.

For his part, Jim takes his time answering, and Elvis sees the way he's playing old Lee like a fiddle. Finally, he speaks.

"I don't think I'll ever be ready."

Lee nods appreciatively and claps Jim on the shoulder. "Good answer." He looks over at Hank furtively again. "You know that you can't trust him, right?"

"Trust him?" Elvis gapes. "Only a half wit would believe anything that snake says."

"Keep your voice down." Lee gives him this irritated look. "Take this." He hands Jim a small device with a grille on its front and a button on one side. "This is a short range radio. It's been tuned to a specific frequency, so don't go fooling around with it. If you get into trouble and you need an out, use it."

Jim holds the thing in his hand, looking down at it for long moments before looking over at Hank. He peers back at Lee, eyes squinted "Who?"

Lee looks at him quizzically.

"Who will be on the other end?"

"Never mind who, just someone that you'll be able to rely on. Other friends that I've made. Friends that don't trust these guys either. Sometimes a little bit of distrust is the safest way... "

"If that's the case then how do we know we can trust anything *you* say?" Elvis keeps his voice low, almost a hiss.

Lee gets this look, like he's addressing a simpleton "You don't."

It's that small piece of honesty that, for whatever idiot reason, actually makes Elvis trust the guy more than anything else.

Before Hank comes back, Jimmy pockets the receiver, keeps his hands in them and walks over to the Company man. David watches him approach, twitchy as always. Hank gives him one of his laconic smiles.

"Alright then, guess we're about ready to move onto phase two. That involves meeting up with some other members of our merry little band." There's a smile on Hank's face that Jimmy doesn't like, like he's withholding something unpleasant for his own amusement. "You and country boy go pack your things and then meet me by the gatehouse."

"Our things?" Elvis lets out a flat laugh. "Hell, we might as well have shown up here naked. Didn't have time to pack."

"Took the liberty of organizing you both some civvies. Had them put on your bunks." He turns and heads off towards his office. "I'll join you boys momentarily, got some errands to run."

Jimmy has a morbid curiosity about what those errands might be, but decides it's probably better that he doesn't try guessing. Lee comes over to stand with Jimmy and together they watch Hank make his way through the camp, until he rounds the corner of a hut and vanishes.

Lee gives the area a quick glance, sees David, bends close to Jimmy and murmurs "Remember what I said."

He gives Jimmy a curt nod before moving off in the same direction that Hank had gone.

Elvis is already following him out and Jimmy has to run to catch up with his partner's long-legged stride "Hey, E! Wait up."

"Out of the fryin' pan, I guess..." Elvis' dour expression belies the brevity of his words.

"At least we'll be out of the camp. That's what you wanted, right?"

"Sure. But who knows who these other jokers are that Hank's talking about." He stops. "Jesus Christ. Hank. Not even the asshole's real name and yet he's got us acting like it's the one his mama landed upon the moment he was born."

They walk back to the bunks together without exchanging any more conversation. What is there to say really? Jimmy can't disagree with Elvis. Truth be told, for the past month, Jimmy's had to put thinking about anything in a holding pattern. There was a certain comfort in avoiding confronting the truth about what came next. The compound had come to represent something of a haven, not just from the outside world, but from himself as well.

Even before the whole Marilyn thing, he had been at odds with himself. His whole life had lacked focus. Maybe that's what he had liked about Marilyn so much? She was someone so similar to Jimmy, but had discovered a drive to make something of herself, despite any naysayers. He smiles, but even as it appears, it falters and dies. But the vultures had gotten her in the end, hadn't they? When they saw that she wouldn't be broken, they had taken upon themselves to do it for her.

Anger flares, and he remembers. He was going to make the bastard pay for what he had done to Marilyn. So what if it came with a cost? Everything had a price. It didn't matter if you were a handyman, a movie star, or a President. There was always someone who would come calling to collect. And Jimmy intended to collect. One way or the other. Maybe it wasn't what Elvis would be down for, but he had the means now.

As they enter the bunkhouse, Elvis gives Jimmy a look, like the thoughts that he had just had were on full display. He ignores the other man, starts packing the duffel bag, jamming clothes in haphazardly. His movements are quick and efficient, almost mechanical as his mind drifted. Mexico had been the first time he had ever killed somebody, after that, there had been the Agency man, Dwight. It felt weird to think how accustomed he was becoming to it.

"Jim?" Elvis has come over to the bunk, his hand resting against its topmost edge.

"What." Jimmy gives him a cursory glance.

"You know that we ain't really going through with this, don't you?"

The pause before Jimmy replies is long enough that Elvis would have good reason to doubt its conviction.

"I know." He lies.

Elvis chews at the corner of his lower lip, but doesn't say anything. Moves back to his bunk and continues packing while Jimmy finishes up. When he's done, he totes the duffel bag and heads to the door, not looking to see if Elvis is following.

PAPER PLANES

Dallas, November 1962

DAVID, FOR ALL HIS QUIRKS, is a pretty good pilot. The little Cessna 172 glides through the sky, with only a bump here and there. From this height, Elvis can see the patchwork grid of the landscape laid out, disappearing into the hazy distance. In the pilot's seat, David seems right at home, unlike how he is normally. Gone is the twitchiness that had dominated every interaction that Elvis had had with the man. Seems like every person had their place of comfort. For Elvis, that was sure as shit not here. Glancing at the compass, Elvis can see that they're heading North East. As they move further from the coast, the land takes on a parched quality.

Long veins of greenery peter out, leaving nothing but broken dips and gullies to break up the otherwise featureless sprawl of desert. He looks back, sees Jim staring out the window, eyes fixed as if he is not really looking at anything at all. Hank sits quietly engrossed in a notebook, scribbling furiously. When he notices Elvis looking, he closes the notebook. Not in a hurried way or anything. He was too cool a customer to let anything like someone intruding on his secret squirrel bullshit rattle him.

When he gives Elvis a tight smile, Elvis doesn't return it. Instead, he turns back and tries to relax as much as he can in the cramped space of the plane. The plane banks to the right and then starts making a long, looping descent. A dirt airstrip with several buildings appears and Elvis can only guess that's where they're headed. David evens out the plane, lifting one wing and then tilting the nose up slightly. The plane connects with the runway and when it bounces, Elvis' stomach lurches a little. The aircraft comes to a stop in front of the wide opening of a hangar.

Elvis is grateful to climb out and put his feet on solid ground again. It's not so much that he has a problem with flying, but the whole way, his guts have felt twisted up inside. Probably on account of the conversation that he and Jim had had right before leaving the camp. As much as he hated to admit it, he hadn't handled it as well as he should've. He got the sense that the other man was closing himself off. That was no good for anything that Elvis might have planned.

Didn't take a genius to work out that Jim had a beef with JFK over this whole Marilyn thing, especially with Hank delivering poison to his ear. Best he could do, Elvis guesses, is to try and work out a way to provide an antidote. Regardless of whether Kennedy was responsible for the actress's death, he was still the damn President. There was no way that you were gonna catch Elvis going anywhere near what Hank and his crew were planning with any serious intent. But that didn't mean that Jim still wouldn't go and take a bite of the apple if he wanted revenge bad enough. Maybe Elvis could talk him out of it, maybe he couldn't, but he had to try if for no other reason than he believed that Jim was better than that.

Jim jumps out of the plane, stretches his legs and starts talking with Hank. David is checking something at the front of the aircraft. When Hank says something to the pilot, David gives him this wave as if he's tired of listening to the Agency man's bullshit. Before Hank can get any cosier with Jim. Hank gives Elvis a little annoyed frown before it slips from his face as if it were never there.

"There's an office at the front of the hangar." He indicates a rusting demountable. "You two wait in there. I gotta go meet up with our partners."

Without waiting to see if they've followed his directions, Hank scurries off. David is eyeballing them, so Elvis gives him a wave and gestures for Jim to walk with him to the office. Jim lights up and follows Elvis.

"Partners, huh? Wonder what you have to do to become a partner and not an asset?" He tries to get a laugh out of Jim, but the other man has adopted a brooding expression. "Come on, man, you need to lighten up a bit. If Hank thinks there's something on your mind... Well, who knows what that cold son of a bitch will do? Might just decide his two 'assets' need to be replaced. Until we can work out how to get out of here without getting shot, I think we need to keep in his good books."

Jim stops. He takes a long drag on his cigarette then lets it dangle next to his leg. He releases a drift of smoke. "Did you meet with Frazini before coming to LA?"

"Huh?" Jim's question hits at Elvis like a jab. He tries to duck out of the way. "Why would y-"

"Just answer the damn question, E! Did you?" Jim has his whole body leaned forward, jaw jutted and eyes screwed tight.

Elvis sighs and lowers his head, scrubs a hand through his hair which has grown long in their time at the camp. There's no way out of answering the question. He gives in.

"Yeah..."

"So when I asked you if you'd seen him, and you said '*No Jim, of course not.*' What was that about?!?"

"I - " Elvis curses, then blurts out. "He wanted me to kill you. You wanted me to tell you that? Huh? You wanted me to say that Frazini told me to clip you for whatever reason?"

"And you agreed to do it?" Jim sucks angrily at the cigarette.

"What else did you think I was gonna do? Bastard's got my balls in a vice... You think I was gonna say "No, Sir. Not my good friend, James Dean." Then he puts me on ice. What would you have done? Besides... You're still breathing ain't you? You damn idiot! No way I was actually gonna do it!"

It's Elvis' turn to get angry, and his voice rises on the last word, rolling and echoing across the open space. At the same time as David looks up and over at them, Elvis stops, eyes locked behind Jim as Hank and his partner approaches.

"Hello, Gentlemen." Frazini is standing next to Hank, who is standing next to Michael. Michael has a cast on his arm, glaring heavily at Elvis. Frazini looks pointedly from Elvis to Jim. "That's the most alive looking corpse I've ever seen. And I've seen a few."

Inside the office, Jimmy is leaned back in his chair, jaw muscles bunched as Frazini sits on the opposite side of a small desk. The big goon that he has with him is standing ramrod straight between Elvis and Jimmy. Elvis keeps glancing sidelong at the guy and Jimmy wonders if he had anything to do with the damage done to the thug's arm. Judging by the way that the guy is staring back with open hostility, the answer seems obvious.

"So... Here we are." Frazini seems relaxed, like Jimmy and Elvis are nowhere near the top of his shit list. "A happy reunion."

"Dom-" Elvis starts, but the goon cuts him off.

"That's Mr. Frazini to you." The thug doesn't even pretend like he's not staring daggers at Elvis.

"Michael." Frazini raises his hands, mimes pushing down the empty air beneath them. "Please... We have important matters to discuss without letting previous transgressions get in the way."

Jimmy narrows his eyes, trying to work out exactly what Frazini is playing at. He sees Frazini's eyes flicker, follows the path of that momentary shift in attention. Hank. He had looked straight at Hank. So that might account for why Frazini was so willing to let whatever beef he had with the two of them be put to bed. At least temporarily. Jimmy wonders exactly what Hank has on Frazini that has turned him so friendly. Hank sees Jimmy looking at him, gives this small nod and another one of his lazy smiles.

"Now, before we get into the nitty gritty. There is one small matter to rectify."

Before Jimmy can react, Frazini has produced a pistol from beneath the desk. He fires without seeming to aim and both Elvis and Jimmy flinch from the noise. The small space is filled with the acrid stench of smoke. Jimmy lowers hands from his ears.

"What the -" Elvis goes to stand, eyes and mouth wide.

Jimmy's heart presses against his chest and his breath tangles in his throat. A bullet hole neatly punctuates the centre of Michael's forehead. One eye had rolled, the corpse giving both Elvis and Jimmy an accusing stare simultaneously. Blood is already pooling around the back of his head and his limbs are bent at an odd angle. Elvis is caught in a half crouch, as if he can't decide whether to sit or stand. The door opens and two men come in, hoist up Michael's corpse between them and drag it out of the office. It leaves a wet smear on the linoleum.

"Sit down Elvis, you're making me feel bad." Frazini has put the pistol on the desk, with its barrel pointed towards them. "Now. Where were we?"

"Are you crazy!" Elvis moves towards the gun, but Hank makes a tutting noise and Jim turns to see that he's casually waving his own weapon at Elvis. Elvis slumps in his chair, head bowed, he's muttering to himself. "What did you do?"

"What did *I* do?" Frazini asks the question with an almost rhetorical air, like it doesn't need to be answered, but then he leans forward and closes his eyes, pinching the bridge of his nose. He reopens them. When he speaks, his voice has grown low, his words peppered with hostility. "You see what I did just there? That was a lesson. For both of you. So, I hope I've got your attention. Fuck with us, fuck with our plans, you just had an up close demonstration of what will happen, in the event that it wasn't already abundantly clear to you." Frazini takes a deep breath, leans on the table before continuing. He's slowed right down, as if he is a teacher showing patience to slow-witted students. "What we have here is a mutually beneficial situation. Your new friend came to us looking for a solution and I saw an opportunity. Call it synchronicity. We decided to aid the cause."

"Synchro-what now?" Elvis gawps.

"It means two things happening which are connected indirectly." Jimmy says the words flatly.

He doesn't really think that Elvis wants to know the definition, but feels like he has to say something to stop from screaming. His guts writhe, the feeling quickly making its way to his head.

"I told you, Dom... " Hank laughs, gestures towards Jimmy with the gun "... This here is one smart cat."

"Yeah, I know." Frazini is watching Jimmy with hooded eyes. He takes a toothpick out of his pocket and places it daintily between his fleshy lips. "So, now the English lesson is finished, please allow me to continue with the rest of class." He speaks around the toothpick. "The Agency needs something from us, and in return, we get something from the Agency somewhere down the line. You two just happened to come along at the right time to make that happen."

Jimmy looks at Frazini, then back at Hank. There's a long silence. Finally, Frazini breaks it.

"Well don't everybody speak at once."

"The CIA is working with the mob to Assassinate the President?" How ludicrous the words sound, now that Jimmy has actually said them.

"Uh uh uh." Hank waggles a finger. "The Agency is not working with the mob. A conglomerate of upstanding businessmen is working with the Agency to excise the moral decay introduced by the President."

"Fine, pitch it however you want. But what makes you think that Elvis and I will actually go through with it? What's to stop us from just walking?"

"You seem to be forgetting just where you are, what we have over you and how it might impact your loved ones!" Frazini snarls, temper flaring, breaking through the casual demeanour. He stands, snatching the weapon off the table. "So stop acting like you're in a position to suggest otherwise."

"Whoah, whoah, Steady there, Dom." Hank gets to his feet, does this huge stretch like he's just woken up from a nap. "No need for threats. We're all in this together." Hank comes closer to the desk, seats himself in a chair between where Elvis, Jimmy and Frazini sit, like he's going to referee. He rests his elbows on his knees, steeples his fingers in front of his face with their tips touching his lips. He takes a deep breath and then releases it. His next words sound as if he's reached a decision on something that he had been considering for a while. "Show him the letter."

Frazini stares Hank out, then throws his hands in the air and reaches into his coat pocket. He pulls out an envelope and drops it on the table. He slides it across to Jimmy. Looking at it, Jimmy hesitates in picking it up. Something about the way that Hank and Frazini are playing this is off. What was in the letter that would change anything? Elvis is watching the three of them. He hones in on Elvis, who sits there watching intently, brow beetled.

"Jim? I don't think you should open that." Elvis leans close, voice low as if he only means for Jimmy to hear.

"Huh?" Jim gives him a glance, barely registering what he is being told.

"Don't open it. I don't like this."

Maybe it's the way that Elvis is warning him off, but now his desire to open the envelope is an almost burning one. He scoops it up, rips open the seal and yanks out a folded piece of paper. As his eyes scan lines of text, he realizes it's a transcript of a recording. A back and forth conversation between Marilyn and the President. A conversation where she's revealing to the President that she's pregnant with his child. Where he's denying it. Back and forth it goes and as he reads, he can almost hear her voice. Panicked. Afraid. Alone. Then he does hear her voice as the other men in the room fade into insignificance and it's just Jimmy and Marilyn.

You see? You see what he did? Now you know... And you know what you have to do.

HAPPY BIRTHDAY

THE LETTER ISN'T ENOUGH. Her voice isn't enough. Even if it does push Jimmy that little bit closer to making a decision. He blinks and recalls. Going back. Back to before she was dead. Back to when there still felt as if there might be a little bit of hope. Something to look forward to. The thrill of being in Marilyn's presence. The thrill of seeing how other people saw her. She was iconic. Was still iconic. Just not in the same way as when her liveliness and beauty ran untamed through the Hollywood jungle. Back then. He recalls.

On a whim she had called him up. Unexpected.

She says *Come fly with me.*

Fly where? He says.

New York. Marilyn replies.

New York? Are you crazy? Cukor's gonna shit if we're not at rehearsals.

Oh, that old fuddy-duddy. Who is he anyway? I'm Marilyn Monroe. And she laughs, all giddy and infectious.

So he agrees. He agrees to fly to New York. She doesn't even tell Jimmy what they'll be doing there. Doesn't even say to him what any of it's for. But maybe he doesn't need to be told, because she is Marilyn, and Jimmy would follow her off the edge of the earth if it means that he gets to spend some more time with her. He likes the way that people stare when he's with her. He likes the jealousy in their eyes. Like they wish that they could be him. And no one had ever wanted to be James Byron Dean before.

The plane trip is a frenzy. A collage of champagne and other things. At one point, caught up in the moment, they're making out. Not like it's a serious thing, like they're attracted to each other. More like they're overwhelmed by the sheer abandon of it all. Living life without borders. Pushing everything away and existing in the tiny bubble of the plane's cabin. It is one of the few times Jimmy can remember feeling unburdened. He laughs. She laughs. They laugh all the way from LA to New York.

But then they land, it evaporates as quickly as the fizz from a bottle of champagne that had been left open too long. New York is grey. A dark empire of towering monoliths. The levity from above the clouds is left behind and overshadowed by the weight of the city. The car drive is sombre in a way that sets Jimmy right back to square one. A place where his nerves are wound so tightly that they are set to snap at any moment. It only gets worse when she tells him.

When Marilyn tells Jimmy the real reason for their trip to New York. That she has this thing. Could he be a darling and look after himself for a while? Maybe go and catch up with some old friends? Yeah, sure. He has his theatre crew from when he lived here before. Mostly off-Broadway, but a few were starting to make a name for themselves outside of that. But dammit! This was meant to be him and her and nobody else. He figures that maybe this had to do with a man, but who is he to question her? He can never go against her. Not when she needed him to be what he was to her. Not when everyone else was not that.

He sees it in her eyes. The expectation that tempers her wild excitement. And he gives her this smile. Maybe the finest performance of his life, because he already feels alone but shows her that he is happy for her. She laughs, and a small patch of warmth blooms in his chest as she hugs him. She holds him tightly and he can smell her sweet perfume as she breathes in his ear a soft...

Thank you.

The car drops Jimmy off at a diner. He jams his hands in his pockets and heads inside. The long curving counter reflects the bright yellow of the dangling lights above. He sits. A woman wearing an apricot outfit and white apron with stains down its front slings him a coffee. He slurps at it, feels the caffeine hit. He gets up, makes a call from the battered payphone on the diner's wall.

Sure, come on over. Liz says. *I'll fix some supper.*

Jimmy exits into a city that holds life only because of the coffee buzz that carries him through its streets. He keeps his head down, unwilling to look up at the towering skyscrapers overhead. He hails a cab and it carries him to Liz's. She looks as perfect as ever when she opens the door. Her big, warm eyes go gooey when she sees him. Removes the smoke that had been dangling from her lips, holds it up in the air as she gives him a one-armed hug. That was the way with Liz. She could always tell when something was up with him, even if it had been months since they had spoken or seen each other.

Inside, they sit down and she pours him rum, puts a record on and then sits down on the floor, curling her legs beneath her on a cushion. A light wood coffee table with dark blue tiles in its top separates them and she deals some cards. She smokes the cigarette elegantly then stubs it out in a turquoise ceramic ashtray. Her apartment is an extension of her. Big posters of French actresses. Jazz musicians. Books cram narrow and high shelves. She leans back in between hands of rummy, studying him.

Who broke your heart this time?

And she wants to know. Not just asking for the sake of it. He watches her watching him and then shrugs.

Nobody. Not in the way you mean.

He doesn't want to talk about it. Doesn't want to pull himself out of her happy company. If he does, then he will be alone again. Maybe he is always alone? Ever since what had happened to him as a kid. The thing that only Liz knows about. Maybe being alone isn't the problem. Maybe being lonely is. That's why it was always that he had to be with someone, even if the company meant nothing. So that he can't hear the nagging voice in his head telling him that he is not good enough. Never good enough.

Jim. Liz says it softly and it brings him out of whatever downward spiral he's travelling. He looks up and gives her a smile, although he thinks she can see that it isn't a smile that holds much joy. She springs up, moves to the record player, switches it up so that the music is more lively. She comes to him and holds out both her hands, grasping his and yanking him to his feet. Together they move. The music, that new band, The Rolling Stones. It's jagged and dangerous, nothing like what he's much used to. But he dances anyway, because it makes Liz happy. Makes him forget.

They finish dancing and he stays a couple more hours. They talk about anything that isn't Marilyn. He kisses her on the cheek at the door as he leaves and she gives him a worried look. He tries for a reassuring smile but doesn't quite land it. As soon as she shuts the door and he's left in the cold of the hallway, everything comes back and he moves quickly out into the street, as if that will help Jimmy escape himself. The asphalt gleams from a late shower, reflecting streetlights. A dog barks, the echoes chasing him back Uptown.

He passes a store-front, sees a big television set. His eyes are arrested by what's on the screen. It's Marilyn and she's dressed to kill. Even in black and white, he can see what makes her a magnet. Her dress makes her look like a Goddess, natural and raw. Tiny diamonds catch the light like captured stars. She stands demurely, not really much like her at all. Next to her is the President and between them is a cake. He starts singing.

Even with the song being the simple thing that it is, Jack butchers it, but the smile Marilyn gives him is so radiant that it eclipses the lacklustre performance. She is looking at him as if he has just promised her the world. Everyone else in the scene is faded, although he can't tell whether it's something to do with camera work, or his own obsessive focus. Jimmy can feel heat in his neck, seething and roiling, the beginnings of an inferno. He snaps. Slams his fist into the window, does more damage to himself than the glass.

Turning, he moves away quickly, the night consuming him as much as his rage.

Next day, they fly back. Jimmy tries not to let Marilyn feel his tension. Her euphoria is even more than it had been on the previous flight. She's joking with him, being affectionate, all of the things that would usually make him act the same, but it's soured by what he had seen. Marilyn and Jack. Something between them. Something that he was incapable of giving her. That knowledge spikes that feeling of loneliness again, like he's headed for a point where she will abandon him.

At the airport, they say their goodbyes, and he acts like the things inside him are not worthy of his attention. She gives him this long and steady look, like maybe she's picked up that everything is less than okay with him. Her hand on his arm is a balm to his anxiety. That feeling of hopelessness lessens. Maybe the thing with Jack will blow over? Maybe things will go back to the way that they had been up until that moment?

That's what he had thought.

Then. But now...

Jimmy's back where all the wrong turns have led him. Back to a present where Hank, Frazini and Elvis are a thing. Where they all want a piece of him, tearing him apart like a pack of wolves. Where Marilyn is just this voice in his head, urging him on to do something that he really doesn't want to, even if it might mean that he brings her some peace. Even if it means that he has nothing left afterwards. Because he owes her. And he owes Jack for what he did to Marilyn.

The three other men in the room are watching him. All of them have different expressions. Hank's is as unreadable as ever, Elvis' brows are pinched and Frazini has moistened his lips, his gaze hungry. Jimmy gets to his feet, looks at each of them in turn before dropping the letter onto the table next to the gun. He starts heading for the door, head swimming and eyes burning.

Where are you going, Jimmy?

"I need some air." Jimmy whispers, although it's unclear whether he's addressing the three men, or Marilyn. Then, he shouts."I need some Goddamn air!"

THE DEVIL WENT DOWN TO DALLAS

JIM IS SITTING UP AGAINST A WALL. That scene in the office at the airstrip had not been pretty. Elvis had looked at the paper after his partner had left the room, read what had made Jim so fired up. At first, he had been of a mind to let Hank and Frazini have it, both barrels. But what would be the point? He knew what they had been about in showing Jim that transcript. Get him fired up to the point where he wanted vengeance. Maybe that's what they had achieved? But looking at Jim now, sitting there watching Hank and Frazini talk shop with the new guy, Elvis isn't so sure.

The new guy had been introduced only as Jack. Who knew if that was his real name. The only truth that Elvis knows he can hang his hat on, is that this whole situation is SNAFU. Didn't change the fact that they were where they were. Dallas. At this rinky dink strip joint that at one time was meant to look like something else, but had faded now. The Carousel Club. Hank says that this Jack character is the owner, but looking at the guy, Elvis isn't so sure. He looks like he has a hair-trigger temper. Elvis might not be the smartest guy in the room, but he understands that business and anger rarely mix.

For the meantime, the guy looks like he's got it in check. Still, his head swivels back and forth between Hank and Frazini, as if deciding who he needs to bow lower to. Again, Elvis has to wonder what it is that the Agency or the mob has on this guy that they've got him caught up in the thing that they're all here to do. He could probably throw a punch at some guesses and hit one or two. The club for one thing. It's shabbiness screams either of laziness when it comes to keeping on top of the maintenance, or a lack of money to keep those sorts of things in check. Was financial incentive the thing? Hank is talking, so Elvis tunes in, despite wanting to do anything but.

"So now you boys have got the basics covered, we should be getting you some tools to work with." He gives Jack one of his oily smiles, but Jack refuses to buy into it. He glowers. "Jack here is in contact with some gun clubs. He's pitched it so that they think they'll be providing the hardware for... what did you call it again?"

"The Carousel Club's inaugural turkey shoot." Jack keeps glaring, but Hank lets out a loud guffaw.

"Get a load of the stones on this guy." He takes a long sip of bourbon. "A regular Bob Newhart."

Frazini cuts in "Nothing finer than putting a bullet in a turkey."

"Alright, alright." Hank gives Frazini this look, like *cool it*, keeps speaking. "The turkey in question will be arriving next week, all ready to be put in the freezer. That'll give you both some time to get acquainted with the area. I'll be giving you some homework. It's mandatory, so hit the books and stay sharp. Dom, you got anything to add?"

Frazini is looking at Hank with a sombre expression, like he's thinking whether he should be pissed off or not. He holds it for a second, then turns to Elvis and Jim. "You two think about getting cold feet, there's something you should be made aware of... We got people covering you wherever you are at all times. You might think that you're on a holiday, but I can assure you that we will be watching. We make the Central Invasion Agency look like a group of schoolboys."

Elvis watches Hank's face as Frazini says this last part. Sees the confident smile slip. Could be something in that hidden distrust that'll work in their favor down the track, but for now, he just nods and acts like he hasn't seen anything. Jim leans forward, studying Jack. Jabbing a finger, he speaks.

"What about him?"

"What about me?" Jack's got a smoker's voice, gravelled and rough.

"They brought you in, showed you our faces. That's more than a little odd in my books." Jim diverts his attention to Hank.

"The way I see it, I'd think that you'd want to keep all of this on the hush? You could've easily got the guns from him without ever introducing us. What's the angle?"

"You really are paranoid, aren't you, kid?" Frazini sneers.

"How's that? You think we shouldn't be?" Elvis allows his incredulity to show. "I mean, begging my pardon, but all things considered, I'm surprised you're as cool as you are. Or is that all an act?"

"Relax guys." Hank has this lecturing voice on. "Jack's gonna be your guide. He's been in these parts going on sixteen years. You couldn't do much better for a Dallas subject matter expert, who better to get you settled in?"

From the look on Jim's face, Elvis can tell that his partner isn't convinced. Can't blame him really. He doesn't like the idea either. One out of turn comment from this guy and they'd both be cooling their heels on Death Row, waiting to be strapped in and juiced. Conspiracy to murder was one thing. Conspiracy to murder the President? Whole other ball game. Hank raises his hand, makes this gesture that Elvis guesses is meant to bring them back to the topic at hand.

"Our friend will be landing at about lunchtime. We made some arrangements. That means his motorcade is gonna be rolling on through via an alternative route to the one planned. He's in town to try and secure his re-election. Tad early if you ask me, but who knows what goes through that man's mind?"

"We'll know soon enough." Frazini mimes firing a rifle, aiming for a joke, but it falls flat. He shrugs and goes back to studying the bottom of his drink.

"You boys will be positioned for a clear shot of the target. Weather conditions for the day are expected to be good. Having two of you means that if one messes up, the other will have him covered. But both of you will be acting as spotters. Plan is to cut down on manpower. Frazini has it organized that there'll be a car to pick you up after it's all done and dusted."

"And then?" Elvis tries to keep the edge out of his voice, but fails.

"Then, you and Mr. Dean here will be taking a holiday down South... Way down South." Hank gives what Elvis thinks is meant to be a reassuring smile. "The Agency has it sorted. You'll have new passports, new names. You'll love it. The climate this time of year is fantastic."

"As easy as that, huh?" Elvis leans back. "A real walk in the park."

Hank is about to speak, but Frazini cuts him off. "Consider the alternatives. Plenty of less pleasant places you could both find yourselves."

Hank sighs, but doesn't say anything. Seems he was done trying to keep the mobster on a leash. Frazini takes another sip of his drink while Hank stands.

"Alright, then. I'm going to set up some reading material for you to look at. Stick with Jack. No doubt, he'll make sure you feel right at home."

Elvis eyeballs Jack, thinking that if this was their host, they were in for a shitty time.

Jack drops them off at a small walk up boarding house in the center of town, tells them that he'll pick them up for dinner that evening. The guy seems irritable. Spending another moment in his company is the last thing that Jimmy wants. Fact of the matter, he just wants to lie down. He's feeling drained and washed out. Thinks that maybe a hot shower and a sleep would go part of the way to fixing things. After reading the transcript, he had felt angry, but that had quickly cooled. Now that he's had time to think about it, he sees that it has proved nothing. He can't afford to be naive in believing that it does.

Sure, Marilyn had said that the President was responsible for her pregnancy, and maybe some of what Jimmy had seen could lend weight to the accusation. But there wasn't enough there to prove it. Elvis follows Jimmy without saying much, lost in his own thoughts as they check in under the names Hank had given them. The rooms are basic. Paint peels from the walls in long strips. An old guy in a fedora sits in short sleeves and tank top behind a small table masquerading as a counter. He reads the paper, stopping only to take their money before going back to reading his paper.

Their rooms are next to each other, both off a narrow staircase that zig zags its way up to the top of the building. Inside the room, the Texan heat is oppressive, caught between the walls and pushed around by a barely operational ceiling fan. A nightstand holds a pitcher of water, but it's brown enough that Jimmy can't stomach the thought of drinking it. The shower is down the hall, but it's lukewarm and doesn't do much to cool him off. He dries, then lies on the bed for a half hour, trying to conjure into existence a sleep that won't come.

Eventually, he gets up, heads out of the room, down the stairs, then out onto the sidewalk. There's a barber shop, a grocery and clothing store, a drugstore and a bar. He picks the bar mainly because he knows that the inside of it will be cool and there'll be something even colder to drink. The sun does its best to impale him as he walks along the paving, but Jimmy ducks his head and keeps walking. He reaches the swinging double saloon doors and pushes through.

Beyond the doors, the bar is a dingy affair. Not that he had expected anything different, but the confirmation is depressing all the same. He thinks back to some of the places that he and Marilyn had frequented, palatial by comparison. Taking a seat at the bar, he orders a beer, swigs it dry in one go and orders another. He should really be keeping a clear head, but part of him wants to aim for blackout drunk, make the whole thing vanish for a few hours. The bartender seems accustomed to such behavior and slides him another drink.

Jimmy eases the throttle a bit. It helps that he can lean into the fact that he isn't the only one caught up in this. Getting blackout drunk was one thing, but putting Elvis in the shit as a result of acting out? Regardless of their differing opinions of the whole situation Jimmy just can't bring himself to throw his partner under the bus like that. He finishes the beer, goes to leave, but orders a third instead, changing his mind about his debt to Elvis. This time the bartender does speak up.

"Got sorrows to drown?"

Jimmy can tell that the guy is on autopilot, like he's saying something that he's said a million times before, the only variable being the asshole he was speaking to. He nods and takes another sip. Marilyn comes calling near the bottom third of the bottle. He feels her voice this time rather than just hearing it. It's a cool touch on the back of his neck and he leans into it, feeling its soothing quality.

Don't you think you've had enough?

Who are you? My mother? His internalized response is belligerent.

Your mother's dead, Jimmy. Marilyn says it like Jimmy doesn't know it already.

And so are you. He flinches as he thinks this. Feels the sting of the hurtful words as if he is feeling what she never will again. A corporeal proxy.

You always did have a strange sense of humor. Her voice is mirthful.

Aiming to escape its familiarity, he puts the bottle down heavily and walks on woozy legs outside. The heat hits him and makes his head even lighter. The sidewalk and the people on it swim into and out of view. He weaves through them. A woman shields her son, giving Jimmy a judgemental stare. He ignores her, keeps walking. He watches faces pass in a parade of ignorance. If only they knew that in a week's time he'd be pasting the President's brains all over the place. What a world where that was the only sane solution to a political problem. What did the French call that? A *coup d'etat?* Something like that, anyway. What does he know?

More people pass and he's a piece of driftwood, floating past them in a secret world all of his own making. He squints, feeling like maybe he will black out after all. The booze? Or something more sinister? Then he squints again because he thinks that maybe he's seen something that he imagined. Squinting a third time makes it real.

Lee.

What was Lee doing here? It's just the back of the guy's head, but he recognises the slender figure, catches a side profile that marks the man. Jimmy is about to call out, but remembers himself. He looks around with exaggerated scrutiny, trying to make out anybody watching, but it's just him and the *maybe* Lee. Jimmy hunches his shoulders, ducks his head and follows.

SUSPICIOUS MINDS

ELVIS IS STILL WAITING FOR JIMMY to reappear when Jack shows up to collect them for dinner. He had gone to his partner's room, knocked on the door, received no answer, and decided to go for a walk. A few hours later, Jimmy still hadn't shown his face and Elvis is beginning to get a worried gnawing in his guts. Jack is pissed of course. He swears and curses and sweats. He jabs Elvis in the chest with a meaty finger until Elvis tells him to stop. The looks he gives the other man says there's a high risk of getting it broken were he to continue. They face off for a few moments until Jack decides that he's better off not going looking for trouble.

"We should call Hank." Jack paws sweat from his jowls.

"Relax. Frazini's got it covered, right? Eyes everywhere and all that shit?" Elvis is toying with the other man. Knowing he shouldn't, but unable to stop.

Jack doesn't respond. Clutches at his hair, panting like a locomotive. Finally he heads for the door. "Come on. We should go to the club."

"Whatever, man, you're driving the car." Elvis gives a shrug, unwilling to let Jack see that he's just as worried.

If Jimmy had gone AWOL, then that spelled bad news for Elvis. Might as well grab a gun and put a bullet in his own skull, let alone the President's. As he and Jack get into Jack's Oldsmobile, Elvis forces himself to take a breath. Had to take the advice he had given to Jack. No point getting riled up over something he had no control over. If he looked at things in the right way, he'd be able to see that he had no control over any of this.

Jack drives them through Dallas' urban sprawl to the club. The exterior is lit up cheaply. A second sign almost as big as the main one proclaims 'Real Pit Bar-B-Q'. There's a line out front, but Elvis wouldn't call it impressive by any stretch of the imagination. Hell, it could be anywhere in downtown Jackson, with just a little bit of that good old Texan flash thrown in for good measure. Jack jerks the car to a halt, fumbles the handle just as unsteadily. He gets out without waiting for Elvis. Elvis was starting to get the impression that old Jack was much more than just a gun smuggler / chaperone. Why else was he so nervous?

The guy was wired and Elvis thinks maybe it's not just the fact that he had lost Jimmy. Perhaps the guy was doing uppers, giving himself a little edge on top of what was already there. Elvis thinks that's maybe a bad idea, given Jack's existing twitchiness. He gets out of the car, saunters after Jack past a big doorman who gives him a once over. Elvis gives the big guy a nod, thinks that he's had just about enough of dealing with this type of asshole.

Through the door, the lights are dipped with the exception of a large spot that picks out a woman dancing on stage. She sports tasseled pasties and her skin gleams with oil and sweat as she gyrates. The music is too loud and Elvis winces as it bites at his ears. Not even good music anyway, some sort of low rent Go-Go shit. Jack is scanning the room until his eyes land on Hank. Before the guy can go and make a mess of things, Elvis heads him off. Hank and Frazini lounge in a gaudily upholstered booth, eyeballing him as he approaches.

"You're alone?" Elvis had seen that dull gleam in Frazini's eyes before, knew that it meant danger wasn't that far behind.

"You guys plum wore Jim out with all that pregnancy BS you landed on him. Cut the guy some slack, huh?"

"Is that so? He didn't go out for a walk?" Now Frazini is looking past Elvis, to a big guy lurking in the shadows near the bar. He nods and the guy starts making his way over. Elvis decides to try a different approach.

"Maybe he did? You fellas would know better than me. Last time I saw him was about an hour ago... When he told me he was feeling unwell. You understand?"

Hank is staring at him. He isn't smiling, but then his face shifts, a weird and stilted transition that makes him look inhuman "Dom, if our man here says his partner is tucked up safe and sound in bed, then tucked up safe and sound he is. No need to make a big fuss. We got a whole week of fun things to get through. There's still plenty of time."

Frazini levels off a flat stare at Hank. Hank ignores him and gestures for Elvis to join them. Elvis doesn't move. "No thanks, think I'll just stick by the bar. Take in the show."

"Suit yourself." Elvis turns, pushes past Frazini's man, standing there like a puppet with its strings cut, unsure of what to do without an instruction from Frazini.

At the bar, Elvis turns, leans back against its edge and watches the crowd. He scans the space, picks up that it's about a quarter Agency types and quarter Mob thugs with the balance made up of regular shmos. He feels like he's standing waist deep in a shark tank and it's only a matter of time before one of them decides to take a bite out of him. He's thinking exactly that the first time he meets her. She sidles up to him, hair swept up in a beehive, eyes made up beautifully.

He plays dumb. Acting like she's not even there, but her perfume is making it hard for him to keep pretending. It smells sweet with a tangy afterbite. Cherries and apples. She holds a drink and watches the stage. When she speaks, her voice has that Brooklyn thing going on where the "ah" sound rolls off the back end of some words.

"You find this exciting?"

Elvis is taken aback for a minute, not sure what she means, then realizes she's talking about the girls on stage. He gives her a sidelong look, captures her full, radiant beauty in profile.

"No. I'm just here for the pretzels." He gives the bowl next to his elbow a nudge and smiles a little when she laughs.

The laugh doesn't have any place being here. It's pure and light and sweet. He locks onto it and turns so that he's at least facing her, side resting against the bar with one elbow still propped there. He looks over, sees Hank watching him talk to the girl, but switches off, not wanting the bastard to ruin the interlude. He's about to ask her name when she beats him to the punch.

"You got a name?"

"Yes, ma'am." He smiles, and for the first time in a while, it feels like he's doing it with no agenda. "Elvis Presley."

"Elvis, huh? You new in town?" Her lips give a wry twist.

"What gave it away?" He's leaning towards her now, just so he can catch another whiff of that perfume.

"Oh, this and that." She looks away, checking out the moving throng of people. "What brings you to a fine establishment such as the Carousel Club?"

"I could ask you the same thing. Surprising to see a beautiful woman in a place like this."

"That line get you what you want most of the time?" She takes a sip of her drink, intelligent eyes assessing him.

"Only with people that dont know me well."

She lowers the glass "Is that so? What about me? I don't know you at all."

"Who says you're gonna give me what I want?" He's stunned, the response clumsy in his mouth.

"Who's to say it's not going to be the other way around?"

And it is the other way around. She's in control and Elvis has to stop himself from gasping at the way she takes over. She's got her legs around him, driving him into the bed, head thrust back like she's caught in a moment of sheer abandon. The dimness of the room reduces her to a silhouette. She's become a shadowy spirit, hell-bent on consuming him. His eyes flutter, not quite remembering the last time, if ever, he had felt this way.

It lasts an eternity and brief moments, time taking on a stretched out and compressed quality simultaneously. In the space of hours, or a few heartbeats, he climaxes and then, she comes too. She rolls off of him. The light catches her face, rendering her a woman once more. She gives him a brief kiss, then reaches for her purse and pulls out a cigarette. As she smokes, she looks like she's taking as much pleasure from the act of smoking as she had from their lovemaking. She finishes the cigarette, lays back quietly, looking at the ceiling of the shitty room.

"You love all the classy places, don't you?"

"We could've gone to yours?" He rolls over, intent on capturing every sharp angle of her face in the event that this is a one time deal. Knows that it probably is, given the circumstances.

"I'm not from around here either."

"What're you doin' here?" He can't work out whether he means with him, right then, or just what she was doing in Dallas in general.

"My boss sent me down here."

A sudden chill lances through Elvis' pleasure.

"Who do you work for?" He narrows his eyes.

She eyes him, lashes only fluttering slightly, then laughs.

"I'm an assistant... What? Did you think I was some sort of Secret Agent?" She nudges him. "Who do *you* work for?"

"A trucking company." It's not a lie.

"Uh-huh." If she is doubtful, she hides it well. "Listen, I..." She stops, as if she was about to say something she didn't want to. "I should go. This has been fun though. More fun than I was expecting to find in Dallas of all places."

She stands, picks up her underwear and crumpled dress from the floor and puts it on, pronounced shoulder blades rolling. It's not until she's fully dressed, looking as perfect as the first time that he saw her, that Elvis speaks.

" Wait!" She stops at the door, holding it half open, dingy hall light spilling onto her face. "Ain't you at least gonna tell me your name?"

She gives him a smile and the rundown space is lit up like fireworks. "Priscilla."

Then she's gone. A beautiful, quick phantom vanished as if she had never been there, only a faint trace of cherries and apples to tell the truth.

I GET AROUND

JIMMY'S HEAD IS STILL BUZZING as he follows the maybe Lee up late afternoon streets. The shadows have started to grow long, painting asphalt, paving and walls with dark stripes limned in gold. Lee takes a right, heads down this alley that looks like you'd miss it if you were walking too fast. Jimmy stops at the corner before following.

The afternoon light dips to nothing. Litter is strewn haphazardly around the narrow space. Jimmy hangs back. There's this vague feeling that Lee wouldn't like it if he knew that Jimmy had spotted him. Questions parade through his mind, all hinged on what Lee was doing in Dallas. More of Hank's covert action shit? Highly plausible. If there was one thing that Hank liked, it was having everything wrapped up in a web. One where all the strands, and the things caught in them, were not immediately visible. Jimmy feels like one of those trapped things. A fly waiting for Hank the Spider to come and devour him.

Well, maybe he could stop that from happening? Maybe Lee's presence here in Dallas was the key to that? Jimmy pushes forward, putting a little bit of speed in his step now, keeping distance between himself and the other man. Enough so as to not alert the other man to his presence, but not too far that Jimmy would lose him. The alley twists and turns like intestines. A couple of times, he does lose sight of Lee. On the last of these, Jimmy nearly blows the whole thing by coming around a corner just as the other man stops inside a doorway.

As Lee turns, a patch of light illuminates his face and dispels any doubts that Jimmy might have had that it was him. Jimmy falls back, almost holding his breath as he ducks into the shadow afforded by stacked pallets and a dumpster. Lee peers back, as if he's heard something, standing there for long moments while Jimmy's breath, light and shallow, sounds in his ears like a steam train. Finally, Lee moves through the door. Even then, Jimmy waits to make sure that the other man doesn't double back. When he's certain there's no risk, Jimmy emerges and moves quietly to the doorway.

Hanging to one side, he peers around the corner, sees a narrow flight of stairs, battered and steep. The stairwell is lit dimly by a light hung high above. The bulb is barely functioning, flickering fitfully as if disturbed by all the activity. Jimmy edges forward, keeping his weight off his feet as much as he can. Even so, the steps creak. He stifles a curse. Jimmy's concern diminishes as he hears voices raised from somewhere above. Their tone is hot. A back and forth of short and sharp question and response. It has the quality and rhythm of a firefight.

Jimmy moves quickly up the stairs, gripping the bannister. He reaches a landing and the stairs switch back. He keeps climbing. At the top of the stairs is a long hallway. He can see a door, partially open, opposite to where he stands. No-one is visible through it, but Jimmy doesn't want to risk being spotted by climbing any higher. He stalls, not needing to strain to make out what's being said. Lee and whoever he was talking to were sure going at it.

"... don't care if they've threatened your family! You know what you have to do, Lee." The voice is older, alcohol and nicotine strained.

"You don't care?!? So why should I do anything that you want?" Lee's voice is agitated, it swings high and low. "I thought you were supposed to have my back?"

"Have your back? This isn't a high school football team. You gotta understand that what we're dealing with here is sensitive shit, if that wasn't abundantly clear already. The Agency finds out what we're up to, that's gonna bring a bucket load of heat down that nobody will want to deal with. Bad enough that Langley found out about your ties with Russia..."

"What did you say?" Lee's voice has dropped too, but it's not calm, it's seething. "Russia?!? That has nothing to do with this.

Even if it did, the only reason I was there was because of you. 'All part of the deal'. That's what you said, right? I help you on one or two things, you help me."

"I understand that, Lee." Exasperation and tiredness fill the other man's voice. "But now we got these other two unknowns in the mix that we don't have any control over, and that's made things difficult. Difficult for me. Bad enough that the organization is copping heat from conspiracy nuts in the gutter press over Blondie's death, but now her boyfriend and some yokel are involved? This is the type of scenario where shit has the potential to get seriously messed up."

"I explained that to you. That had nothing to do with me. Nothing to do with them, either. That was the Agency, playing more of their games."

There's a lengthy silence followed by the clink of ice on glass, then the sound of a leather creaking and a sigh.

"If the public finds out about this interagency cat-fighting and the shit both parties are up to, there's gonna be a reckoning that makes judgement day look like a tea party." A pause filled with the tinkle of ice, expansive swallowing. "You know what happens when something like that goes down, Lee? They try to find a patsy. Look at you, and look at me. Out of the two of us, which one do you think the organization would back if it came to it? Hell, Son... All you've got is me to watch your back, and to vouch for you when the chips are down. I'll do that... You can count on it. But if you come at me with excuses for why you can't do what you're obligated to do... Well, let's just say, you won't need to worry about your family receiving threats anymore."

The silence between the man's last words and Lee's response is filled with hostility. When Lee answers, his voice is barely breaking a whisper "So what do you want me to do?"

"When it comes to it, you make sure our boy Jack has his brains where they're meant to be." More creaking. "You do that, you'll be well looked after. Understood?"

There's a sharp scrape, the sound of furniture moving against wooden floorboards. Jimmy quickly turns, starts moving back down the stairs. As he reaches the landing, he hears:

"Don't come back here again, Lee, not until this is over."

Elvis has his door ajar when he hears footsteps coming down the hall. He sees Jim passing his room through the crack and gets up from the bed. The Dallas heat has cooled off, but as he comes out, he sees a large stripe of sweat-dampened cloth on the back of Jimmy's t-shirt. He watches his partner hunch and fumble in his pocket for his room key.

"Did you forget we had dinner plans?" Elvis tries to keep his tone light, even if he's feeling anything but.

Jim jumps a little, drops the key he had retrieved from his pocket, quickly stoops and swipes it off the floor before turning. His eyes are bloodshot.

"Something came up." He's speaking in his usual mumbled and casual way, but there's something defensive in his response.

"You gonna give me some info on just what that something might be or do I gotta guess?" Elvis leans one shoulder against the doorframe, folds his arms.

"I saw Lee." Jim watches Elvis' face, locks onto it with this keen expression.

Unfolding his arms, Elvis straightens and moves closer to Jim.

"Lee?" His brow creases. "What the hell..."

"Something to do with... some organization? Russia... uh... I don't know..." Scrubbing the back of his head, Jim turns, unlocks the door and opens it, enters the room and seats himself heavily on the bed, springs creaking. He hangs his head for a few moments. When he looks up at Elvis, his eyes are like tunnels to nowhere. "I think Lee's gonna try and kill us."

"Kill... Now hold up there, Jim." Elvis moves into Jim's room, shuts the door behind him. "You're not thinking straight. Why would someone train us in all the stuff that Lee has, just to waste all his hard work by killin' us?"

Even as he says the words, Elvis regrets it. Jim's eyes narrow and a sour look creeps onto his face. Can't blame him for reacting that way really. Especially considering all the crazy shit they'd been dragged into lately. Was it so far-fetched that there was yet another angle playing out that would most likely end up with them dead? If Jim said that Lee was here, that Lee was here specifically to kill them, then maybe Elvis should give him the benefit of the doubt? But it's too late. Something in Elvis' refusal to believe has sparked a response that feels like it's been simmering inside of Jim for a while.

"You don't get it, do you?" Jim is speaking levelly, as if explaining something to a slow-witted child. "You never get it. People like you and me, hell, even people like Marilyn, we don't get the luxury of choice. We just get our faces pushed into the dirt and then held there until we understand that we have to do what we're told. Lee's no different. He's got his face pushed down as much as the rest of us, doing what he's told to do with this slim hope that maybe he'll eventually be set free."

Elvis feels the back of his neck burn, feels the weight of everything pushing hard upon his shoulders. It's an unfamiliar sensation when he usually feels in control. What Jim was saying? That completely made a lie out of everything that Elvis thought of as truth. And yet, there is an honesty to it that Elvis can't find fault in. He goes to speak, to maybe try and laugh it off like he always does, but Jim isn't finished with him.

"You might blame me for bringing you into this, but think back. Mexico. It began then. Maybe even before then. You made what you thought were your choices, but were they ever really yours? Think back to the last time you made a decision that wasn't just a reaction to some other thing." Their eyes are locked and Elvis can feel the haunted depths of Jim's stare tugging at him like a magnet. "Even if you decided to run right now, how far do you think you'd get before you reach the realization that it's just another decision that isn't yours?"

Elvis stays quiet and in that moment, his mama is there, not trying to comfort him, but present as a dead witness.

He's right, baby boy.

I know, mama.

"So what do you wanna do about it?" Elvis lets the silence hang before finishing. "Take him out?"

Jimmy has lowered his head again, giving the floor a long stare that could mean anything. Finally, he answers.

"No." He looks up, brow set in a determined line. "No, I think we're going to have to get ourselves out of this a different way."

LITTLE GREEN BAG

AFTER ELVIS LEAVES, JIMMY TURNS OFF THE LIGHT and lays tangled in the sheets as the streetlight outside the window flickers fitfully. Maybe he has half a plan in his head, maybe he doesn't. Either way doesn't matter that much. What does matter is making sure that Elvis at least thinks that Jimmy has an idea of what they were going to do next. With Lee in the mix again, and with Jimmy having only half a guess at his agenda, everything that is certain has suddenly vanished. He had told Elvis that he thought Lee intended to kill them, but something about that didn't add up.

Sitting up and swinging his bare legs over the edge of the bed, Jimmy slides out the bedside drawer and sets it down beside him. He reaches into the exposed cavity of the vacant night stand, fumbles for the lump taped to the underside of the night stand's top and extracts it. The device's matte casing catches the dim light struggling in through the window. Jimmy turns it in his hands. Lee had said that it was a radio. How much truth to that was anyone's guess, the thing was smaller than any radio that Jimmy had ever seen. It had some writing on the bottom but it was indecipherable. Japanese maybe, if Jimmy had to hazard an uninformed guess.

If Lee did plan to take out Jimmy and Elvis, why go to the trouble of giving them this thing? Was it a fail-safe to make sure they stuck to the plan? They decide to use it and it alerts whoever is on the other end that they're trying to skip out. No. That didn't feel right. What Jimmy really thinks, backed up by hearing Lee's conversation with whoever he had been speaking to, is that Lee has gone rogue against Hank and his crew, if he had ever been allied with them at all.

Seems that whatever the Agency had lined up didn't fit in with Lee's plans. Maybe by helping Jimmy and Elvis, Lee was looking to give himself a better chance at success in achieving whatever it was he was really about. Jimmy frowns, gives the radio another heavy once-over before returning it to its hiding place. If nothing else, the risk Lee had taken in giving it to Jimmy in the first place spoke volumes about his intent *not* to kill them. Maybe that risk was a whole lot bigger if he was playing both sides against each other.

Jimmy gets up, grit sticking to the soles of his feet as he pads to the window. He lights a cigarette and looks down at the street below. The black sedan that had been parked across the road earlier was still there. Jimmy can see the dim shapes of whoever was huddled inside, sunk low in their seats. Some of Frazini's men? Whoever they were, Jimmy knew that he and Elvis only had one shot to make a right judgement call on what came next. Killing the President was one option, but the more Jimmy thought about it, the more he wondered what that would even accomplish.

You're doing it for me.

Marilyn is there again with Jimmy, looking out the window at the car. He wonders if she is ever not there, haunting him. Finishing the cigarette, he moves away from the window, returns to the bed and flops down. He shuts his eyes, the beginnings of a headache forcing its way into the space just behind his right temple. Marilyn tries to join him, but he shuts her off. That was half the problem. Too many demands being levied against him. Marilyn. Elvis. Hank. Lee. Why couldn't they just all leave him alone?

You got yourself into this mess. That was an accusation Jimmy had levelled at himself, and he couldn't refute it.

He *had* gotten himself into this. He had convinced himself that he was doing all of this to find out who had killed Marilyn... And to exact revenge. But was that it? Maybe? Or maybe it was something else? Jimmy flinches in the dark, unwilling to hold the torch too close in case it reveals something he doesn't want to see. Of course, he knows the answer, but is afraid. Afraid to hold himself accountable. If he does that, there is no guessing how deep the hole is that he'll fall into. Probably deeper than what he was capable of climbing back out of.

Maybe that was why he had liked Marilyn so much? Her problems had seemed so much more significant than his own. Real world problems. *Important* problems. Why did he think that? Because she was a candle that drew in all the moths? As for Jimmy? Well, he was a nobody. A loner who drifted through life with acquaintances over friends. Too difficult for anybody to really want to know or love. And when somebody did get close enough? They burnt out on who he really was. His frenetic energy. His incessant need to belong. To be somebody's someone.

He draws the cigarette down to nothing then grinds the butt into the ashtray on the nightstand, rolling his back to it and shutting his eyes. No point worrying about something that was too far gone to change. No. Better to just let it lie and play out the hand that life had dealt him. That he had dealt himself. Who knew? Maybe everything would fall in a heap without him having to do anything. As he drifts off, he hears Marilyn singing. A lullaby or some such nonsense. With sleep blurring everything, her voice becomes that of the mother that he had lost. He grabs the pillow and shoves it over his head, hoping to drown out a tune that he doesn't want to hear.

Next morning, Elvis is sitting in the small and crummy downstairs dining room when Jim finally decides to make an appearance. His hair is tousled as it usually is, but Elvis can see that the other man hasn't slept much. Dark circles ring the hollows of his eyes and he yawns expansively. He slumps in the seat across from Elvis, orders a cup of coffee, and scans the local paper. Elvis takes a sip of coffee, watches Jim over the cup's rim, sees the way his partner's eyes devour the words. News of the impending arrival of the Commander in Chief fills columns.

Elvis wasn't much of a reader himself. Not to say that he wasn't interested in learning new things, but he preferred a more hands on approach to life. That was better. Grabbing something with both fists and devouring it. The martial arts thing, his music, hell, even this. He'd be the first to admit that he couldn't pin the blame for all of this solely on Jim. After all, he could've just hung up the phone. But he hadn't. Because part of Elvis had grown bored cooling his heels in Tupelo. There was nothing there for him except noodling on his guitar, busting his hump driving trucks and chasing small town girls drawn from an ever dwindling pool.

Jim's call had been a life preserver, even if that wasn't immediately clear. It had yanked him out of a self-imposed slumber. What Jim had said had been mostly right, but Elvis didn't one hundred percent agree with him. Sure, life could control you, but that was only if you let yourself play the victim card. And Jim was a victim, of that there couldn't be any doubt. He had done this to himself. Always allowing himself to get pulled into things that he seemed desperate to escape from.

For Elvis' part, he had no intention of letting anyone bully him into doing something that he didn't want to do. Kill the President? There was no way on God's green earth that Elvis planned to do something so stupid. That good ole Agency boy, 'Hank', was playing them for a fool. No way Elvis was anybody's fool. Hank, Frazini, and anybody else tied up in this little plot could go hang. Elvis had come to that decision last night. He'd also come to another decision. He was gonna do everything in his power to pull both he and Jim out of this mess in one piece. And if they died trying? Well, he'd given it his best. That was all he could do. Right?

"You, okay?" Elvis keeps his voice low, giving the dining room staff quick glances, unwilling to trust anybody he didn't know.

"Yeah, it's just... Uh... I don't know." Thumping the paper with a loose fist, Jim looks up. "This whole thing. All I wanted was answers."

"And you got 'em, so..." Elvis gives a small shrug. "What else do you want?"

"Justice?" Jim's stare is empty, like he's not buying his own bullshit.

"You said it yourself last night." Elvis keeps his voice gentle, wanting the other man to know that he was still on his side. "That sort of thing is in short supply these days. Justice. Truth. Freedom. It's a dry well, Bubba." Jim huffs air from his nose, looks at JFK's smiling mug dominating the page in front of him. Elvis taps the photograph. "And that guy? Well, he's just a puppet that got away from his strings. Now, his masters have come calling to tie him back up again. Any. Way. They. Can. You really want to help 'em?"

Jim's eyes are spears now, suddenly alert and bright. They impale Elvis. It's like his words have become an anthem. Elvis rocks back in his chair, eyeing Jim cautiously, uncertain of exactly what he had started. Hopefully nothing terrible. Finally, after what feels like an age, Jim answers.

"No." Jim flinches after he's said the word, like he's heard something that he doesn't want to, but then appears to regain his composure. "No. I don't."

"Alright then, well... only one thing for it. Let's sort the sons of bitches out."

SPINNING WHEEL

THEY'RE NOT EXPECTED AT THE CLUB until after lunch. Jimmy doesn't know what can be accomplished in that time, but Elvis' words had solidified something that was already building inside of him.

Lee.

Lee was the key to all of this. After all, Jimmy was pretty certain that the Agency didn't have any idea that Lee was in Dallas. If they didn't know that, then what else didn't they know about? More questions that didn't have immediate answers. Both Elvis and Jimmy huddle at the window in Jimmy's room, looking down on the street.

The black sedan is still parked where it had been the previous night. Now, there's only one person inside of it. Jimmy can't quite get a good look at whoever it is, but has to assume that it's somebody different from the previous night's occupants. The day shift. Even with that information, there was no way of knowing how many eyes were actually on the place. Elvis moves away from the window, laces his fingers behind his head.

"We're not gonna get very far with Hank's spies casing the joint." He puffs his cheeks, sits slouched on the edge of the bed.

"Might not belong to Hank. Could be Frazini's guys?" Jimmy half mutters the words, thinking about options.

"Frazini. Hank. Same same." Elvis grunts. "The minute we show our faces out there, you can bet whoever it is will put the word out that we're going off plan."

Put the word out.

Jimmy moves quickly to the nightstand. He yanks out the drawer carelessly in his rush to get to the device and it spills its contents to the floor. A bible, a pack of cigarettes and a hip flask of bourbon. Jimmy ignores the mess. The duct tape makes a tearing sound as he reaches in and tugs at it. He peels the tape off the back of the radio, feeling the sticky residue tack beneath his palm. Elvis gives Jim this look like he thinks his partner has gone mad. Jim studies the device, turning it this way and that, locates what looks like the on switch. He flicks it and static fills the room. He quickly switches it off and looks about uneasily.

Elvis says nothing as Jimmy moves into the bathroom, shuts the door and turns the faucet on. He toggles the power button on the device. In the smaller space of the bathroom, the static seems louder. He squeezes the button on the side, takes a breath then speaks.

"Hello?" Jimmy pauses, then gives the device a shake. When it remains unresponsive, he speaks into it again. "Uh... it's Jim. Jim Dean. Anybody there?"

Long moments become even more drawn out. Jimmy's nerves spike. What if this was the trap he feared it was?

What if -

"Dean? What're you doing? I thought I - " Lee's voice is wired, giving an even higher pitch than usual.

"Shut up and listen to me. I know you're in Dallas. We need to speak."

"I don't -"

Jimmy cuts him off again. "There's eyes everywhere. Uh, How do we get out of here? Where do we find you?"

Jimmy's words race each other to escape his mouth.

There's hissing static again before Lee speaks, his voice sounding wary. "Go downstairs. Head out back through the kitchen. There's an alleyway. Follow it to the left, then take the first right. Head straight out to the street. There'll be a car there waiting to collect you. Make it quick. You've got five minutes."

The radio falls silent and Jimmy doesn't hesitate, switching it off and jamming it back into its hiding place. Elvis is on his feet, eyes a little wider than usual, watching Jimmy's quick movements.

"What's goin' on?" When Jimmy doesn't stop, Elvis grabs him by the arm. "Tell me."

"You should stay here. In case Frazini, Hank or anybody else shows up. I'm gonna meet with Lee... Talk this out and see what he's got to say. If I'm not back in a couple of hours, I guess you'll have to figure out the rest by yourself." Jimmy moves to the door, swings it open.

Elvis grabs him by the arm again. "Uh uh, I'm coming with you. Weren't you the one that said Lee wanted to put us both on us ice? You could be walkin' into a trap."

Jimmy shrugs out of Elvis' grip and gives him a smile. It feels easy and relaxed, and its presence surprises him "We're already in a trap, E."

Elvis tries to speak again, but Jimmy is already gone.

The clerk has his back turned to the foyer when Jimmy comes down the stairs. Even so, Jimmy's cautious to walk casually towards the kitchen as if he belongs there. Grimy tiles, pots and stove-tops mark his path as Jimmy passes through the narrow kitchen and out a poorly maintained screen door. He swings left in the alley, dodging a stray cat that hisses at his legs. The smell of rotting garbage slaps at his nose. Barely literate graffiti festoons the cracked plaster. Jimmy moves quickly, eyes hungrily taking in the space around him. No sign of anybody. It surprises him a little, but he gives thanks for small blessings. About time something went his way.

Taking a right, he stumbles into an alley that could barely be called that. It's narrow and water has collected in holes in the uneven asphalt that has grown stagnant and pungent with midges swarming the water's surface. Jimmy sees a rat scurrying for some hidden refuge. He ignores it and keeps forging for the glare of daylight coming from where the alley intersects the street ahead. As he approaches, he slows, unwilling to exit onto the street without certainty that the car will be there to collect him. He peers from the gloom, slowing to an uncertain shuffle.

No car that looks at all like it might be waiting for him. Jimmy keeps hanging back, wondering if this is the part the bullet with his name on 8t will finally catch up to him. More time passes and he looks back up the alley, bites the inside of his gums. Maybe if he just heads back now, he can... There's an engine's low growl and a silvery blue Impala appears. The driver looks up at him from the car, brimmed hat pulled low, shades obscuring his eyes. He gives Jimmy a brief nod.

Jimmy gives the street another back and forth sweep with his eyes and then rushes forward, moves to the rear passenger door and gets in. The car pulls off at an even pace, as if it's going about ordinary business in an ordinary world. The driver throws a strip of cloth into the back seat.

"Cover your eyes." Jimmy hesitates and the man speaks again. "Do it, or I drop you off here and now, and you and your buddy are on your own."

The driver's accent is hard to place. It sounds like British by way of the Midwest. Jimmy grabs the cloth, fashions it into a blindfold and ties it around his eyes. Without seeing the driver, he still feels the sense that he is being observed. Like a kid on an outing with their parents, Jimmy slumps in the seat, wishing that he had thought to bring his cigarettes. His fingers twitch and the fabric of the blindfold is itchy against his eyes. They drive. After some time, the car goes from smooth asphalt to dirt. He rocks slightly. They drive some more.

An eternity that is probably ten minutes passes and the quality of light visible through the blindfold changes. The car comes to a halt and Jimmy thinks that maybe they're in a barn. With the engine off and the windows down, there's a strong smell of hay and livestock. He remembers it well from Indiana. The door next to him opens and he jumps. Then he hears talking, low and indistinct and is still undecided on whether he should relax or not.

"You can take that off now." Jimmy recognises Lee's voice. Soft. Considered almost.

Yanking the blindfold from his eyes and getting out of the car, Jimmy blinks despite the dimness of the space around him.

He had been right. Faded red wood, stalls that stand empty but for stacks of hay gone bad. The rough ground of the barn crunches beneath his scuffed boots as he shifts his feet. Lee steps back, like he's exercising caution. The driver leans his ass against the hood of the car and lights up. Jimmy stands in front of Lee, blindfold dangling from his fingers.

"Well?" Lee folds his arms.

Everything about the guy speaks of impatience. He has this intensity about him that makes it hard for Jimmy to get a read on intent. His stare is direct, a beacon in the gloom that Jimmy struggles towards, trying to articulate exactly what he wants. Hard when he barely knows himself. Even so, he forces himself to quieten his nerves

"You first. What are you doing in Dallas?"

"I think that's pretty obvious." Lee smirks without humor.

"Is it?" Jimmy takes a deep breath. "Lee, I know about you. I know you're working against the Agency with... Someone."

The smirk falls away from Lee's face and he steps back. Suddenly, there's a pistol jammed into Jimmy's face. It's close enough that he smells the oil used to clean it.

"What did you say?"

Jimmy opts not to hesitate, thinking maybe that his survival hinges on what he says next "It was by accident. I saw you... Or I thought it was you at least. I wanted to know what you were doing here, so I followed you. To your meeting with... I don't know. Whoever it was." Lee is breathing heavily and the driver has put his cigarette out and has come around the car, standing with his hands by his sides. Jimmy thinks that it wouldn't take much for the man to act. He remains very still, but keeps talking, trying not to flinch away from whatever came after he had finished. "You're here to stop them from killing the President, aren't you? To stop *us* from killing the President."

Lee looks past the gun at Jimmy, head cocked to one side, squinting. In the stillness of the barn, there's sweat dampening the hair at his temples. His stare bores into Jimmy, like he's assessing and challenging what he's just been told. He lets out a low noise, almost a satisfied hum and lowers the gun.

"And if I was? What would you do?"

"Tell you we're on your side. That we had plans that don't necessarily fit with whatever the Agency is working towards. That we could work together to make sure our plans and yours turned out alright."

Lee uncocks the pistol and slides it into the waistband on his pants, nestling it against the small of his back. He turns and paces. Jimmy watches him, aware of the driver who stands like a statue, emotionless and taking in the scene through eyes still hidden by his sunglasses.

"You know, I wasn't sure about you. You or your friend." Lee swings back, movements edgy. "That was a big risk you took, using the radio. The Agency has ears everywhere"

"I took precautions."

"Not enough, I'm certain." Lee frowns. "You'll be exceptionally fortunate if they haven't come for you and your partner by now."

Jimmy jerks "What?!?"

"You think this is just a fly by the seat of your pants operation?" Lee continues to pace. "What kind of effort do you think it takes to kill a President? This is a long game, played over years. Probably began before Kennedy even started running for his first term."

"Why?"

"Why what?" Lee stops, peers at Jimmy.

"Why are they doing it now?"

"Kennedy's proving to be unpredictable. The people in the know don't like that, so they're taking measures to ensure that control is reintroduced." Lee pauses, then presses on, as if he has reached some decision point. "I'm working with a coalition that aims to prevent that. The predictability desired by our mutual acquaintances doesn't work in the coalition's favor."

"Is it the Feds? Is that who you're talking about?"

Lee looks irritated at the interruption "a better that you don't know. Just leave it as what I've said it is. A coalition of willing participants. Not that different from those we're working against. We stop the Agency's plan, however, we may be issuing in an era of peace that the world would not see otherwise. Do you see what I'm saying?"

Jimmy chews his gums, eyes searching Lee's face for untruths, but there are none. The man has a blank honesty to him, like a notebook waiting to be filled up. A thought occurs to Jimmy, one that he might not have, had he not witnessed that quality of truth in Lee.

"And what about Marilyn? What was her part in all of this?"

"The actress?" Lee shrugs. "Who knows? A warning maybe?"

"They told me that the President had her killed."

"Maybe he did? Who knows?" Lee blinks, slight confusion present in his odd stare, his words sounding almost dismissive.

Jimmy feels hot, the collar of his t-shirt too restrictive. He knows. Knows that Marilyn was collateral. But he had been clinging to that knowledge like a sailor adrift at sea. The fact that even if he didn't exact vengeance, at least one person knew the truth about what type of man the President really was. She had been pregnant! A complication that needed to vanish. That was the truth that Jimmy had allowed himself to buy... Because he had needed it. To muddy the water with other possibilities only added a new dimension that makes Jimmy feel dizzy. He reels, but Lee seems oblivious to his distress, continues as if that part of the conversation had never occurred.

"So now I've explained it to you, what is it that you want?"

"I want to help you."

"What makes you think that I need your help? What makes you think that I want it?" Again, Lee's tone reduces Jimmy's words to unimportance.

"I heard you, when you were talking. You're scared." Jimmy takes a breath, trying not to let the nerves show. He gives the driver a pointed glance and knows that he's on the right track when he sees a hint of doubt tinge Lee's expression. "You're caught in the middle of this just as much as Elvis and I are. We help each other, maybe we all get out of this in one piece."

Lee shifts from foot to foot, gives the driver another look shaded by uncertainty. Finally, he nods and even though the driver doesn't move, his posture shifts, some of the rigidity leaving it. Lee slumps a little and Jimmy can see the tiredness that he carries for the first time. He moves a little closer.

Lee gives Jimmy another long look and it's impossible to tell what the other man is thinking. He waits. Willing to wait for as long as it takes for Lee to decide that working together is the best option. Finally, Lee sighs.

"Alright... But first you're going to do something for me." Jimmy doesn't respond, waits for Lee to lay out the price. "You have to find out exactly how they plan to kill the President."

A WHITER SHADE OF PALE

ELVIS IS BACK IN HIS ROOM when the Agency guys come for him. The two men are big, each wearing clothes that speak nothing of their background. Apart from their size, Elvis thinks they could blend right into the background if they wanted to. He hasn't seen the two before, which lends a little weight to his guess that there's probably more of Hank's goons in Dallas than what either he or Jimmy know about. Elvis gives both men an easy smile as they crowd the doorway.

"Morning fellas, can I help you?"

They stand there. Of course Elvis knows that they expect him to go with them, but he's guessing that if he does it's gonna be straight to a shallow grave. Still, what were his options? He might be able to take one of them out, but two? The odds just weren't that much in his favor. Better that he go along for the ride and see if he can get out of it along the way. Even that wasn't a bet he'd like to make, but as Elvis stands, sees how the guys loom above him, he knows it's the only play he can make.

In the car, Goon One and Goon Two look like adults crammed into a child's toy. Elvis picks up the smell of sweat from both and cracks a window. Goon two is in the back seat with him, gives him this long glance, as if to say *Did I say you could do that?* Elvis gives him a big shit-eating grin back. He knows it will piss the guy off, but can't help himself. He guesses that Hank had taken the liberty of having the boarding house room bugged, curses Jimmy for being so rash.

As they drive on, Elvis frowns. They're not heading towards the club at all. He cranes his neck, tries to work out where they might be going. If it was towards the outskirts of the city, that would most likely make sense, but instead, they were heading further in. Warehouses spring up. That might be even worse. Warehouses were typically out of the way enough to be good for activities that didn't need a lot of attention. He goes to speak, but Goon One brings the car to a halt and gets out. Goon Two gives Elvis the nod to do the same and Elvis does as he's told. No need to cause a ruckus now.

They both start walking towards a large warehouse clad with rusted sheet metal. The rest of the industrial park appears deserted, weeds forcing their way through cracked asphalt. A hot wind has sprung up and scours the urban wastes. The only sound is boot heels on the ground. Elvis squints against the bright glare of the sun, tries to make out whether there's anything in the immediate vicinity that will help him out of this jam. He comes up empty.

Goon One pushes his way through a squealing metal door and Goon Two gives Elvis another nod, prompting him to follow before bringing up the rear. Beyond the door, shafts of sunlight streamer a broad, open space. It's completely empty except for some chains hanging from a gantry crane overhead. Elvis eyeballs the chains and swallows. His nervousness turns to mild confusion as they swing a right and head up some stairs that hug the wall immediately adjacent to the door. At the top of the stairs is a wall mounted office with a wooden door, paint hanging from it in strips.

Through the door, the office has been crammed with desks in close proximity to each other. Men and women in shirt sleeves crowd the working space. Elvis looks around, frowning now. At the back of the office space, a familiar face appears, standing up as Elvis and his two companions loiter in the doorway. It's Priscilla. He watches cautiously as she approaches. That she has a smile on her face goes a long way to making him feel less like he's about to get iced. He smiles back, but it lacks a lot of his usual confidence.

Her smile drops away as she looks at both men, gives them a curt nod and their hulking presence vanishes, departing mountains from behind Elvis. She gestures to a chair sitting crammed up against the desk. Elvis apologizes to the man sitting immediately behind the seat and tries to sit without jostling him too much. Priscilla takes her own seat, leans back in the chair and her warm smile returns. She places her hands deliberately on a folder set before her, crammed thick with paper.

"Hello."

"If you wanted to see me again, you could've just asked me out on a date." Elvis gives her a relaxed smile, even though his heart feels like it was gonna railroad its way through his ribcage.

"Where would be the fun in that?" She shifts in her seat, head cocked a little, watching Elvis intently. Finally, she opens the folder and starts studying its contents as if she didn't already know what was in them. "You've been a busy boy."

"Your boss know you've been compiling info on innocent US Citizens?"

"Innocent? That's a stretch." She sifts through the papers, then looks up and her liquid eyes are predatory. "You mind telling me what you're up to with the CIA?"

Even though it shouldn't, the question catches him off guard.

"You go first. Who're you with?"

"The NSA."

"Is there anyone else that the Government decided needed to be in on this little party? That's one hell of a guest list."

"Oh, we weren't invited." Her mouth creases a little. "But it's our job to make sure we know what's on the menu. So here we are."

"So I'm guessing you know what Hank and his posse are up to then."

"Hank? Is that what he's calling himself now? That's cute." She closes the folder, pushes back her chair as much as the space allows and crosses her legs. "Mr. Presley... We're in the business of information gathering, and what we've gathered so far on this little fiasco is... Alarming. There are numerous pieces of intelligence that we've compiled that could be used quite effectively to indict you on a list of charges designed to ensure you never see the light of day again."

Elvis leans back, bumps the guy behind him, but doesn't apologize. He folds his arms, "Well now, that's quite an accomplishment, because the way I see it, I ain't done nothin'."

"Plotting to kill the President is not *nothin'*." Priscilla's stare is unflinching.

With someone other than Hank talking about it, it feels more real. Perhaps it's the way she said it with ultimate certainty? Like it was a thing that could actually happen, instead of the half-cooked conspiracy that it felt like when delivered by the Agency man. Elvis dips his head, like he was a kid that has just been chastised by the teacher. He scrubs both hands across his face, lets out a long breath. He only had one shot to convince her that he and Jimmy weren't about to do anything of the sort. He takes a deep breath and releases it.

"Well Miss Priscilla, you got me dead to rights, it seems. There's just one thing missing from what you've put together."

She leans forward, rests her chin on steeped fingers, watching him with a cat-like intensity "Oh, do tell, I'm all ears."

"Jimmy and me, we're just innocent bystanders. Caught up in this mess for no other reason than we were in the wrong place at the wrong time. Y'all can just keep on pointing the finger, because you got it aimed in the wrong direction, y'hear? Anyway, if you're so sure that the Agency is gonna do what you said it's gonna do, I'm guessing you would've put a stop to it already, am I right? That you haven't, and that I'm here... Well, that tells me you need me more than I need you."

For the first time, the confidence slips from Priscilla's face, she shifts awkwardly and, for a moment, her youth becomes apparent. Elvis doesn't allow himself to show any smugness at pointing out what he had. The only way this was gonna play out in his favor was if he approached it with an element of humility.

"Mr. Pres-"

"Priscilla, I think we're a bit beyond Sirs and Ma'ams, don't you?" He gives her a level look, and flashes back to seeing her in an entirely different light. "Or was that just something you Intelligence types do to get 'Assets' warmed up? With all due respect, that's the second time I've been screwed by a Government Agent, although I enjoyed our encounter a damn sight more than my little tussle with Hank."

"Alright, Elvis, let me paint a picture for you. The NSA deals with data, and right now, that data is saying that there's a few things going on that could potentially destabilize the US position in the global amphitheatre. We cannot allow that to happen. However, we lack the agency to change that without causing a significant amount of destabilization at a national level. There's a potential they already know, but we are hamstrung. We are operationally incapable of becoming involved without the proper authority, and by the time we get it, it'll be too late. We will just have to approach this covertly. Beg forgiveness rather than ask permission"

"And that's where I come in? You want me to take care of NSA business?"

"Yes, essentially." Priscilla picks up a pen, almost as if she hadn't realized it, starts tapping it on the desk. "You'll need to do what you can to ensure that the Agency, or whoever is orchestrating this thing, does not succeed."

"What makes you think I'm even capable of somethin' like that? I mean, right now, I'm here when I should be back in my room awaitin' further orders like a good little soldier. You don't think Hank's gonna work out somethin' stinks? He had goddamn people parked outside of the joint all night. They would've seen you pick me up for sure."

"We took care of that."

"Oh, I thought you were... How did you put it?... 'Operationally incapable'?" Elvis retrieves a toothpick from his pocket, slides it between his teeth.

"In this instance, we were able to act. You can do quite a bit with information if you know how to leverage it properly."

"Convenient." He smirks. "Alright then, say I help you? What's in it for me?"

"We overlook your involvement in the whole thing and you walk free." Priscilla frowns, as if the answer is obvious.

"I could just do that now... You ain't got nothin' on me."

"And then you wind up as fish food when this whole thing is over, courtesy of your friend, Mr. Frazini."

Elvis knows that what she's saying is true. Had thought about it already. No way around it, Priscilla had him on the hook. Probably better to be the fish than the worm.

He shrugs "I guess you got me."

"I'd prefer if we collaborated on this as allies rather than you feeling as if it was a hostage situation, Mr. Pres.... Elvis."

Elvis takes the toothpick out of his mouth, slides it into his pocket, rocks the chair back to its original position "Well, seein' as you asked so sweetly, Priscilla."

BEST WEAPON

THE DRIVER DROPS JIMMY BACK where he was picked up. Going through the alley, Jimmy feels the back of shirt stick to his back. He can only wonder if what Lee had said was true, had they come for Elvis while he was gone because he had messed up in using the device? He feels a brief flare of guilt that quickly turns to frustration. If Lee hadn't intended him to use it, why the hell had he given it to Jimmy in the first place? In amongst everything that he had learned, he had forgotten to ask. Bad enough that he was being asked now to effectively undermine a conspiracy formed by one of the most labyrinthine intelligence organizations on the planet.

Jimmy wonders what Marilyn would make of all this. Her ghost had fallen quiet since he had made his decision. In some moments, Jimmy was glad that she was gone, in others, he missed her. Thinking of her, he half expected the ghost to make an appearance, just to prove Jimmy wrong, but it doesn't. Maybe that was because he lacked the evidence to prove one way or the other what had actually happened to her. The uncertainty that he has been left with about the perpetrator of her death nags him. It follows him out of the alley, through the kitchen and back up to the rooms.

Stopping outside Elvis' door, he knocks tentatively. Silence. Jimmy feels a dropping sensation in the pit of his stomach. He forces himself to remain calm, unwilling to buy into more paranoia until he is absolutely certain that what he suspects is the truth. He raises his fist to knock again, but before his knuckles can strike against the shoddy wood, Elvis appears at the top of the stairs. He looks out of breath and a little wild-eyed. He gestures for Jimmy to follow him. Together, the two men move swiftly back down the stairs.

At the base of the stairs, Elvis looks like he's about to speak, but Jimmy glances towards the front door, nudges the other man's arm subtly. Hank is standing at the entrance of the lobby. He is studying them speculatively. Elvis fumbles a bit with his hands, as if he doesn't know what they're used for. Jimmy steps away from Elvis and gives Hank a quick nod.

"Well, if you two boys don't look like a couple of kids caught with their hands in the cookie jar." Hank lets out a good-natured chuckle. "Whatever have you been up to?"

"Just got back from breakfast." Jimmy says quickly.

"Uh-huh." Hank tilts his head, looking from Elvis to Jimmy and back again, the doubt on his face almost a pantomime. "Little late in the day for breakfast, isn't it?" Finally, he shrugs his bony shoulders. "Well, no matter, looks like you got back just in time. We've got a few things to go over before the main event. You two ready to roll?"

Jimmy doesn't hesitate, starts walking towards Hank. He forces his breath to even out. Even so, he can almost feel the tension rolling off Elvis in waves. Where had the other man been? There were too many threads to follow and it makes his head reel. He gives his partner a quick glance, sees Elvis with his hands crammed in the pocket of his jeans, head dipped low.

Outside of the boarding house, the familiar black sedan waits. It's empty of occupants and Jimmy wonders at Hank's confidence in not bringing any protection. Was this more mind games on the other man's part to set Jimmy and Elvis on edge? It doesn't make much difference what the real reason is. Jimmy wouldn't be surprised to learn that there were snipers watching their every movement. Maybe that was all it was? They get in the car, Hank taking the back seat after Jimmy and Elvis pile into the front.

Hank directs them, not to the club, but in the opposite direction. Jimmy looks out the window as Elvis drives. Dallas has this weird vibe going on. A mix of rural and the future. Skyscrapers break through trees that look like they would be right at home on a farm somewhere. They pass over bridges where green-watered creeks flow beneath. Pedestrians are few in the midday heat, but the ones that are present eye the sedan suspiciously.

Jimmy gives the rear view mirror a quick glance, sees Hank sprawled in the back, both arms spread wide, windows down, wind ruffling the messy knot of his full beard. He's wearing his usual khaki shirt and Jimmy thinks that for a guy who's trying to pull off being casual, his clothing kind of comes off as a uniform. Hank's aviators shift a little, looking straight at the mirror and Jimmy looks away quickly. He reaches into his pocket, extracts a pack of chesterfields. He offers one to Hank but Hank waves it away, goes back to staring out the side window. Jimmy shrugs and lights up.

Elvis' hands are white-knuckled on the steering wheel. The mix of Hank's relaxed posture and Elvis' tense one makes Jimmy feel squeezed in the middle. He sinks into his seat and tries to ignore them both. They drive for another twenty minutes, weaving deeper into the heart of downtown Dallas. There's a sound of aircraft overhead and Jimmy tilts his head slightly so that he can see out and up through the window. A light aircraft is coming in to land and Jimmy sees that their final destination appears to be an airfield.

"Just left up here, Slick." Elvis does as instructed, turning the car towards a gatehouse set at the end of a side road adjacent to the main one.

He pulls the car to a halt and Hank gets out. He gives them both a quick look through the window. As he approaches a gatehouse, Jimmy notices a man in a well-tailored suit standing waiting for Hank. The two talk for what feels like an eternity, the suited man looks over at the car every few seconds. Finally, he points past the gatehouse to a cluster of low buildings that huddle together against the larger curve of hangars.

Watching Hank, Jimmy sees the Agency man's confident posture shift into something else for what feels like the first time. He's not saying anything and the suited man just stares him down. Finally his shoulders dip a little, and his hands go out to either side in a *I guess so* shrug. He shakes his head but the suited man has already turned, walking past the gatehouse towards a gleaming jet that sits waiting in the distance on the runway.

Jimmy peers at the jet. There's a symbol on the side, it's kind of circular but Jimmy can't make out what it's supposed to be. As Hank approaches the car, Jimmy switches his attention. The Agency man gets into the back seat, leans forward a little. His smug smile has found its way back onto his face as he claps spindly fingers on their shoulders.

"That there was the boss-man, says that we are green on Operation Turkey-Shoot."

"You didn't look too happy about it." Jimmy doesn't look back at Hank, just watches as the jet starts moving back down the runway.

Hank removes his hands. Jimmy can see his eyes, dim behind his aviators, but visible all the same. They narrow.

"Is that so?" Hank watches Jimmy in the rear view mirror, then snorts. "You still got one of those cigarettes for me?"

Jimmy doesn't stop looking at Hank in the mirror, pulls out the pack and tosses it into the back seat. The Agency man catches it effortlessly, pulls out a cigarette and lights it with a gold-plated zippo with some government seal on it that Jimmy doesn't recognize. Certainly nothing Stateside, that was for sure. It disturbs Jimmy in a way that much of everything else hasn't. Makes him aware that Hank, or whoever he really was, has probably done this plenty of times, in plenty of other countries. The scope of it overwhelms him.

Hank gives Elvis the nod and the boom gate swings up as the car approaches. The gatehouse has heavily tinted windows and Jimmy can't see the occupants as they pass. Beyond the gate, they turn down another side road until they reach a carpark that sits just next to the low buildings that the suited man had pointed out to Hank. Hank gets out and starts walking towards one of the buildings, not waiting to see if Jimmy and Elvis are following.

Elvis follows Jimmy and Hank into the buildings. Hank uses what looks like a playing card to gain access through the front entrance. He taps it against a small metal tile set into the wall, and a green light flashes at the tile's top right hand corner. Whatever happened to good old fashioned lock and key? Something about that small detail makes Elvis think, more than anything else, that he was well out of the shallows and into the deeps. The solid door, made from what looked like a combination of steel and glass, swings open. Beyond the door is air conditioned, but colder than anything that Elvis had ever felt before. There was no reception desk, just a long, straight corridor, bracketed on either side by floor to ceiling windows, as heavily tinted as the gatehouse had been.

Hank has the keycard on a retractable lanyard, yanks it out and lets it snap back. The snapping noise makes Elvis flinch each time it breaks the oppressive silence of the passage. Whoever had funded this place, the design makes the NSA Dallas set-up look like a kindergarten. Now that they are inside, Hank strides more than walks. Jimmy's little dig at him about the sharp cat in the suit had seemed to rattle the man, but now he seems to have recovered. Whatever was going on there, Elvis doubts that he'll ever find out.

They reach the end of the corridor and a set of double doors constructed the same as those at the entrance. Another tile and Hank taps the card against it. The beep is loud in the narrow passage. As the doors swing open, seemingly of their own accord, noise floods out, further breaking the stillness of the passage. The noise itself is a loud hum, like you might get from an overworked generator. Through the doors, several tables, part of the building itself it seems, rise straight out of a concrete floor.

The tables have lighted surfaces and are spaced around the room at regular intervals. It could be Elvis' imagination, but the persistent humming seems to perforate the floor and send faint vibrations through the soles of Elvis' boots. Bright fluorescent lighting makes the room harsh, and Elvis shivers as they enter. How was it possible that this place could get any colder? Yet it was. It has the unpleasant quality of a butcher's meat-locker.

The tables themselves are square with their surfaces lit softly from within. The whole space seems clean and sterile. Hank wends his way through the tables until he reaches one that seems to hold the info he requires. It reminds Elvis of a light box in a doctor's office, except instead of x-rays, the tables held what looked like aerial maps. He had seen a few of those maps over at Hoagie Williams land development office, except these maps looked like they were part of the glad that made up the table top, some sort of weird television set up. Each map was an overhead shot of a city. Elvis wasn't gonna be so naive as to believe the city was anywhere but Dallas.

Hank stands looking down at the maps with his hands braced against his hips. He taps one that shows three roads built into a shape that kind of reminds Elvis of King Neptune's trident with the prongs heading towards a group of buildings at one end. The image grows larger and Elvis takes a step back, like it could bite him while Jim peers closer at it. Elvis moves back closer to the table cautiously. Railroad tracks run across an overpass at the trident's base and there's what looks like a memorial off to one side. In front of the memorial is a low hill that slopes down towards the road. There's a wooden fence and a dirt car park wedged between the slope and the railroad tracks. The Agency man bends slightly at the waist, taps a building just to the right of the memorial.

The building is non-descript, several stories high, nothing about it to mark it out as being anything remarkable. Elvis peers at it, trying to see if there's anything that he's missing. Hank taps a window on the top floor on the far right corner. He leaves his finger there, looks up at Elvis and Jimmy. He knows that he should be looking down at the table, but Elvis can't stop looking at Hank's aviators. He still wears them, as if he finds the fluorescent light too bright, and their rims catch the light and make the glasses gleam.

"You boys will be up here, one spotting, the other making the shot. Only way we can pull this off. You'll need to make about three shots, just to make sure that the job gets done. Jackie boy will be coming past in an open top. We had a bit of push back on that, but we got it sorted. We've also made sure that you'll be provided with enough opportunity to make your shots. Wind direction and speed is set to be favourable on the day, but that position can only aid you. We're not expecting anybody up on that floor at the time. We've cleared your presence there as security consultants. If anybody does show up, however, you know what to do." Hank rattles off the information as if he's reciting instructions on how to bake a cake.

Jimmy has been quiet since they entered the building, but now he does speak up "Who would show up?"

Hank's lips quirk, as if Jimmy had told the funniest joke. He gives this little tilt of his head. "I don't know, James. You tell me?"

Jimmy's face flushes beet red and his voice comes out as a bark "How the hell should I know?!?"

"I don't know, James, how would you know?"

Elvis feels the hair on the back of his neck lift. Both men were edging around saying something dangerous. It was only a matter of time before one of them said something which would open a can of worms. He thinks about what Priscilla had said to him, that nothing could come out that exposed the NSA's involvement. He holds his hands up.

"Hey! Hey! Cool it, you two!" Hank swings his shielded gaze on Elvis and he immediately regrets saying anything. He can see himself reflected in the lenses. "I mean..." He lets his words trail off into a mumble.

Hank shrugs.

"You're right. We've got work to do." He traces a route coming down the central road leading into the top of the trident. He then moves his finger right along the road that borders its top and then down the right-most prong of the trident, beneath the building that he had first indicated. He stops his finger just down from the window. "Here is where you'll have the best opportunity."

"What about that tree?" Elvis cocks his head. Damn thing was right in the way of where Hank had said that they'd be taking their shot. "You giving us magic bullets?"

"You don't trust the experts? You'll see when you get up there."

"We get to go up there beforehand? Have a look around?" Jimmy has perched against a neighboring table, goes to light up another cigarette, but Hank stops him. Jimmy shrugs, puts away the packet as Hank answers.

"No. This is gonna be a one shot deal. We can't risk exposure by someone catching on that you were up there any earlier than on the day."

"So, we're goin' in blind?" Elvis raises his eyebrows. "Job this important, you'd think we'd be gettin' in there early to make sure it all goes off without a hitch?"

"Not possible. Sorry." Hank becomes even more close-lipped and Elvis thinks that's been the case since they entered the building.

He looks around the room, trying to take in more detail. Apart from the tables, the walls are exactly like the passage, floor to ceiling glass, tinted as dark as a Mississippi Midnight. Now that Elvis looks at the walls, he sees them for what they most likely are. Windows. Who was behind them? Watching. Listening. He shrugs his shoulders, uneasiness filling the pit of his stomach. He tries to shake it off, but it stays put. He had to get a grip on himself, he was becoming as bad as Jim. To take his mind off things, he turns to his partner, gives him a long look.

Hank looks between the two of them. "So, what do you think?"

"Does it matter what we think?" Jim's voice is flat. Resigned.

"No, I suppose it doesn't." Hank straightens, heads to the door and beckons for them to follow. "Come on, let's get you two sorted for weapons."

As they follow behind Hank, Elvis gives Jimmy another look. His partner's eyes look even more forlorn than they usually do. Elvis had never quite understood that quality. The only time that he had come close was perhaps when Mama had died. He wishes that she was here. Maybe he didn't always listen to her advice, but the woman had been his rock, and her absence makes Elvis feel as if he lacks anything substantial to hold onto. As they follow Hank out of the room, Elvis can't shake the feeling that somebody was watching them go.

EYE OF THE TIGER

THEY GIVE THEM CARCANOS fitted with telescopic sights. Two, just in case something 'doesn't go according to plan', as Hank puts it.

"Not that anything like that is gonna happen, am I right, boys?" The Agency man is sitting in a folding chair, drinking whiskey while Frazini sits across from him playing Solitaire. There's a bustle around the room. Agency spooks and mobsters alike. It's a hive of activity, and Jimmy shifts uncomfortably every time someone moves a crate in a way that makes an unexpected noise.

Frazini doesn't look up from his game, but snorts "With these two? Who knows what could happen? Let's just say, you're more confident than I am."

"We need people who can think on their feet." Hank gives Jimmy a smile, and Jimmy represses a shiver. He switches his attention away from the Agency man.

It's odd looking at the weapons. That something so plain could somehow have the potential to irrevocably change the course of things. Important things. It's not lost on Jimmy what's happening here. He thinks back to what Lee had said about changing the course of history. All it would take is for something to occur outside of either Elvis or his control and that would be it. That it could happen quite so easily was what caused Jimmy's chest to tighten.

He thinks back to that first morning after Marilyn died. It makes her death, and Jimmy, feel small. How could he have possibly thought that solving Marilyn's murder would change anything. Taking in the hustle that was happening around him, the number of moving parts to it, astounds him. Elvis is sitting against a wall, eyes closed. Jimmy still hadn't had a chance to quiz him on his whereabouts earlier that day.

"I'm going for a walk." Jimmy says it loud enough that he hopes he gets Elvis' attention.

"Don't stray too far." Hank's voice is light, like he's shed his earlier mood and is now looking forward to something that he finds particularly pleasing.

Outside, the moon is bright, painting the buildings in silver. Jimmy goes to light a cigarette, remembers that he had left them back inside and jams his hands in his pockets instead. He wanders, moving between the buildings, looking with curiosity at the huge letters adorning the sides of the buildings. They are painted in neat and precise strokes.

OAI.

He tries to puzzle out what the acronym could stand for, but it remains a mystery to him. Reaching the fence that segregates the runway from the rest of the facility, he grips his fingers through the fence and looks out into the Texan night.

Why are you not going to help me, Jimmy?

Marilyn's ghost is almost tangible beside him. The moonlight seems to create her spirit from thin air. He trembles at her presence, longing for her to leave him alone, but feeling indebted to her. The way she waits for him to say something reminds him of the promise that he had made to her. The one about not believing what they said about her.

Thing is, he doesn't know what to disbelieve. So much had been said. She was simultaneously a spurned lover, a succubus, an avaricious harlot and a dear friend. Shouldn't he just settle on that last one? After all, that was his truth for her, what she had been to him in life. But he can't even allow himself to trust that. To trust himself. He hadn't known her. Not really. Maybe no-one ever had? Maybe that's what she was? A chameleon. Ever shifting her colours to be whatever someone needed her to be. Had that been what had gotten her killed?

They killed me, I told you.

"I know!" He almost shouts the words, quietens his voice a little. "I know, dammit."

Balling his fist, he pounds it uselessly against the fence. He jumps at the sound of footsteps behind him, he spins.

"Who're you talking to, Jim?" Elvis stands there, handsome despite his obvious exhaustion.

It was funny. This thing the Agency was getting them to do should require utmost concentration, however, Jimmy felt as if they wanted them both tired. Tired so that their judgement would be skewed enough that they wouldn't think twice about what they were doing. Wasn't that Hank through and through, wasn't that-

"Jim?" Elvis has stepped closer, placed a firm hand on Jimmy's shoulder as if to steady him. He looks into Jimmy's eyes steadily, concerned. "Let's talk, okay?"

Jimmy takes a breath, grateful for the interruption, but uncertain of how to express it. He takes another breath, releases it into the mild night air "Sure."

"Not here." Elvis gives a quick backward glance at the open hangar door, at the noise of preparation coming from it. "Over this way."

He lopes off into the dim space between buildings, giving a quick look over his shoulder to make sure that Jimmy is following. Jimmy looks back, half expecting to see Marilyn there, accusing him with her once alive eyes, but there's nothing except moonlight and shadows.

Elvis waits for Jim to catch up. As the other man joins him, Elvis doesn't say anything straight away. Looking at him, pale face, and a noticeable tremor in his hands, Elvis wonders if Jim is even gonna make it. What if telling him about Priscilla and the NSA being involved will be enough to tip his partner over the edge? Still, it's unfair not to tell him. Whatever else happened tomorrow, Jim had a right to know the number of ways this thing could play out. Priscilla had guaranteed immunity for them both, but she had also said that they lacked any operational capacity outside of their data gig.

How did that translate into getting them out of the pinch that he and Jimmy had become caught in? Well, the way his new friend had put it? He and Jim just had to get to an agreed meeting point after making sure the President kept his brains in his skull. No big deal. Elvis almost laughs thinking about it. After she had said that part, there was a whole other thing about what them doing it would mean for the country. For the future. That's the way she had said it. In amongst all of it. What was the phrase she had used? Predictive data analytics.

Data analytics? Hell, that was a whole foreign concept to Elvis, but Priscilla had made it sound like it was the second coming of Jesus H. Christ himself. Well, whatever it meant, Elvis was more inclined to trust the woman over that son of a bitch, Hank. Bastard was partnered up with Frazini after all. What better reason could you have than avoiding helping out a bunch of political crooks and gangsters? Just about anything would be better than that.

Jimmy is swaying now so Elvis makes him sit down on some crates stacked between the buildings. He slumps against them, watches Elvis squat. Crouched down as they are in the shadows, hopefully no-one would be able to make them out, but with this place? Who knew? What Elvis felt was that it was a mixture of something out of science fiction and a regular old storage facility. Before he lays it out for Jim, Elvis gives a furtive look back towards where they had come, making sure that as much as he had control, no-one was eavesdropping.

"Listen, we ain't got much time. While you were out this morning, I took a little trip."

"I know, what about it?" Jim still looks like a ship about to capsize, but at least Elvis has his attention.

Elvis leans in close, whispers "You heard of the NSA?"

"NSA?" Jim blinks. "Of course, but..."

"No time for that." Elvis grips Jim's arm, squeezes it, begging silence without asking for it. "They're cutting us a deal. All we gotta do is screw over these guys, and we got a chance to be home free. That fit in with what your buddy Lee had planned?"

Elvis wasn't sure about Lee, but if it helped them get to where they needed to be, he guessed he'd have to swallow his suspicions. At least for the time being.

Jim nods.

"Was he working with the Feds?"

"Uh... I think... I don't know... "

"What do you mean, 'you don't know'?" Elvis frowns. "He either is, or he isn't."

"Well, he... Look, never mind. The NSA? You think they're good with their offer?"

"We got any other options here, Jim? You really think Hank is the best offer we got?"

Jim pauses, probably not because he's unsure, but because he wants to be certain that whatever they do doesn't end up with them dead. The chances of that happening were escalating every minute between now and when the Agency expected them to pull the trigger. After what feels like forever, Jim answers.

"No."

"Good. So we're on the same page with this?" Elvis takes a huge breath, not realizing until that moment that he'd been holding it. "Cause if we ain't, then-"

"We're solid." Jimmy nods weakly.

Elvis gives a tight grin. Holds his hand out to Jim. His partner grips Elvis' hand almost as weakly as he had nodded. Not perfect, but it would have to do.

"Come on, we better get back before that asshole comes looking for us."

LIVE AND LET DIE

DRIVING THROUGH PRE-DAWN DALLAS without worrying about who was looking over their shoulder feels weird. Someone was definitely still keeping tabs on them, of that there could be no doubt, but for this brief moment, they are alone. The day has dawned clear and mild, the heat of the last couple of days dropping away as if it had never been. The weather had seemed to hold a strange portent, like it was building to something. Now that it had settled, the tension in the air had seemed to depart with the heat.

Elvis hangs his arm straight out, wrist hanging loose against the top of the steering wheel. They park the car up in the car park next to the railroad tracks, just where Hank had told them to. Getting out, Jimmy looks at the tracks. There's a couple of box cars pulled up, doors slightly ajar on one. Most likely there's hobos inside, but there's no sign of them. Sleeping no doubt, given the early hour.

Jimmy has a light sweater pulled over his usual white t-shirt, hair ruffled a little by the light breeze. He follows Elvis through a patch of weeds growing wild and tall, watches his partner scan the area, cautious as always. For Jimmy's part, he's just tired and edgy. The sooner they're done with this, regardless of how it all pans out, the sooner he can rest. Maybe that rest would be inside a coffin, but Jimmy can't shake the feeling that he's operating on borrowed time anyway.

The streets are deserted with the exception of a city maintenance crew, but they're absorbed in their work. The men stand huddled around a manhole cover, all looking down as if whatever is inside holds the answer to some divine mystery. Elvis gives them a long stare, but Jimmy touches his back lightly, nods him forward. They had hours yet until the President rolled through the plaza, but Jimmy wanted to get set up. Part of him thinks once that happens, at least they'll be in a position to work out what other games Hank might be playing.

Elvis gives him this quick look, sidelong almost. Jimmy wonders what that was about, but holds his tongue. Most likely the other man is just as nervous as him, but Jimmy can't help to wonder if it's something more. After all, what had the NSA really talked to Elvis about? Had his partner told Jimmy everything? Or was there something else he was holding back? Unwilling or unable to share it.

The building turns out to be a book depository. Imagine that? History changing from here, of all places. As they reach the door, Jimmy notices Hank's absence more keenly for the first time since they had set out. Part of the plan all along, Jimmy guesses. Hadn't the Agency man said that at the start? That the whole reason he and Elvis were being used was to ensure plausible deniability if things went South.

Well, guess what Hank? There's a chance that might happen, just not in the way you expect.

Unless they were dealt a shitty hand, in which case, Jimmy guesses it won't much matter, either way.

They come to a door with a lock that Elvis picks without too much difficulty. Say one thing about Hank, he had made damn sure that they had been given the tools to get the job done. Through the other side, the bottom floor of the depository is silent, stacks of boxes creating obstruction over a clear line of view. In one corner, there's an office, but it's dark. They head quietly to a flight of stairs and head on up. As he and Elvis climb the steps in the pre-dawn light, Jimmy's legs feel weak. At one point, he stumbles, but Elvis puts his hand out and steadies him.

There's noises coming from all around, the sounds of the building itself waking up, bricks and mortar shifting with temperature changes. Remembering what Hank had said about what they would have to do if someone found them, Jimmy prays to a God he doesn't believe in that it doesn't work out that way. No way he wants to take out an innocent just for being in the wrong place at the wrong time. Especially if they're not going to do anything. If only Martin and Liz could see him now. Thing is, the whole situation has a feeling of make believe to it. Every step that carries him upwards, Jimmy's feeling like he's climbing up to a stage, about to give a performance.

They hit the sixth floor and Jimmy scopes it out. Much like the first, if truth be told. More boxes, more mouse and bird shit, some birds roosting up in the rafters. It looks more like a storage area than the bottom floor, like people came up here only if they needed to dump something. That worked to their favor, although Jimmy supposes that's the whole point of the Agency picking the place. Elvis leads the way to the window Hank had told them to set up at. As he starts unpacking the gear, Jimmy stands for a moment at the window, looking down at the triple stripe of roads and the city slumbering beyond.

Light splashes against the bricks, concrete, asphalt and trees, painting what it hits with orange. High up, thin clouds streak the clear sky. What if this was the last sunrise that he got to see? What if it was the last sunset that Jack Kennedy ever got to miss? Well, either way wouldn't matter that much. Marilyn hadn't even got to see *or* miss anything. Hadn't even been aware that when morning came calling, she wouldn't be around. Jimmy clenches his teeth, his eyes stinging. He had a chance right now to set things right. Sure, this all worked in Hank's favor if he did, but he had to take that chance.

Elvis looks up from unpacking and frowns.

"You okay, Jim?"

"I will be." But if he tells himself the truth, Jim doesn't know that he will.

As dawn arrives too quickly for Elvis' liking, he settles back. Jim is still staring out the window. Been stuck that way for the past hour like he's a statue. For his part, Elvis is alternating between watching Jim and looking back at the entrance to the stairs. All it would take is someone to come lurching up there and it wouldn't matter which way things played out. He and Jim would be as good as cooked. Elvis had taken the liberty of moving some boxes around to block their set-up, but still wasn't satisfied. From time to time he gets up, looks down the stairs and then comes back. Finally, unable to bear the weight of the silence, he comes up beside Jim and looks down on the road and grass below. He raises an arm, rests it crooked against the brick by the window.

"You gonna tell me what's playing on your mind, or you just gonna bottle it up until you explode?" He half snarls the words, not intending to, but the frustration had escaped before he could get a leash on it.

"Nothing."

"Don't give me that shit!" Elvis leans to one side and spits. "You're a moody son of a bitch at the best of times, but this is different. And don't say it's to do with any of this BS either."

Jim gets that sullen look that he has, turns and gives Elvis a helping of squint "You think that letting Kennedy get away with what he did is the right thing?"

"I thought -" Elvis holds back from answering straight away, wanting to get the words right before he goes and makes the hole any deeper. He straightens, runs his hands through his hair, then shrugs. "Does it matter what I think? You seem to be pretty certain about what you want to do."

"It does matter. Because if you don't have an opinion on this, then I guess I never knew you as well as I thought I did."

"Thing is, Jim, you don't know me." Elvis turns on him. "You and me? We're just two fuck-ups that got thrown together... Both times. The thing down South and now this."

"You came into this of your own free will." Jim's voice has a hostile quality to it that Elvis doesn't like. His partner is coming off like a caged wildcat.

"Yeah, I did. That's what we do where I come from. Someone needs help, you go help them. But that was back before any of this other shit. And you know what? I could've run at any time between then and now, but here I am, sitting in a shitty storage room, waiting to try and stop the President from getting put on a slab. Is that what you're doing here, Jim? Because the way you're talking right now makes me think that it ain't."

Jim starts a little at the accusation, straight brow dropping, mouth screwing up. He jerks forward, jabbing a finger in Elvis' face. "You think I wanted any of this? No. Who am I to try and change the way things are gonna work out. Didn't we already have this conversation? I told you, we don't have a choice. It's just you and me, with a whole heap of people higher up the food chain waiting to either push us another square on the board, or take us off it completely. Does it matter who we end up making a move for? Way I see it, we can't win this game whichever way we swing it. Might as well do some good in the process."

"And you think killing a man is any kind of solution? Don't you think there's been enough of that? You're here now. You *do* have a choice because you chose to be here. You *chose* to do *this*. Whatever it is you're thinking of doing." Elvis stands back, breathing heavily.

Jim looks at him, eyes wet, then shakes his head and turns away "And if I do decide to do what Hank wants, what then?"

Elvis doesn't want to answer, but thinks he owes Jim at least that simple honesty "Well, I've already made my choices about what'll happen then."

"Why not just call it now?" Jim doesn't turn to face Elvis, and he stares at the other man's back. "You got a gun. You can stop me."

"Because I'm not sure you've landed on what you'll do." Elvis sighs. "Dammit, man, why you gotta be like this? Can't you see I'm trying to help you?"

"Help?" Jim's laugh is bitter. "I'm beyond that."

Elvis says nothing. Thinks instead, *I hope on all that's holy that isn't the case.*

Hours pass with Jimmy alternating between dozing and taking turns with Elvis to watch the doors. After their exchange, they had both fallen silent. There wasn't much more to say, not much more to do but to wait until Jack and his entourage came rolling into the plaza. He thinks about what Lee had said, about what killing Kennedy actually means. He wonders if the decision to put this into motion kept Hank awake at night the way that it had kept him tossing in his sheets? He feels more alone now than he had in his entire life. Even with Elvis sitting nearby, Jimmy feels cut off from the other man.

And then, there's not much time left for anything because it hits a quarter past noon and there's only another fifteen minutes until go time. Elvis comes up beside him, holding his rifle. Jimmy picks up his own and checks it over, just the way that Lee had shown him. It was a funny thing to think that the man who had shown him how to shoot properly was also the one asking him not to pull the trigger. But Jimmy knew why it had been done like this. Because it was better to know who was looking through the scope than have to rely on an unknown.

The minutes stretch, becoming something insubstantial. Even with the mild temperature, it's hot up here. The muffled sound of people filing out of the building to go and watch Kennedy pass travels up the stairs. Elvis settles into position, kneeling. He gives Jimmy a brief look, unreadable. Jimmy doesn't need to try and interpret it though, they had said enough earlier. Jimmy takes the rifle and raises the scope to his eye. He swings it left and right, looking up Main street for a glimpse of the motorcade.

They would swing right and come down Elm, that's what Hank had said. Jimmy's hands grow slick against the rifle's grip. More time passes, but it's changed in quality, moving a lot quicker. He catches a glint of sunlight on glass, sees the first car appear.

Closer now.

He sees people lining the street. A child on someone's shoulders. Women screaming out Jack's name. Yes. That would make sense. He was a ladies man. Maybe the ultimate one? They all loved Jack. Jimmy forces his breath to slow. Hears Elvis say something beside him, but his heart is thudding too loudly in his ears.

He tries to force himself to stop, but the surge of his heart beating assaults his ears. He opens his eyes wide, jams it against the scope until it hurts. Now that he's looking, he sees men dotting the crowd. They wear suits, varying shades of grey. Instead of watching the approaching vehicles, they appear to be looking back at the depository. Jimmy reels, steadies himself. He feels Elvis touch his shoulder but shrugs it off. He mutters something but it has an animalistic snarl to it that makes it unintelligible.

Closer.

He breathes in, and holds it.

Through the magnified view, a God's eye, he sees Jack's face. He's squinting against the sun, but is still handsome. He waves, leans over to whisper something to Jackie. She's wearing purple and black, smiling, but it appears a little forced. Little details that make the scene come off like a movie through the scope. It evaporates the space between Jimmy and Jack. There's a flash somewhere off to his right and Jimmy frowns. He swings the rifle instinctually.

Lee's face appears. He's in a window struggling with someone. They hold a pistol between them and then there's a flash. Lee's mouth goes into this big O shape and then he's falling back, arms raised, bent at the elbows like he's trying to turn them into wings. He clutches at his throat and falls out of sight.

"They killed him!" Jimmy hears himself mutter, then he says it again, louder this time. "They killed Lee!"

He keeps looking through the scope. Lee's killer turns. Turns and looks straight up at Jimmy, face looming in the scope's lens. It's Hank and he's shouting something, pointing towards the road. There's a roar of engines from below and a gunshot, this time from off to the repository's right, near the memorial. There's a loud percussive boom right next to his ear. Jimmy jerks, but manages to keep his eye to the scope. There's another shot, from the memorial, and this time brick shards ricochet near his face. He falls back, yelling. He sees Elvis grimace, take aim and fire. The shot rolls out, long and low like thunder, and is followed by screams from below.

The motorcade is speeding now, along Main street, straight down the centre of the plaza. Jack is ducked down low in the back seat, shielding Jackie with his body. A black suited Secret Service Agent lies sprawled in the road behind the car, bleeding out, clutching his stomach. More shots ring clear across the azure Texas sky, but the car is going at high speed now and there's some sort of fire fight happening over near the memorial. Elvis is grabbing at Jimmy, pulling him from the window and towards the stairs.

"He got away!" Elvis' eyes are wide, sweat streaking his forehead. "Come on, man! We gotta get outta here!"

Jimmy gives one final look back, heart pounding, head swimming with too much adrenaline. He flees after Elvis towards the stairs.

PRESSURE

ELVIS HEARS JIMMY SHOUT SOMETHING about Lee. About Lee being shot. His mind races, but he ditches the binoculars and grabs his rifle. He picks it up and swings it in one smooth motion. First thing he sees is Hank framed by a window, face scrunched angrily and breathing heavily. Seeing no immediate threat, Elvis swings the rifle and sees two cops by a fence. Both men are holding weapons that don't look anything like Elvis has ever seen before. Nothing like what beat cops should be carrying anyway, that was for sure. He sees one take a shot at the motorcade and a Secret Service agent who had been scrambling over the back of the President's car falls from it like discarded litter.

Elvis takes a breath and holds it, lines up the shot and fires at the cop. A small mark appears beneath the man's right eye, and then there's a spray of misted blood and brains out the back of his head. The assassin falls, and his partner's concentration is broken. He swings the rifle towards where Elvis and Jimmy are positioned, takes a shot, but it goes awry. The bullet punches into the brickwork. A large section of wall evaporates as if it had never been there. Elvis' eyes go wide, but he returns fire and his bullet catches the cop in the throat. The man falls away from the fence, grabbing at his ruined larynx on the way down.

Elvis hears screaming coming from the crowds lining the streets below but ignores it. He grabs at Jimmy, yells in his face that they had to get the hell out of here. When Jimmy remains motionless, Elvis gives up and bolts for the stairs. Before he reaches them, he hears someone coming up and stops. Looking around, he sees that there isn't any time to move back from the door. He's still trying to figure out what to do when time runs out. The guy who steps through the door is dressed in a striped t-shirt and jeans. He looks like he could work there, and Elvis pauses.

When the man spots him and smiles, that's when Elvis realizes that he's not an employee. The gun appears in the man's hand as if he had conjured it there. He starts raising it without saying a word. Elvis lunges but never reaches the man. There's a loud *bang* in the closeness of the room. The guy staggers back, eyes a little wide, clutching at the side of his neck like he'd been stung by an insect. The smile is still on his face but it slowly shifts from self-assured to *what the fuck?* Elvis turns and sees Jimmy with a pistol in his hand. He turns back, the guy holds his hand out, palm first. It's completely red and he takes one unsteady step forward, then falls face forward to the floor.

Damn lucky that Jim didn't put a bullet in Elvis with that shot. He skirts the assassin's body, gives it a quick glance on the way to the stairs. Any bets it was one of Hank's clean up crew, coming to tie up loose ends. Just like how Priscilla had said it would be. No time to consider that. Elvis reaches the stairs and starts taking them two at a time, not waiting to see if his partner is following. Reaching the bottom, he looks for a rear entrance to the building, but with his head swimming, can't recall where they had come in. He heads for the front instead. Jim shuffles up behind him and Elvis grabs him just before they hit the street. He delivers a slap, hard to Jim's cheek and holds him up by the shoulders.

"Listen." Jim is looking from right to left as if he doesn't recognize where he is. Elvis gives him another slap, harder than the first. "Listen to me, Jim. We gotta play it cool now, y'hear? Hank and his crew are gonna be out there scouting for us. More of the same of that dude upstairs. We play it cool, we are home free. We didn't do nothin' wrong, man. It was all Hank. We just stayed right out of it. Jack didn't die. That's all that matters, you got me?" Elvis deliberately keeps the two cops he had shot out of the mix. No point muddying the waters any more than they needed to be.

Jim nods mutely, responding without Elvis being sure that he fully understands. It's enough. He guides his partner out, scoping the crowd for familiar faces. Doesn't really know what he'll do if he finds one. Long hours upstairs has given him a cramp. He curses as he tries to shake it out. People are scrambling, but he keeps calm. A woman is running back and forth, hands plastered to her face, crying. Her voice is a quavering siren, rising and falling in hysteria.

"They tried to kill him! They tried to shoot the President! Oh Godddddd!" Elvis pushes her out of the way and the woman gives an indignant squawk.

Elvis guides Jim forward, searching for any sign of Priscilla or her crew, but comes up short. Jim is wigging out like he's dropped some bad acid. Nothing for it but to get him off the street. Elvis sees that the people are all swarming in the opposite direction from where the motorcade had vanished. He grabs Jim, heads against the crowd, walking hurriedly until the mob starts to thin out. They round a corner and Elvis sees a silver Catalino with its windows down. He looks around for an owner, but the street is deserted. Elvis jumps in the front seat and yanks down the sun visor, lets out a high-spirited yip as a key falls into his lap. He gets out and opens the back door, shoves Jim inside and watches him lie down across the bench seat, curled up into himself. Jamming the key into the ignition, he starts the car, the engine turning over a few times before roaring to life. As he pulls away from the curb, he hunches his shoulders, half expecting a bullet that never comes. He stays that way until they're well out of the city centre. He heads Southwest. Any direction would do, just so long as it got him and Jimmy as far away from all of this as possible. If Frazini or Hank found them... Well, Elvis didn't want to think about that.

He sees a sign for a movie theatre, a half sphere of stars jutting out above the entrance. The place looks shoddy. Perfect for lying low. He pulls up, gets out and yanks Jimmy from the rear of the car. Maybe he's being naive in hoping that Priscilla will come looking for them? After all, hadn't she said she would be there? It's a long shot, but he's counting on her to keep her end of the deal and get them out of Dallas. If she didn't? Well, he'd just have to work that part out when it came to it. Hitting the open road was too risky for now. No telling what Hank would have waiting for them on the way out of town. A special little parting gift.

They stumble into the foyer like a couple of drunks, Jimmy's arm draped over Elvis' shoulders, but the kid sells them tickets without asking any questions. Maybe he hadn't heard that the President had nearly been assassinated. Elvis grabs some popcorn. Not even sure why. Just doing it on autopilot. God knows, he doesn't feel anywhere near hungry. Inside, they sit at the back, hunched in their seats. Jim shivers while Peter O'Toole leads an army on the screen. Elvis tries to feed him popcorn, but Jim is staring straight ahead.

Elvis would slap him again, for no other reason than he doesn't know what else to do, but he thinks Jim is beaten enough. With his heart still thudding, Elvis sinks into the seat and tries to ignore the broken man by his side. He runs a hand across his face, trying to decide what to do next, but doesn't come up with anything solid. The way he saw it, they couldn't go anywhere with Jim being in the state that he was. Maybe Priscilla would come? Or maybe he was kidding himself?

Then there was Hank and Frazini. Any bets that the two of them were already scrambling to find a scapegoat for this mess. What that meant for Jim and Elvis, if they survived this, was that they had better get used to looking over their shoulders for the rest of their days. Unless, by some divine intervention, they somehow managed to get their sorry asses out of the country and away from this mess, and even then, there were no guarantees. The Agency had a long reach, of that Elvis has no doubt. Thinking about all the ways in which they were screwed is starting to hurt his head, so Elvis settles in and starts watching the movie.

It feels ridiculous that they should be here, less than thirty minutes after being right in the thick of an attempt on the President's life. As he watches the images flicker across the screen, Elvis tries to follow the plot, but it's lost on him. Something about some Brit who was too smart for his own good getting involved in something that was bigger than he was. Wasn't that rich? Whatever, man. All Elvis knows for certain is that they can't camp here for long. They needed to scoot, and fast. He looks back over his shoulder at the entrance. With his attention divided, he doesn't notice the emergency exit to the right of the screen open until the flood of daylight from outside hits his face.

It's stupid he knows, but he turns towards it with a little thrill of hope. Childish almost. Like he's half expecting to see Priscilla or one of her people standing there. Instead, Hank is there. Of course he is. Why would it pan out any other way? Damn spook had an almost supernatural ability to make himself appear and ruin everybody's day. Elvis can't see his face, framed as he is by the daylight beyond the half open door, but he recognizes the man all the same. The bow of his lanky legs, the scraggly whiskers sprouting from the thick beard. Hank stays there, looking up at them, then approaches as if he doesn't have a care in the world.

Jimmy feels as if someone has kicked in his ribs, the pressure against his thudding heart intensifies. It gets worse as he watches Hank approach. All he can picture in his head is Lee's face. The man's oddly calm demeanour stretching into pain, disbelief in his eyes. Of course Jimmy could be painting all of these details into the scene. His mind was unravelling after all, wasn't it? He knew that. Maybe it had been doing that the whole time? He tries to breathe and finds that it's like someone has put a gag in his mouth, not enough air to fill his panicked lungs.

He starts wheezing and hears Hank laugh "What's wrong with him?"

Jimmy has enough focus to see that Hank holds a gun in his hand. Of course he would have that. He was going to kill both Jimmy and Elvis right here and now. It made sense. Lee had made a try at taking Hank out, and when that had happened, it had validated whatever suspicions that he might have had about Jimmy and Elvis. Elvis doesn't answer and Jimmy is incapable. Hank looks at him with this look on his face as if he had just come across some spoiled food in his refrigerator. He snorts out a low chuckle.

"Pathetic."

"Just leave him the hell alone." Elvis' voice is low, the words delivered through gritted teeth.

"Alone?" Hank takes a moment to wave the gun around the theatre. "How much more alone do you want to be?"

"What do you want?" Elvis' voice keeps dropping out, like it's coming through static. "You can't blame us for that shit back there. Turkey shoot? More like the Goddamn turkeys were the ones pulling the trigger."

Hank cocks his head to one side, quirks his eyebrows in an expression of pity that lacks any sincerity "Come on? You really gonna play it that way? Like we don't know that you and Hollywood here haven't been talking out of school? Who was it?" Hank keeps the gun pointed in their direction, but taps the air with its barrel, like he's selecting from an imaginary list. "The Feds? The Commies? Or.... Oh yeah... That makes a lot of sense. That skirt you were talking to at the bar? You didn't fall for the NSA's pick-up line did you? What did they offer you? Let me guess? Getting you out of this mess? That was it, wasn't it? And you fell for it like the dumb redneck that you are. You really have to stop thinking with your Johnson, Elvis."

"And what about you, man? You gonna ice us so that you have some kind of explanation for this shit show you've created? Tie us to Lee, somehow? Just a bunch of crazies looking to change the world?"

"Well, now that you mention it, yeah. You dumb fucks really think you can take out Agency people without it coming right back at you at twice the -"

Jimmy lurches to his feet and Hank's command of the gun suddenly becomes more rigid. Jimmy knows how stupid it would be to attack the man so instead he says what's been plaguing him this whole time. If he's going to die here, he wants to know the truth. Maybe it was futile, but he has to try. For her. It was always for her. So he asks the only question that really matters to him.

"Marilyn." His voice sounds like something out of a Hammer Horror film, cracked and dead. "Tell me... You killed her, didn't you? You did all this to get to Kennedy. You set it up so that you could blackmail the President into doing whatever the hell it is you people do when you're not trying to kill him. When he broke ranks, well, you had to change your plans.."

Hank frowns, then purses his lips in confusion. He looks to Elvis. "Can you believe this kid? You're both about to be ventilated, and all he wants to know is what happened to that blonde whore of his." He scratches the back of his head with his free hand. "I'll give you credit, you're a persistent little asshole, aren't you? You really want to know what happened to her? Will that make you shut your mumbling mouth about it? Jesus Christ! You wanna be an actor, you gotta learn to enunciate, dammit!"

Elvis shifts in his seat, but Hank jerks the gun towards him.

"Sit still. You wouldn't want me to have put one in you before we got the best part, would-" Hank goes to reach inside his jacket but never makes it.

The emergency exit opens. Hank spins but only makes it a quarter of the way around before a bullet catches him in the mouth. He lets out something that might be a scream if he wasn't now missing his tongue. Another shot takes him in the chest and a wet gasp escapes from his lips as he slumps between the seats. Jimmy jerks backwards as gore sprays his face. He claws at it, a mimicry of Hank's death throes. He falls to his knees and vomits. There's nothing in his stomach to release and he starts dry heaving. He hears Elvis scrambling behind him, his partner's hands on his back trying to pull him down.

"Elvis?" Jimmy hears a woman's voice, tight and urgent.

He feels Elvis shift, wipes ineffectually at his face, blinking through the mess caked to his skin and hair. Elvis is still crouched, looking towards the emergency exit.

"Priscilla?" Elvis' voice is shaking in a way Jimmy has never heard before. A mixture of tension and relief. "That - that you?"

"Who else did you think it was? I told you I'd come get you. You really made us work for this. You should've stayed put. If it wasn't for this dumb bastard, I'd have never found you." Her voice hitches, growing more tense with each moment. "Come on! Dallas PD are on their way and it's going to be very difficult for me to explain this mess to them without creating a complete nightmare for everybody involved. I'm going to be in enough trouble as it is."

Jimmy feels Elvis' hands grab him under the arms and hauls him to his feet "You won't get any arguments from me, darlin'."

HEARTBREAK HOTEL

THEY LET HIM HAVE A SHOWER AT LEAST. They've taken Elvis somewhere else in the mostly empty office block that the NSA was using as some sort of base of operations. Jimmy shivers despite the coarse blanket thrown around his shoulders. He reaches out a shaking hand and takes a glass of water from the battered looking table in front of him. Big windows line the room, and occasionally people will come and look in at him and then leave. They brought him a hamburger, some fries and a new packet of Chesterfields. He takes one out and lights it up, draws deeply. He closes his eyes. He had been close. Close enough that he could've almost grasped it. Maybe he would've taken Hank's bullet if he could've just found out what had happened to her.

It's okay, Jimmy. You did your best.

But his best had not been good enough. And that had been the case his entire life. He had failed her when she needed him. He opens his eyes, taps the cigarette against the rim of the ashtray. A shiver passes through him and he turns his head. He sits very still when he sees who it is looking back at him from the other side of the glass. The President, John Fitzgerald Kennedy. Jackie stands beside him, big eyes downcast, hand clasped in his. Priscilla stands in the background. They watch him as people attending an art exhibit might study a sculpture. JFK gives him a brief nod, grave eyes the color of storm clouds. Jimmy can see what Marilyn had seen in him. The President turns and says something unheard to Priscilla, disengages from Jackie, and then leaves. Jimmy half expects Jackie to follow, doesn't quite know how to react when she doesn't.

The First Lady comes to the door, pauses with her hand resting on its handle, and says something to Priscilla. The NSA Agent nods her head briefly and turns on her heel and leaves. Jackie pushes open the door, comes through and sits across the table from Jimmy. She is more beautiful in person than any Newspaper or Magazine photograph could do justice. She nods at the packet of cigarettes that sits between them.

"Do you mind?" Her voice is so polished it could gleam.

Jimmy is shocked to silence, feeling like he is witnessing a dream. Between the events of the day and this moment right now, he half expects to wake up in some Dallas jail cell. He shrugs, and then immediately stutters a response.

"Sure... I mean, Of course." He feels his cheeks grow warm.

She takes a cigarette from the packet, and Jimmy offers her a lighter. He's surprised that for the first time in hours, his hands are not shaking as he lights her cigarette. She draws in a sharp breath, then tilts her elegant neck and releases the smoke in fine tendrils. Hell, even the way she smokes is classy. She looks through the glass, and then turns her attention upon him. Her eyes look wounded, but strong.

"Agent Beaulieu informed me that you and your colleague are responsible for saving my husband." Her tone is throaty, made even more so by the nicotine. She looks down, like she is preparing herself for something that she doesn't really want to talk about. She finally seems to find a reserve of strength that enables her to forge on. "The least I can do is repay you for your efforts. I understand you had some questions about an... Acquaintance... Of my husband."

Jimmy feels the weight of tiredness drop from him like a heavy curtain, suddenly alert and breathless. He nods his head once, quickly, thinking that if he spoke, she might flee like a startled deer. She takes another drag and this time when she releases the smoke, it's funnelled into a spear.

"I know my husband is not always the best at being... Discreet. Your friend Ms. Monroe was one of those indiscretions. I had the pleasure of discussing such things with her." She picks her words carefully, a diplomat navigating a difficult negotiation. "In fact, she and I spoke the night she passed. Just before, in fact."

She watches carefully, seeming to gauge his reaction. His mind races as he sorts through everything she is telling him. He tries to identify some element of her story that won't mesh with what scant evidence he has. He falls short, the shock of realization that she is telling the truth making him slump back in his chair. He lets out a low breath.

"The book. It was never him that she was going to talk to... It was you. She rang you that night. Didn't she?"

Jackie hesitates, then nods, a slight tremble on the first word that quickly vanishes. Her commitment to telling him her side seems renewed, even though she owes him nothing at all.

"She... She told me that she was pregnant with my husband's child. As you can imagine, this was quite a shock to me, but it was not a surprise that she and my husband had been intimate." She reaches across and pours water into a spare glass from a jug in the centre of the table, takes a long drink before continuing. "Ms. Monroe went on to tell me that my husband would leave me for her. That was her belief. Her hope. It was then that I realized how much pain my husband had caused not only me, but Ms. Monroe as well."

Jackie ashes the cigarette and then grinds it into the ashtray as she stands, pushing the chair back. The fluorescent light frames her like an angel of judgement. Her eyes are hard and flinty and it's seeing her like this that makes Jimmy feel that she is more powerful than her husband ever will be. She looks at Jimmy with an unflinching stare.

"I felt it was my duty to advise Ms. Monroe of my husband's frivolous nature with women, and that she would be better off resolving the issue without deluding herself any further. I was very saddened to hear of the manner in which she chose to do this."

"But the-" Jimmy grips the edges of the table, leaning forward across it as if he can stop her from saying what she has already just said.

"There's a recording. I can arrange for you to be able to hear it if that will help convince you? It's not easy to hear, as I'm sure you'll understand. It's unfortunate that you've been led to believe that my husband had some involvement in this tragedy beyond the obvious. When I learned of this, I felt that it was only appropriate to correct this misinformation. My husband would have spoken with you himself, however, there is much that requires his attention given the circumstances. I'm very sorry for your loss, Mr. Dean, but I hope my explanation has gone some way to assuage your misgivings. Ms. Monroe was a very troubled young woman, who had to deal with a lot of unfair attention focused on her personal life. The public feels that they own us, and that with ownership, a debt is owed. It's one of the many unfortunate by-products of the society in which we live, particularly when you possess a measure of fame."

Even if every fibre of his being wants to scream at Jackie, to tell her that she had been lied to, as much as the rest of them had, he finds that in that moment, he cannot. Her honesty is too bruised, too similar to his own, to deny. He looks down at the table, but before he can look up at her again, he hears the door open and then close, and she is gone with all the swiftness of a phantom. He allows a sob to escape. Just a single one. A fragile thing that dies as soon as it is born. He looks up at the ceiling, eyes burning from tiredness, anxiety and grief.

I'm sorry Jimmy. Marilyn whispers. *I'm so sorry. I just wanted someone to love me.*

But he can't answer her, as much as he can't forgive her. Because there is nothing to forgive.

EPILOGUE

Cuba, 1964

ELVIS IS SITTING AT THE BAR, arguing with Hunter about the likelihood of Kennedy's third term running into a fourth. Above the bar, a television set is bolted to the wall. You had to take what the state-sponsored news fed you with a grain of salt but there was no denying how things looked like they would go. Kennedy is flanked by his brother and the new VP, McCormack, who had been appointed after Johnston's ticker had bummed out the previous Fall.

Hunter takes this big drag from his cigarette. He's a weird cat. Dresses like he's gonna go hunt big game on a savannah. He smokes through this dainty cigarette holder and talks with the eloquence of an academic and the profanity of a sailor. Why

Castro let Hunter in was anyone's guess. Hell, why he let Elvis in was anyone's guess.

Apparently, the Beard had taken a liking to him, that's what Ernesto had said after their first meeting. In any event, he was certain that opinion would change quick-smart if Fidel ever got wind that Elvis was packaging up intel for the NSA. Priscilla had given him that warning last time they had spoken. He hasn't worked out if she is worried about him, or about losing an asset.

"Look there, man." Elvis points at the television screen. At the three men on it. Priscilla had told him that they are being called the Unholy Trinity in places where it counts. "Old Jack's got the whole country in lockdown after Dallas. You need a permit if you want to take a dump, let alone get in or out of the country. You tellin' me that you really believe it'll ever stop? Kennedy goes, it'll be his little brother who takes the reins. They're setting up a - a..." He tries to remember the word Priscilla had used. It comes to him and he blurts it out. "Oligarchy!"

Hunter is shaking his head rapidly like he's listening to Jazz only he can hear. Elvis had been to enough of his parties to know that was generally what he liked to listen to. A little Miles Davis to get the juices flowing. Elvis didn't get it immediately, but it had been growing on him. Yanking a notepad from one of the numerous pockets on his suit, Hunter slides it in front of Elvis, taps the scrawled writing.

"And you look here. I've been writing about this sort of thing for a while now. There's a definite agenda, Hound Dog, but it's much bigger than what your simple worldview can handle." *Hound Dog*. That's what Hunter has taken to calling Elvis for whatever reason. "If they could get that close in Dallas, they'll get close enough to him some other time. All it'll take is some strong-willed, iron-hearted extremist with a solid enough agenda, and everything he's planned will come unravelled. Mark my words!"

Elvis wants to tell him exactly what he knows about that, but guesses it wouldn't be the smartest move. Hunter takes a swig of rum, and Elvis doesn't get a chance to respond anyway. Seems like Hunter is hell bent on delivering one of his rants again.

"You're missing the point, Hound Dog, and frankly, I'm disappointed. What you should be realizing is the whole system is rigged. One person's Oligarch is another's esteemed leader. Kennedy goes, they'll just do the old switcheroo and put in someone who's a bit more malleable. The state gets what it wants, after all."

Which was maybe why Priscilla had sent him down here in the first place? What better way for getting some projections on how things looked like on the other side of the jump than to visit Cuba. Elvis feels tired. Tired of the conversation with Hunter. Tired of being down here away from Pop when he was so sick. Tired of what was happening in the States. He gives Hunter this shrug, like maybe the problem is bigger than what some dumb conversation in a Cuban bar could work out.

He's about to take his leave when the phone rings loudly. No-one looks up, but the bartender takes the call, shouts out Elvis' assumed name. Elvis raises an eyebrow. Priscilla wouldn't call him here, that was damn sure. He weaves through the old guys playing cards and picks up the heavy black receiver. As with everything in Cuba, the connection is a little shaky. There's a hiss of static, and then he hears Jim's voice.

"Hi, E." Elvis pauses before answering, recalling what happened the last time they'd spoken like this. Truth is, Elvis hasn't heard from Jim since Dallas. It had been bad enough that time. "E?"

"Yeah... I'm here. How've you been, Jim?"

"Oh, well enough." Jim sounds okay, a lot better than that last time, but Elvis knows that wouldn't be too hard. "I'm not doing too badly now that the President is looking after most of my bills. What about you?"

How Jim found him is beyond Elvis "Well... It's a job... Better than driving trucks, or that last thing, that's for damn sure."

There's another long pause and Elvis wonders if he should say something, when Jim speaks again.

"Listen uh... I just wanted to, uh... Well, I never thanked you. For helping me." His voice sounds heavy.

"Naw, man. You don't have to-"

When Jim speaks again, it sounds rehearsed, but even that doesn't stop Elvis from hearing the effort that it takes him to get it out.

"I put you into that mess, and it was the wrong thing to do. I had no right to expect that from you. If I had just accepted what happened to Marilyn, instead of imagining conspiracies then-"

Elvis looks around the bar, leans into the nook where the phone sits, and lowers his voice. Even here in Cuba, there were no guarantees that the President didn't have eyes and ears. Even Priscilla's protection would mean nothin' if Jack decided that Elvis was becoming problematic "Now wait just a minute, Jim. You might've got it wrong with Marilyn, sure, but don't go thinking there wasn't a conspiracy. You're forgetting that we nearly got hoodwinked into killin' the President."

Jim jumps on the last word, almost like it's a lure and he's a fish just eager to bite at it "I would've done it too... If not for Lee. I was gonna do it. I shoulda done it."

"You..." Elvis lets his words taper off, because he already had that idea, but didn't want to give it any more strength by saying anything else.

"He got her pregnant, E. He got her pregnant and then threw her to one side like she was garbage. And all because she posed a risk to his power. You tell me he didn't deserve that bullet."

"Listen, Jim... It's done now. Hank's gone... Frazini... well, you know how those guys handle anything that puts them at risk. But you and me? We're free." He keeps it soft, partly because he doesn't want anyone to hear, but mostly because he wants Jim to know that he understands. "It's over. We made our choices." There's a long hissing silence, broken only by the poor connection. Elvis turns, looks back and sees some guys looking over at him. The way they're staring makes the hair prickle on the nape of his neck. "Listen Jim, I should... Uh... I need to go."

"You take care of yourself, E."

"You too, Jim."

"And E?" Something in Jim's voice stops Elvis from hanging up.

"Yeah?"

"Remember what I told you about choices?"

There's a click and the line goes dead. Elvis holds the phone for a few moments longer, staring at nothing. Jim's words ring in his ear, sounding more like a warning than anything else. Finally, he hangs up the phone. Turning, he makes his way back through the cluster of Cubans engrossed in drinking and swindling each other out of what little money they have. Outside, Havana is a beautiful, humid mess. He runs a hand through his dark hair, already feeling the sweat laced through it. He starts walking, no real direction in mind. Soon, he is swallowed by the city, thoughts of Jimmy Dean dancing from his mind.

THE END

ABOUT THE AUTHOR

AK Alliss writes. Anytime. Anywhere. Scifi, Fantasy, Noir and anything else that grabs his attention. Breaking barriers from the mainstream genre tropes and introducing rich and intriguing characters to accompany readers on their adventure.

Author of the coming of age novel, 'A False History', the Ouroboros Cycle Scifi saga (FR[A]ME, Future's Orphans, and Gravity's Truth), The Pattern Codex Science Fantasy epic (All The Dead Stars) and the domestic psychological thriller, 'Kill Your Darlings'.

'Jimmy Dean's Last Dance' is his seventh novel.

Want to learn more about the elusive AK? Find him on Social Media or wherever good books are sold.

Twitter: @AkAlliss
Instagram: @AKAlliss
Facebook: Facebook.com/AKAlliss

CPSIA information can be obtained
at www.ICGtesting.com
Printed in the USA
BVHW040933080222
627678BV00014B/218/J

9 781737 822806